Anything for Love

Anything for Love

Sheila Rann

WARNER BOOKS

A Time Warner Company

Warner Books, Inc., 1271 Avenue of the Americas, New York, NY 10020

 A Time Warner Company

Printed in the United States of America
First Printing: July 1995
10 9 8 7 6 5 4 3 2 1

Library of Congress Cataloging-in-Publication Data
Rann, Sheila.
   Anything for love / Sheila Rann.
      p.   cm.
   ISBN 0-446-51830-1
   1. Motion picture actors and actresses—United States—Fiction.   2. Man-woman relationships—Spain—Fiction.   3. Women—Psychology—Fiction.   4. Americans—Spain—Fiction.   I. Title.
PS3568.A573A82   1995
813'.54—dc20
                                                          94-32015
                                                          CIP

Book design by H. Roberts

To the dearest of my heart, my children
Adam and Jaclyn Rann
for love and support

Acknowledgments

Special thanks to the gracious and exemplary editors of Warner Books, my terrific agent, my family and all the friends and colleagues who listened and inspired, the city of Barcelona for being the perfect setting for my story, dancing—forever my joy—but mostly, to love.

Anything for Love

*P*rologue

June 1962

But something was wrong this night ... Bethy's scream shot out of the pain. Inside her there was scorching, breaking ... broken open. Why wouldn't he stop? This couldn't be happening ... She must be dreaming, only a nightmare. When Bethy woke up, they would bring her the warm drink to soothe her, and rock her back to sleep ... Finally, the air. It was light, she must be awake now. Everything would be all right now ... She could feel herself being lowered into the bath. Its warmth surrounded her. But why was the water red like this? Blood. Her blood. The pain still searing through the middle of her body, her head would explode from it ... "Shh, Bethy Dolly," she heard the voice above her ... No, it couldn't be, she'd heard wrong. She wouldn't look up. She crumpled over, a broken ballerina doll in the red water. No! No! It was only a nightmare, only a dream. Still she heard it again, "Bethy Dolly, shh."

One

June 1992

Barely fifteen minutes ago, I dropped my luggage with the doorman of the Hotel Colón and ran across the square, shoving through the crowds in front of me, forgetting who I was. I had no ties. I didn't feel like Elizabeth anymore bounding up the steps of the cathedral two at a time ... I was somebody who could run without looking back. The Gothic spires surrounded me, drawing the same ominous shadows on the broken paving they had that day I first saw them twenty years ago. It seemed another lifetime ... another woman ... she'd even had another name, Bethy, eighteen, a pale, blond ballet dancer daring the world in tattered jeans, arriving in Barcelona to dance in the corps de ballet of the opera of Teatro del Liceo. And there on the left, the ancient stone path shortcut she ran through on her way to meet too many lovers. I raced through it again now, feeling the rhythm of her long-legged gait.

Down a hill and through the cobblestone maze of Barrio Gótico, I knew exactly which narrow streets led to Café de la Opera, and followed them until they opened on to Las Ramblas de las Floras, Barcelona's teeming promenade of flower and bird markets and constantly moving crowds. I found my café exactly where it had been. Dusty gold walls were still hung with mirrors etched with the gods of love and music and the morning air was already hazy from European cigarettes. How could it still be the same? A girl with wide-spaced slanting eyes sat sharing wine with a dark young man. I listened to the girl's laugh. She drew me in with a low voice that flaunted her unaccountability. She mocked me with her smile. It was my smile as it used to be . . . unaffected by gravity.

I retraced my invisible footprints to the café's terrace on the Ramblas. "Buenos días," a tiny Gypsy girl greeted me. I gave her some newly exchanged pesetas and chose a table on the side, but I could not sit still. I paced through the nearby tables, reabsorbing the early sounds and colors of the Ramblas before the day mixed them into thousands of others, until I stopped short, surprised to feel myself blushing. I was standing at the table of a man of about twenty-eight, with sun-streaked, rock star hair waving around the shoulders of his black tee. A shadow of a beard completed the effect. He looked as surprised as I was, then cheerfully recovered, all proper politeness on the outside, but his eyes traced every line of my body. He was adorably boheme and somewhat macho, just my type, from before of course. Certainly not me now. But his eyes were such a startling pale gray, I couldn't look away from them. I had to be mistaken . . . the excitement of the trip . . . In their colorless reflection for a moment, I saw myself so young. I saw Bethy.

I made myself walk back to my table with practiced New York cool, but when I got there, I gave an unnecessary amount of attention to stirring the tiny espresso, mixing and splashing and compulsively half looking back at him until I burst out laughing at myself, little tears squeezing out from trying to keep the laughter in. It really was funny, after all I'd done and become, here I was, only a few minutes in my old café again and right back to blushing when a gorgeous man appeared.

"Hello again, Bethy," I greeted myself. Bethy was the girl I used to be. Today, she hides inside me, stubbornly waiting for her moment again, cleverly disguising herself in women's clothes, looking serious, accomplished. I never know whether to rejoice or mourn that unlucky girl, but I always envy how free she became and the risks she took, chancing anything for love, never understanding how quickly you could lose everything.

I'm a successful filmmaker now, businesslike, a workaholic. I've nicknamed this stage of my life Elizabeth the Woman, and take my sixteen-hour days in stride, flying regularly from New York to L.A. I appreciate any opportunity to work and am always more than punctual because L.A. studio executives don't like to give independent filmmakers too much time. After my meetings, I take the red-eye home, exhilarated or depressed, depending on how my presentation went, but always ready for an early shoot or another meeting the minute the plane lands. My friends boast when they introduce me, "Meet my dear friend Elizabeth, she's America's hottest new filmmaker." They back it up with, "You must see Elizabeth's fabulous new film, *Firenze*. You know, the Oscar winner! You'll love it!" The minute I walk away, they lower their voices to whisper to each other, "She's been lucky with this film, but we'll see how she does with the next one."

I dress the part in appropriately dark business suits for meetings with financial backers, and jeans and loose shirts for days on the set. Once in a while, for the treat of a New York downtown TriBeCa night, I like to go all out with a silky low-cut black tuxedo and odd pieces of shiny designer jewelry, and think of myself as striking, though by no means a great beauty. I'm five foot seven and thin enough still to fit into this sky blue dress for my trip to Barcelona today. It's high-necked, just above the knee, with modest lines, but it needs a lean hip to wear. I have straight blond hair, styled in an easy-to-care-for blunt cut, falling below my shoulders. I call it my Swedish look, except that I have brown eyes and a full mouth. And I'm very fortunate to have the kind of skin that doesn't need makeup. I appreciate it more now that I never have time for anything other than lipstick.

Tomorrow, I'll be starting preproduction meetings here, on a major film about the '92 Olympics. But it was a year ago that I started thinking about coming back to Barcelona to produce the film for Studio Goya y Ximínez. Everybody hailed this new opportunity as "her chance to create her own *Chariots of Fire*," and I know that should have been enough reason to come back. For any filmmaker. But the truth is, something else was driving me, and I had to understand it. It was something that I'd long ago crushed away deep into an inside pocket where nobody else would ever see it, and I could always look the other way. But maybe a secret can only spend a certain amount of time compressed in a human being before its edges begin to unravel and its cold gnawings begin to turn the mind. My secret had begun its swelling through. It began slowly at first, in the dark before morning, trapping my mind with dreams before I could wake and push them away. Later as I'd go through my day, determined to work, trying to smile the dreams away as only dreams, the secret would be there again, hiding, waiting in some corner. Oh, it had always been somewhere, even during those long-ago ballet years when I'd lived in Barcelona as Bethy.

It was there that she'd freshly hidden the secret away. But its edges began to unravel in Bethy too, and she had to bind them up tighter. She was the best at glossing and painting over the past, changing its form until she was successful at forgetting what was true and what was not. Now as the secret gnaws its way back into my memory, great chunks of it are missing.

I had to find them. At thirty-eight, enough time had passed that I felt strong enough, but I'd have to go slowly. Working in

Barcelona again would be perfect, putting me in the center of Bethy's path yet giving me the necessary distance and protection.

The timing was right. Early last year, after *Firenze*'s success at the film festival in Cannes, Spain's well-known but still new film company, Studio Goya y Ximínez, telephoned me from their Barcelona headquarters with a colleague's call of congratulations and an invitation to come to Barcelona to co-produce a new film with them. The new project would be a full-technical-scale, no-holds-barred, financially sound film production. Quite different from *Firenze* for me. I created *Firenze*, doing everything myself, from conception to direction, right on through marketing. But despite my devotion, I was surprised as anybody when my low-budget film became an international sensation. *Variety* hailed it with a front-page, bold-caps headline that read, "SUCCESS, UN-HOLLYWOOD STYLE." The story went on to celebrate "a major artistic work with no names, produced by a new film company run entirely by one woman." I read it again and again to make sure it was happening to me. Audiences formed long lines for the chance to see *Firenze* in first-run movie houses around the world, and I began to follow my film like a roady, giving interviews on prime-time television everywhere, even to *The Wall Street Journal* in the role of celebrity executive. "I couldn't be happier," I told reporters in cities around the world. It was true.

But their questions always demanded the same answers: "Tell us about your romance, Elizabeth, who's the man you love? Who's the man who loves you? Elizabeth, Elizabeth, you must have a lover."

These are only typical reporter's questions, I'd tell myself, but each time I heard them the same freezing of the early-morning dreams would start in my chest. I'd push it away, smiling at the cameras and answering, "I'm so excited about the Olympic film I'll be doing next. That's my new romance."

Later, in my hotel room, I would acknowledge the true answer, that I'm always alone now, an island. I'd try to tell myself that it's because I've been so busy these last years. I no longer notice if it's by choice or by habit that I've joined our new heroic breed of American loners, the BMSs, the Beautiful Mateless Supergirls, roaming our big-city ranges like the lonesome cowboys roamed their Wild Western ones, ridin' herd with our first-class airplane seats for trusty mounts. "Here's to Elizabeth," my friends toast me over cocktails at our occasional girls' nights out, "she's mega-talented and she's worked her A off."

"Ha," another points out, "she's only been able to do it because she didn't have some husband to take care of!"

Funny, we all think to ourselves, how it used to be the other way for us. That wasn't so long ago. Then we laugh and exchange knowing looks, but all the jokes we make can't cover the longings for love I'd never admit to.

You see, I've become the polished role I play so well now that none of my friends or any of my colleagues could ever guess the story of Bethy. It's only lately in those black hours before morning when the night demons are their strongest that I dare to listen to it myself. I say dare, but that's not the truth. Bethy won't sleep anymore. She demands I hear every detail.

The Bethy dreams first started a little over a year ago, a few months after I'd finished *Firenze*. In the beginning, I couldn't say they were dreams, but more of a wisp, or a fleeting sensation of past colors without words I'd look back on in the late afternoon. I'd wonder, had I dreamt at all, or were these only thoughts passing through me at the moment. As those wisps became longer, and began to stretch through my night, Bethy's voice was always muffled. I'd dream she was calling to me from down a stairwell and the bouncing echo distorted her words too much for me to make them out . . . she'd call to me from a long tunnel, but roar of trains and the screech of wheels drowned her words . . . we were at a crowded party and she wore a black silk strapless dress and her long blond hair gleamed . . . we held fluted glasses and spoke, but the noise of the guests and the music of the room obliterated her words . . . she'd spoken to me in a Spanish I couldn't understand, the words never made sense, and she'd spoken in English too low to hear . . . When she began to come to me as a little child, she called herself Bethy Dolly, and wore her blond hair tied up tight into a ballerina's bun, entwined with a spray of tiny pink flowers. She was pale and thin in her black ballet tights and sat with her head down for long periods, refusing to speak . . . Lately she comes to me as a young woman again and her words are clear enough for me to understand, but I never wake up till she allows it.

Two

"Señora, excuse me, señora," the waiter of Café de la Opera interrupted my thoughts trying to speak his best English. He was placing an unordered espresso in front of me. "Compliments," he explained, pointing to the man with the pale gray eyes who'd looked at me so conspicuously before. I nodded an unsure acceptance. I'm unpracticed these days in meeting handsome strangers in cafés. There was no need to worry though, the stranger stood and left, walking through the terrace on to the Ramblas. Maybe just being gracious for my embarrassment before, I thought. I watched the stranger go, tall and lean, bouncing forward on the balls of his feet with a lithe athletic rhythm, the arms swinging naturally, a flexible body, long muscles in the legs ... maybe a tennis player ... head held high ... almost like a dancer. I still have my dancer's habit of sizing up bodies. At Teatro del Liceo, male body watching was a pastime.

I looked across the Ramblas at the old Opera House. It was shuttered except for the box office, which was doing a brisk business for tonight's performance of *Lulu*. My thoughts drifted inside to the grand stage and how it looked to Bethy under its spotlights of white and blue ...

Bethy and her fellow members of the female corps de ballet would stand in the wings every night and watch Luíz, the premier male dancer, do his bravura jump variations, the male corps behind him, all bounding off the floor, their thighs taut with long sculptured muscles outlined by their white tights, and their high tight rounded buttocks above. "El gitano," the Gypsy, all the girls called Luíz because of his dark looks and animal energy. And "tu amor," your love, they'd giggle to Bethy. "Sí, Luíz, amor, y ballet."

"Yes, Luíz, love and ballet forever," Bethy repeated. In Barcelona, all her dreams were coming true.

After her morning ballet class, if she wasn't required to attend a later rehearsal, she'd dare to give up her dancer's diet for a long Spanish lunch. After lunch there were exquisite treasures to look at in tiny shops hidden away in cobblestone alleys and the port to explore with its ships and surly sailors with their dangerous looks. She'd look back at them now and then, dreaming how jealous Luíz might be.

In the early evening, she'd join all her new friends at Teatro del Liceo, to prepare for the performance. The dressing room set aside backstage for the corps de ballet was one long chaotic blaze of a lighted mirror table with open tubes of lipstick, sticky pots of purple eye shadow, cracked compacts of rouge, and used tubes of everything. Every inch had a dancer in front of it making up. She'd sit between two girls melting black wax in a spoon and applying the warm smelly stuff to their eyelashes with a matchstick. When the wax dried each eyelash looked an inch long. It was there that she practiced her new life by retelling her old life.

"My father was a famous violinist," she told them in well improved Spanish as she melted the wax too, "and my mother was a ballerina from Russia. Her name is very long in Russian, but everybody called her Marya. I did too." When the dancers looked surprised at this, she'd explain, "Well, Marya was very young. She was tall, but because she was so thin, she looked even younger, we were almost like sisters. Daddy called us his little girls."

The dancers had checked and knew that Bethy's story about her famous family was true, and they were eager to hear more. Bethy went on, "We lived in a big apartment on Riverside Drive in New York City. Marya gave me my first ballet lessons at home in the Russian method. Daddy set up a ballet barre for us in his music room, and every day after school he played his violin for us while we practiced. The sunlight would shine through the windows and I would pretend it was the spotlight for Marya's dance."

After the evening's performance at Teatro del Liceo was finished, Bethy would tell them more about her famous parents. Across the street at Café de la Opera the dancers would gather around her to listen. "Daddy was originally from Austria. He met Marya in Leningrad during a concert exchange tour. She was only sixteen and already dancing at the Kirov. They fell instantly in love, but Russia wasn't like now, where you could just leave. Daddy had to sneak Marya away to Romania in a truck. From there they had to find their way to Yugoslavia where they'd be able to cross the border. The same night they arrived in Romania they swam the Danube together by moonlight to her freedom."

The dancers cheered, and neighboring tables of opera patrons raised their glasses to Bethy too. Everybody loved the story of her romantic Daddy and his Marya and the moonlight.

Still, Bethy knew that later on, as soon as she'd left the café with Luíz, the dancers would be asking each other questions about her. They knew her parents were both dead now, and they'd be much too sensitive to ever ask her how it happened. "She obviously loved them so," she knew they'd end that part of their speculation.

But they'd have other questions. Bethy had been stopped cold by these one night at the Café when she'd been about to turn the doorknob to enter the ladies' room. "Why did Bethy come to dance in Spain, where she makes so little money and dances in the back line of the corps?" she overheard one girl inside ask another. "It doesn't make sense."

She heard another dancer confirm her history with, "Did you know that Bethy was also accepted to a famous ballet company when she was only sixteen, the New York City Ballet?"

"And she's been dancing solo parts for over a year, just like her mother did," the first dancer confirmed. "And with good reviews. I know that for sure."

"And with all her connections," still a third commented, "she was on her way. Why would she stop her career to leave and go so far away to join such a small company where nobody sees her? It doesn't make sense."

Bethy stole away quietly from behind the closed door before any of them could ask her. She knew that later that night, as always, she could forget all her real answers in the bewitching Gypsy arms of Luíz.

"Bethy, my dearest," Luíz said to her one night after he'd fulfilled that wish for her with her wildest dreams of love. "Please, I need only you to work out my new dances on. Nobody can do my leaps like you. You dance like the Russians. Even our best lead ballerinas don't have your Russian training. Please say you help your Luíz. Ah yes, I see it. The theater will be packed, and Bethy and Luíz will triumph together. Ah the flowers mi amor."

And it was true ... at first ... The theater was packed for their triumph, and the miraculous reviews and the flowers surrounded her ... until Bethy found herself dancing less and less. "It's because of these little injuries lately, it happens, normal, nothing serious, I'm out of my teens, that's all, I'll be back on stage very soon," she'd told the reviewers. But everyone knew it was from that awful injury she'd sustained flying from a height into the Gypsy Luíz's arms in his most celebrated ballet, where human projectiles were perfectly normal.

"Nobody can dance like my beautiful Bethy, I love you,"

he'd rushed to assure her, tormented with pain from the twisted knee, backstage at the packed house during intermission while her understudy was hurriedly getting ready to replace her in the second act.

Right after the accident, Luíz carried her everywhere in his arms to her never-ending delight. "Please stay with me, I care for you every minute," he insisted, and he took her to his apartment and made sure she did all the exercises the doctors prescribed to strengthen and heal the knee. At night when he went to perform, she busied herself writing down and notating every step and movement of all the roles in the ballets he'd created on her. "My darling," he exulted when he came home with special foods from La Bouquería for her after the performance, "you have done the best job for your Luíz! My work would be lost without you." Again they made love.

When the knee exercises and the shots began to work, and the knee was almost strong, she busied herself in the rehearsal hall, teaching her parts in Luíz's ballets to other dancers, both so that she would have understudies when she could dance again, and so he could make films of the ballets for the repertory.

"My angel," he kissed her, "only God could have sent you to me. Soon the knee is strong, and you dance on stage with your Luíz. But not yet."

"I'm sure it's fine now," she told him at the end of each month that went by.

"No, no, I am afraid you hurt yourself again. Please, you must be patient for your Luíz. I must protect my Bethy, mi Prima Ballerina." And he brought her to ecstasy again.

It was a Monday morning months later when Luíz told her that the company directors had decided that the small undemanding part he'd made in his new ballet for her, to celebrate her recovery, would go to a new young dancer.

Bethy's heart stopped. She couldn't believe what she was hearing, some mistake, it wasn't so. "But it's your choice who dances the parts in your ballets. You promised me that part over a year ago, everyone did."

"This girl is new here in Barcelona. But she has a name in France. The directors wish to try her in some small part only to see," he patiently explained.

"But you've promised me . . . you love me . . . even yesterday . . . How could you not know what they were planning?"

He looked away and wouldn't look back. "Things have changed with the company now. There is new directors. I have not the same powers. My love, I do not know how to tell you this, but they change casts for everything starting next week, and your name is no longer on any lists."

She lost all feeling in her arms and legs, and was she standing or sitting . . . or was it day or night? She was only twenty-five! True she hadn't danced on stage in over a year. How could it have been that long? The days working with Luíz had slipped by so quickly. They were so in love. "But surely I could get back into shape somehow," she reasoned. "I'll work hard. I'll starve to lose the weight. You know I can do it." Weren't her words coming out? Couldn't Luíz hear her? Luíz was walking away.

The next week her name was not on any of the lists. She searched them twice a day to make sure . . . some mistake . . . some explanation. Did she exist at all? She cowered away to dutifully do her barre exercises, not in her usual place in the company class with the new girl from France, but alone, in the cold rehearsal hall of Teatro del Liceo.

"But I only wanted to love him," she cried aloud to her mirrored double. No words echoed back in the empty hall. "You've certainly tried," she answered herself, "but now you've got to be realistic." She raised her leg off the barre into a not-so-perfect arabesque.

Bethy took her heel in hand to raise her leg high above her head, and held it there for a moment admiring her still extraordinary extension, but when she let go of the leg, she couldn't keep it there. The injuries had won. Her body was failing her. It was true. Her magic was gone. She had to find another magic to replace it immediately, or she would not live. Ballet was her entire identity.

But dancers, especially the ones who grow up in the corps where every port de bras or tilt of the chin to the lavender gel above must be exactly the same, are trained to take direction and execute it perfectly without question. To be successful they are quick studies, and do not ask questions, because fresh competition is always waiting in the wings. This is what saved Bethy.

When she got her expected pink slip from the company, she'd already investigated what to do. She went out and found her first nonballet work as a bilingual gofer with an American film company shooting in Spain. It wasn't dancing, but there was something about filmmaking that fascinated her, and the camaraderie of the film crew was what she needed most.

Not long after her first day, the American producer called her into his office. "We're behind schedule here and we're going to need another location scout. Can you handle it?"

Bethy knew this city she loved, inside out, and did her job so thoroughly the producers thought she'd worked even harder than the twelve-hour days she'd put in.

"We're going to make you location manager," the grateful Americans rewarded her. "There won't be an increase in pay right away, because it's kind of more of an apprenticeship." They knew it wasn't easy to find someone so cooperative at such low pay, and she knew better than anybody how to cut down on the extra pesetas that were always charged to foreigners. Bethy agreed to the new title, and worked at her usual one hundred and fifty percent.

Soon came other American film companies to take advantage of the economic benefits of shooting in Spain, and they needed a reliable bilingual contact. With them came the wonders of

American overtime pay and the things she could buy with it—a new place to live, clothes, food, wine . . .

"Even cocaine," Bethy excuses another new fascination. For the days that dancing still haunted her so much that she had to work extra hard to forget. **"And some Valium to keep it all under control."**

Two years later Bethy was much sought after by American and British film companies. She was on the set by six A.M. to oversee her shoot, and worked late into the night to prepare for the next day. To anybody who would have questioned the drugs, she would have replied, "What else can I do to keep up with the amount of work I have? I have to work, don't I? And I only do a little . . . Everybody does it . . . You should see how much these American film guys do." But nobody asked; she was very discreet.

The banter of Bethy's new American colleagues about how they missed their hamburgers and french fries, and their Mets and their Dodgers, made her realize how long she'd been gone. "Did you hear what happened on that set last week in New York?" and "Let's get together for lunch in L.A. next week," they'd jovially say to each other. And "Look me up when you get back," they'd all say to her when each project was over, and hug and kiss her goodbye and make sure she had their addresses.

She was twenty-eight when she got up the nerve to think about returning to America. She now had solid professional referrals from the American film companies she'd already worked with, and impressive contacts with their international backers.

In the next years, bettering herself from job to job in the time-constricted rigors of the American film industry, dancing itself was forced to push back into time. She never dared visit Madame Verosha, the ballet teacher who'd loved her and been her coach and mentor, but her dancer's discipline stayed to serve her well, as piece by piece she struggled every day to change. Even a new name . . . Elizabeth. "This time I'll succeed," she promised herself. "I'll make films in America, and England and France and Italy, and when I'm famous enough, I'll deserve to forget everything about Bethy Dolly. But if I fail . . ."

Finally I, Elizabeth, made it easier for her. Elizabeth, the respected new filmmaker with a studio in a loft on lower Broadway, in her hometown of New York City, thankfully had little time to worry about the tormented, dancing Bethy she left behind. And with time Bethy eased away from me. The things I've won in the film industry are hard-fought. They take constant nurturing. And in turn they give me a different opportunity for a dancer's perfection and obsession.

Since my good fortune with *Firenze*, new colleagues invite me to power lunch uptown at the Four Seasons, or power breakfast at the Plaza. Over gourmet food, they offer me first-look at the best new scripts. They know what my work requires—nothing too commercial, characters or place is key, nothing tightly written, open to my own improvisation—I've worked hard for my own style.

In the early Barcelona days, Bethy's most important meetings, the ones with her jealous lovers, always took place over a common Spanish Rioja, here at the Café de la Opera, and ended in sparse rooms with love beatings and passionate lovemaking, to beg her forgiveness. She was always, but only, paid for her time in the most exquisite orgasms from the most exquisite young men, and could hardly keep track of the counting.

Today, I'm paid for my efforts from far less young and exquisite, but far more profitable men, and much of it in foreign currencies as I negotiate film distribution channels for *Firenze* with theater chains from Milan, Italy, to Lagos, Nigeria. A major international bank keeps track of the accounting. In those last moments before dawn, when the night demons pull Bethy back to her place in the past, and I get up without much sleep to start my day as Elizabeth, I go through my calendar of meetings and think what irony for both of us that part of being Elizabeth is knowing how to negotiate with dangerous self-centered men and come away very much the richer for it.

And then I close the appointment book and try to sleep for a few more hours, but it doesn't work anymore. Bethy used to be bound by the perimeter of the night, but now she follows me into the day . . . persistently, passionately with our secret hidden . . . she holds out something more to me and its draw is too strong . . . I follow her.

Three

"Hola qué tal?"

"Bien, muy bien, y tú?"

"Bien, y tu esposa, como está?" . . . Sounds of friends greeting friends were all around me. The morning sun had moved higher in the sky over the terrace of Café de la Opera, and summer colors and tourists were filling the small spaces between the full tables. As I changed my chair's direction, moving back a little into the shade of the awning, the gray-eyed man in the black tee I'd blushed over before walked back into my view. The table he'd sat at earlier was now occupied. A man and woman who'd just entered the café, their eyes searching everywhere for an outside table, waved hello to him. Their expression said, "No tables again." Others waved to the gray-eyed man too. A waiter rushed by, apologizing to them all in different directions with a gesture that confirmed there weren't any tables left inside either. They all seemed to recognize each other. This café always had regular patrons. Bethy and her ballet friends were once part of its scene, cheerfully knowing everybody. If they didn't, they made a point of meeting them.

"May shee set down?" the gray-eyed man pointed to one of

the three extra empty chairs at my table, looking a little embarrassed himself this time.

"Well . . . I . . ." I wasn't sure what to say.

"I theenk . . ." the man shyly struggled with his English.

I caught my breath and smiled inside. His English was awful and my Spanish mostly forgotten. We couldn't "communicate." At long last I'd be spared those lengthy, disastrous discussions about who we were, where we were from and what we were doing here. Free at last from that obligatory New York and Los Angeles opening convention of explaining your life to every new man you meet, that initial sizing up and speaking out that men and women do in those places. From the first second, trying to determine what good you will be to them and what your vulnerabilities are. Language always spoils any real opening communication between a man and woman. It only sets up mistaken first impressions of future scenarios and subtle competitions that convolute everything to come. What could it hurt if I agreed to share my table with him? I could always leave if I changed my mind, and I probably would soon anyway. "Por favor, sit down," I answered simply and we sat quietly at our rickety café table.

Once a stream going down to the port, long ago paved over to a mile-long street, the Ramblas was now a sea of energy in front of us as it filled with morning people, rushing and dashing, stopping only for a millisecond to buy flowers, a café con leche, a croissant. Seventeenth-century European gargoyled granite architecture and graceful Spanish balconies looked down on us, and young people in jeans ran by on their way to classes at the university.

A Swedish couple with backpacks walked onto the café terrace and asked in perfectly dictioned English if they could "please occupy" the two empty chairs at our table. The gray-eyed man and I agreed, and we all sat without a word. The mixed sweetness of fresh cut blooms, Turkish tobacco, and traffic exhaust around us was exactly as I remembered.

Not too far from us, engrossed in watching a mime troupe perform, stood the American man I'd sat next to on the overnight flight from New York to Barcelona. I'd first noticed him in the boarding area lounge surrounded by a charmed contingent of female airline personnel. He'd seemed a little too comfortable with their attention.

Steven Brandon, the former Olympic skier, was now a journalist and TV commentator from L.A., an intriguing almost forty, and traveling with his overpossessive, teenage daughter.

"Yup, that's me, the same Steven Brandon from the *People* magazine story on famous bachelors," he'd tried his best to make light of it when we were comfortably in the air. But I'd noticed he didn't flinch too much when he continued with, "What can I say? . . . That's the way they sell magazines . . . Look, will you talk to me anyway?"

His daughter had shot me a piercing look and ordered earphones for them for the movie.

Our seven-hour flight had gone very fast. In spite of the cockiness of that first impression I'd had of Steven, he'd really turned out to be very nice. He had the most wholesome laugh I'd ever heard from a man. Not loud, not soft, just an honest enjoyment that caught me up in it too. He was broad shouldered but lean. A young Olympic skier's body grown into full manhood. And his brown hair had a tracing of gray on top in an honest way, not on the sides in a debonair way. He had clear blue eyes in a square-jawed face.

About two hours into the trip we started to talk about fate, you know, the way people on airplanes talk about everything. The drink cart had worked its way past us through the narrow aisles and we'd been among the first to be de-stressing the day with little individual portion bottles of Absolut on the rocks.

"Sure, sure," I was still kidding him about the *People* article, "a mass magazine bachelor who believes in fate."

But Steven appeared serious, "Don't you think it's fate that sat you next to me on this plane?"

"Not at all," I laughed, "it was the Iberia flight attendant at the gate."

"Fate's messenger," Steven stated logically. "Fate works in strange ways by placing people in strange positions. That Iberia flight attendant was put behind that desk for the specific purpose of putting you and me next to each other on this plane."

His getting around of it delighted us so much we laughed again.

His young keeper buried herself in her flight magazine.

The stewardess delivered our little flight dinner trays. I'd ordered a special "healthy-choice" dinner and was looking dismally at its cellophaned fruit.

"Would you care to have some chocolate cake for breakfast?" Steven joked, handing me double fudge, inside and out. We'd passed several time zones and no longer knew what time it was.

"It must be dinner somewhere," I accepted with an appreciative smile.

The keeper gave me a "How gross can you be!" look, and turned up the volume on her earphones.

I tried to eat the melting chocolate cake as neatly as I could, although I don't know why I wanted her approval of my manners. When some crumbs fell, the keeper gave me an even more condescending look, and turned to look out at the clouds.

I think Steven was more relaxed to be free of her gaze too.

"I hope you don't believe the publicity stuff. You know, that magazine story about me, all that," Steven said. "Nobody'd pay for a magazine that tells the truth."

"Oh really? What's the truth?" I asked.

"You want my truth?"

"Sure, why not?"

"The truth is when I was a younger guy, traveling the world

after winning the silver in the Olympics, I had a lot of girls, and the truth is, I did do some wild things … I was a kid, I didn't have any fear yet. That life stopped years ago but the publicity from it never does, and now that I'm a network guy they use it to promote me to attract a female audience."

"How slimy can they get?"

"That's the networks, they never claimed to be a charitable organization, and they're going to do it no matter what I say because they get the publicity and I'm still a good guy image for them."

"It's all very neat, huh? Commercial!"

"Look, those running around, wild days were fine for me when I was younger, but I have absolutely no interest in them anymore."

"So, you're really having a sort of good guy's reverse mid-life crisis, is that it?" I barbed.

"It's not a crisis," he answered honestly, "it's just new choices for me. I see new opportunities for myself at this time of my life, and I've made a lot of changes when it comes to women. If I were to get involved with a woman now, it would probably be a more serious relationship."

He was starting to lose his lightness, too, now. I pulled us both back to it with, "Ohh, that notorious "R" word, huh?" But then I really meant it. "I hate that word, 'relationship.' It ruins the romance of it. Overstated, overused, it sounds clinical, psychiatric."

"Yeah, psychiatric, I agree," Steven laughed and his appreciative smile was more than photogenic. It made me feel witty, bright. "Relationship does sound like problems are coming, and usually some are," he agreed. "But what else would you call it? Commitment?"

"No, please, that's worse. You wake up in the morning and say, 'I have a commitment,' it sounds like you have work to do. I have enough of that."

"How does love affair sound to you, Elizabeth?"

"Love affair is much better. It keeps the romance in it," I mused. "You say 'love affair' and you can see them kissing in Paris or Rome."

"Or Barcelona?"

"Or Barcelona."

"But I've already had enough love affairs in my life," Steven said, determined to move our conversation into serious territory again. "I need a deeper connection. I've never really taken the emotional risk."

We sat quietly looking at each other for a moment, strangers on the brink of saying more than they should and not knowing why.

"There must be something in the air up here tonight, Steven," I said as the flight attendants put out the lights and the movie we'd both seen on another flight started. I didn't believe that Steven the Famous Bachelor's "emotional risks" would be as sincere once on the ground, but I have to admit how comfortable I felt sitting next to him in the air. The blankets and pillows came around, and we lifted the armrest to give us more room. Our little individual portion size bottles of Absolut began to take their toll and we fell asleep. The next time I opened my eyes, even Steven's daughter had stopped keeping guard and had fallen asleep.

"Why don't you ride with us into Barcelona?" Steven offered, the complete gentleman, helping me with my luggage at customs. "I've got a limo coming."

"No!" the daughter answered for me. "She has too many bags. They won't fit." The poor nervous girl went on to recite all the complex travel plans she'd arranged for just the two of them. No outsiders, the eyes said, so don't you even think it! She finished, "Dad and I are going to be very busy together, and we have to take notes on our favorite places for my two best girlfriends from Beverly Hills who'll be here next month."

Hopefully their fathers will escape, I almost quipped at her as I declined the invitation. "I'll be staying at the Colón," I said instead. "I'll call and invite you to dinner."

"Promise?" he asked.

"I promise."

"Good, 'cause now I know where you're staying and if you don't call, I'm gonna come lookin' for ya!"

How cute he is, I thought, and took the card he gave me with the Avenida Palace phone number written on it and slipped it into the inside pocket of my purse. The poor young girl was beside herself, but she really didn't have to worry. I wasn't going to chance anything with anybody who had as long and colorful a reputation as Steven the Famous Bachelor.

Now as I sat here in my old café with the gray-eyed stranger and the Swedish couple, that plane conversation with Steven only hours ago seemed to have happened a world away. I looked into my purse to check where I'd put his card. When I looked up again, he was crossing the traffic-choked street with his daughter, turning off the Ramblas and disappearing into the colors of a sidestreet winding toward Barrio Gótico.

The waiter had returned to our table and the gray-eyed man was reaching for his check and mine, too, which now had the Swedish couple's bill on it. While we all protested, he paid it good naturedly. The Swedish couple thanked him and left the two of us sitting. After a while my generous table mate stood tall above me, inviting me to join him for a walk on the flower-filled Ramblas. What a beautiful day! It was the time of day in early summer in Barcelona before the cloudless sky would begin to beat through the soft morning warmth, before the wall-to-wall metal of the traffic would reflect it back and the cracked sidewalks and tarred streets would steam it up from beneath . . . I stood to join him in the crowds of the Ramblas around a bird vendor, inspecting dozens of colorful birds from all countries, happily chirping in their clean little cages . . . Long-ago male murmurs of "Qué guapa, guapísima," beautiful, beautiful, which had once greeted long-legged Bethy when she walked on the Ramblas, began to be heard as the crowds passed by me. "Qué guapa, guapísima, qué guapa, guapísima." The male voices were becoming louder and more rhythmic till they were almost a vibration in the moving crowd. The pale-eyed man smoothly wrapped his arm around my waist, was it to protect me from all those other men or was it just to stake his claim, I really didn't know, but I was surprised to feel a high-pitched corner of an old feeling of risk peeling its way to the front of my mind . . . "Danger," its long-ago low voice enticed me. I walked with the man up the Ramblas turning into Barcelona's famous La Boquería, the huge, covered fresh food and produce market. Bethy always treasured walking through La Boquería.

Inside, the food smells, textures, shapes and colors excited me. My gracious stranger from the café bought us some red grapes from a stall that seemed to be made of mountains of them, until a running child tipped them all over. We bent to help the vendor gather his flying and rolling avalanche of red, chasing them along the floor like millions of red marbles, laughing like children. The stranger put his hand over mine and lifted me to my feet. When we were standing our laughter became freer, and flew on to freer still as we shared in the hallucination of red. Thousands of juicy red strawberries danced with thousands of ripe red tomatoes, glowing red apples and red sausages of every thinness and thickness. Raw red carcasses of meat rose to the air, pulling with them whole fishes that turned from pink to orange to red. Clams, oysters and shellfish of every shape, and smells of cheeses, and purples of plums and grapes cavorted in a riot of red. Shades of greens, from the lightest olives to the darkest leaves, became the greenest greens we'd ever seen.

The noisy Boquería was packed with shoppers, vendors, aristocrats and beggars, but we were anonymous in our own rolling capsule of colors and sensual promise. Somewhere along the way I found out that his name was Carlos, and he was an artist with regular gallery shows in Barcelona and Madrid. I couldn't care less who he was or what he did. I was ecstatically free from the monotony of personal history and accomplishments. "My name is Bethy," I told him to hear how it sounded again. I tossed my hair into a stream of sunlight as she might have. "I'm traveling." Our bodies traveled as one through the stalls and bars of the market, and our feet found the same footsteps.

The Bouquería was cool and damp, and when we finally wove our way back out to the Ramblas I was amazed at the blanket of heat that met us. It was only midmorning. On this new planet, my blue dress with its proper long jacket needed to be exchanged for anonymous light cotton. "Will you wait for me here while I go back to my hotel to change," I asked Carlos in my best Spanish.

Carlos answered in the most outrageous combination of Spanish and bad English with even a touch of French that he would accompany me every inch of the way because he could never again bear to let me out of his sight.

"Carlos," I laughed, "you say that as if I'm the only woman you've ever said that to." And then in English, safe that he couldn't understand, "Even Bethy wouldn't have believed that from a stranger on the Ramblas, but just for this one morning, Elizabeth will."

We wound together and started our walk back to the Hotel Colón, down the narrow medieval streets that wind off the Ramblas de las Flores to the fifteenth-century Avenida de la Catedral. My spiky heels made the most wonderful clicking sound on the ancient cobblestones. I'd always marveled that somehow you could walk long ways in Barcelona, in the highest of heels, without tripping or hurting your feet. Now the crowds in the old city flew in and out of tiny cafés and bars. Everything was madly accelerated until the winding procession of people and streets opened on to a sunny square in front of a little ancient stone church. Here was another Barcelona I remembered. Lazy cafés, red-tile roofs and filigree balconies with fresh carnations were everywhere. The people sitting in these cafés were here to spend the morning or perhaps the day. The sun was fierce but I couldn't leave now, couldn't risk losing this mirage. I slipped out of the jacket of the dress and we sat down in as much shade as we could find, at a postage-stamp-sized table under a tree where the waiter absentmindedly ignored us. My business mind wondered, "Do these cafés ever make any money?"

In the next café, which was close to ours, Steven Brandon was also settling in. His daughter had found them a table that hadn't even been cleared off yet. She parked him there, under the canopy, while she took charge of racing waiters, and getting menus, then hurried back to diligently keep guard of him.

I was happy to see Steven again. Three times in one morning I thought as we exchanged the now formal waves and smiles of recent plane companions and professional colleagues. The keeper's exchange to me was merely a scowl.

Carlos and I went back to deciding on naranja or citrón, until I noticed a striking German woman I'd seen earlier on the Ramblas. She'd appeared to be doing some kind of sedate hooking, but it was marginal so you couldn't be sure, and now she was inching her way through the crowd, over to Steven's table. Almost a classic beauty with very light skin, big blue eyes and lots of dark hair, she didn't look like a prostitute; maybe she wasn't, maybe she was only a beautiful young woman who was daring or rebellious enough to dress in a tight black skirt, with a black satin bustier and black lace stockings. "My name is Soosi," I could hear her purring in provocative accents. She pronounced Steven, "Shtephen." It sounded sexy. I felt like killing her.

A handsome young student appeared, quickly seizing the opportunity of Soosi's distraction to begin entrancing "Shtephen's" daughter. Would the keeper be sufficiently diverted to allow Soosi to do whatever it was she was up to? I watched this foursome play out the drama before me. Soosi was progressing slowly, but the handsome student and the daughter had found the instant friendliness that those who are still children can.

"Sure, you can go with him to meet the other students at their table," Steven was saying to his daughter.

The delighted girl left and Soosi moved in.

Carlos watched me watch Steven and turned my face back toward him. The pale eyes narrowed with Latin jealousy and I felt my adrenaline rise . . . Bethy's voice was almost too far away to hear, but the low laugh she'd begun in Barcelona unmistakably mocked me, **"Yes, it has been too long, hasn't it, Elizabeth?"**

Carlos raised my hair off the side of my face and his hand caressed my neck right under the ear. Then it possessively moved down my arm, stopping at the side of my breast.

The low voice inside became closer and the laugh carefree, and my eyes purposely looked over at Steven again. What if I did try out Bethy's old teasing game on both of them? See how it felt?

But it backfired. Instead, I became the one suffering from jealousy over Steven's absorption with the German girl's creamy skin, and I'd already gone too far with Carlos. His hand hovered right under my breast. My eyes riveted to Steven . . .**Bethy laughed on.** Carlos smoothly turned my body toward him, again away from the view of the café, and his hand moved down to grip my waist and spread low on my abdomen, the little finger digging in dangerously lower. His lips feathered down to the nape of my neck, and the other hand began to threaten my inner thigh. My buttocks tightened and everything wanted his touch. I felt the wet excitement inside and the sweating from the heat outside, or perhaps the other way around.

Steven's arm was around the German girl's bare shoulders and her silky dark hair brushed his face, but he couldn't take his eyes away from Carlos and me. **Bethy's laugh mocked louder.**

"Here's to today, Carlos," I said, disengaging myself and toasting this midsummer day's dream with the red wine that had appeared and been poured. "Yuk, sour house wine," I groaned at first, but after a few swallows it tasted better than any of the expensive aged wines I'd soberly take minute sips of at noon in the trendy business restaurants of New York and L.A., and I happily started to lose all concept of what time it was.

Shouts of "Bravo," "Olé" and staccato clapping brought me back. Two flamenco guitars had joined the jazz group in the center of the square and the occasional melodies from *Porgy and Bess* were replaced with abstracted phrases from Granada. When an old man joined in with castanets and a throaty Gypsy chant, the café patrons enthusiastically showered them all with coins from all nations.

The black satin Soosi had practically moved into Steven's chair now and was opening one welcoming lace leg. I became furious at him and her. What surprising emotions I was feeling today. "This is stupid," I confided to Carlos. "Why should I be jealous? It was only a flirtatious conversation on a long plane ride. Only that . . . I hardly know him. And I'm never jealous. Even Bethy would never give in to jealousy. And that Soosi, whatever she's supposed to be, she's got a right to do whatever it is she does. Why am I fighting myself not to go over there and whack her?"

"Sí," Carlos agreed, not understanding a word. At least I was giving him all my attention. He protectively put his arm around me, gray eyes sparkling again.

I swallowed more house vinegar and made a decision to put Steven out of my mind forever, not spoil one millisecond more of this beautiful day. "Camarero, champagne, por favor," I called to the waiter, and fused into the flamenco jazz rhythms, feeling perfectly cool now in the scorching midday sun. I've always been very good at mind over matter.

Carlos and I took our bottle of champagne and walked over

near the musicians. "Aquí, Aquí," they shouted as the bottle passed from player to player for long swigs. I ordered another, which disappeared as quickly as the first. What a time we were all having. Carlos and I danced the flamenco, and when the music was over, we danced and sang out of the square. When we reached the little stone church, I looked back to see Steven watching me leave for what seemed like a long lonely moment, but maybe it was only my own feelings of hope.

Carlos and I wound deeper into the cool shade of Barrio Gótico. Narrowness blocked the sun from boring through the shadows of fifteenth-century buildings, and a wall of metal shuttered the shops for lunch and afternoon siesta. The old hanging night lamps watched over the emptiness. We stopped at a crooked corner. "Te quiero, Bethy." Carlos moved his hands over my thighs.

I pulled away, pulling back to myself, the haze of sun and wine clearing, but Bethy's voice inside became demanding, insistent, forcing, I could hear it clearly. It was exactly how she'd sounded in the dreams . . . **"Remember how happy we were for that short time we loved? Remember . . . that short time we loved."**

"Te quiero, Bethy," Carlos said. Somehow the pale eyes knew. "Te quiero, Bethy," he repeated.

I leaned my body to his and moved my hands over his chest and arms. His chest was muscular and hard, but it somehow seemed transparent . . . I could pass through . . .

"Remember? . . . that short time we loved . . ."

"Te deseo, Bethy." The pale eyes seemed flecked with red . . . I had to be mistaken. Again our feet walked in the same footsteps.

Carlos led me past an ancient fountain that crumbled without repair. An old man drank from a faucet on its side and on its ledge a flute player sat accompanying us on our way. One more alley of a street and we stopped at the narrowest doorway I'd ever seen. I felt like Alice about to fall down a rabbit hole into some bizarre Wonderland because I couldn't imagine what else a doorway this narrow could lead to. We passed through. On the other side was a wild garden of lilacs fronting a multi-angled structure with giant skylights. We walked through the garden and entered his artist's studio.

Four

I felt lost in space. It was impossible to tell where the room began or where it ended. A hexagonal balcony jutted out somewhere high above, and looking through its wall of glass, I could see the Mediterranean, or was it the sky. Sea-reflected sunlight bleached out the already whitewashed walls so that one could only imagine if they were actual boundaries or simply high crystalline transparencies on which paintings were suspended. Translucent pastel canvas, almost a wash, blended into the pale shimmering pastel dots reflecting off the sea. My Wonderland was an abstracted indoor version of an outdoor Monet with only angles of confusion for subject, and Carlos's paintings had no structure at all. I could feel my own structure losing its form and spreading out into the dazzle of this room without boundaries. When did light ever have so many colors? I floated renewed. Myself again. The dancer.

I knew that if Carlos and I had spoken the same language, or spoke at any length at all, this extraordinary lightness could never have happened. There'd be too much conversation and exchange of thoughts we'd dutifully pursue. Words, words, melding and countering other words. Nuances and innuendos, poses and projections to chain us down. Intellectual repartee to guard the chains. We'd discuss Carlos's work and accomplishments, his theories, opinions, strivings, tryings, conquerings. I'd give my views on his views. We'd discuss his shows, his future plans, his background, his art education. Is he famous, does he want fame? My work, awards and new film would enter the conversation and lead to my background, theories, strivings, tryings, conquerings. We'd get to know each other in an intimate intellectual way, have a meeting of the minds. Later we'd become lovers, have arguments.

But for this moment I was young and free again. What did I care for the world of achievements and disagreements? No. I didn't have to waste one precious breath of energy on the aging of words, not one thought to think of thoughts in common. And Carlos made no attempt at reasons or words of any kind. At long last, lack of communication. How I'd longed for it. I passed through the ether, up the circular stairway to the balcony, and just for a minute I thankfully dared let Elizabeth's hard-fought vigilance wrapped in words pass outward to the Mediterranean. It was only a crack, but Bethy quickly pressed through.

The sunlight was so bright off the water, that when I looked back to the room, it had disintegrated into a mass of dancing dots. After a while I began to make out Carlos, standing in front of me. His naked body took form out of the dotted sparkle around us, as beautifully taut and athletic as I'd thought when he'd first walked out of the café. Gracefully sloping shoulders and defined chest muscles were covered with the same smooth golden skin and soft down Bethy had worshiped in her affair with her ballet partner, Luíz. The same long arms that had once lifted her and laid her into his bed reached out. I saw the same young thighs she'd once wrapped her own thighs around in a million ways. And Carlos had the same high tight rounded young dancer's buttocks. His arms stretched further toward me, reaching back into first nights of miracle passion, and the blues and browns and amber colors of another time replaced the dots of brightness around me . . .

. . . It is the very first night after the ballet that Luíz invited Bethy home. The soon-to-be lovers are walking through the Old Quarter of Barcelona holding hands across the pitch black cobblestones of the back alleys. They stop in an alley before the building he lives in and stand face-to-face, features blinded to each other by the shadows. Luíz's hand reaches out to trace her cheekbones, then moves down to caress the outside of her mouth, his fingers go inside to trace all the moist inner parts, the lovers kiss with bonded tongues retracing all the places he touched. She follows him upstairs and listens to the turn of his key in the apartment door . . .

. . . Once inside, Luíz lights one red candle dripping its last tallowed traces of light into a china dish on a lone table in an almost bare room. Before its play of shadow on the wall, he begins to undress her as if he is unwrapping a precious present, and the delicate wrappings are part of his gift. He carefully removes her jacket, and kisses the inside of each willowy candlelit arm from elbow to wrist, then slides her skirt over her buttocks and thighs, and follows it down, reverently kissing the thin iridescent skin underneath. He kneels and lifts each pointed foot over her skirt, and his hands move up to feel her calves and thighs . . . his sounds of passion escape him as he presses his fingers into her buttocks, sending ten pleasure points of pain to join her sighs . . . he undresses before her, exposing the golden-lit sinewy thighs she's watched for months on stage, conquering the air with their leaps—she'd dared to dream of them at night. His compact dancer's body is fluid and lithe with its still boyish grace, she'll be free from the suffocation she feels with the bulk of full-grown masculinity. She sees the high taut rounded dancer's buttocks with deep grooves on each side, the places she'll grip to press him into the screaming anticipation of her body and mind. She stands rapt as the magnificent Luíz, the star of the ballet, kneels again before her and holds her tight in worship. His rivers of kisses flow up her body . . .

. . . He lifts her to his hips, and holds her tight to him before he lays her gently down on the dark Paisley bed and bends to her breasts with his tongue and his teeth. Time becomes measured for her only in his sucking of her nipples until she grips him tight to press his body into hers forever. The lovers' bodies fuse into the night shadows of the room, and she feels for the first time the mad surging dance she'll dance forever with Luíz and love . . .

. . . For weeks the new lovers are spellbound by each other. At night, the grand orchestra of Teatro del Liceo plays only for the flight of the eyes of each seeking across the stage through the swirl of dancers for the eyes of the other. And after the performance and into the next day they lie on Luíz's bed spiraled to each other in waves of madness and tenderness . . .

. . . Then suddenly it changes. Last night he'd ignored her and now as they wake, she sees a different tension in his body. She moves close into his chest, longing for his warmth, but instead cold hands take her and draw her down the stairs. His key opens the lock of a tiny apartment filled with shelves of cobwebs and tearing costumes of the ballet and matted wigs and tubes and jars of makeup of every color and consistency. Sunlight streams through the broken window panes between the smear of blackness lighting thick diagonals of dust . . .

. . . She watches Luíz's dark Gypsy eyes rim with a fiery red as they lock to hers. He holds her wrists tight, bruising them and forcing her down to the floor . . . His hands are like ice. Panicked, she tries to stand, but he holds her wrists in the handcuffs of his own, pressing her down further till her hair slides in the dust. His eyes stare down overpowering her, boring into her mind . . . No! this couldn't be . . . it must be a nightmare

... only the dream ... this is her lover, her tender Luíz ... yes, it's only for the moment, and soon it will be over ... He caresses her cheek gently now, and the blond hair streaked with black dust, and she knows she was right ... "My love," his voice is a breath, allowing her to her knees and his eyes force further into her and she accepts their will, hypnotically compelled, feeling herself becoming eager to follow anything that will unfold before her ... He continues to stare down at her until she feels her last trace of fight leave her ... He allows her to rise, she stands, drawn only to the world of the dark Gypsy eyes ...

... Luíz takes a yellow silk matador's cape from the burdened shelves and wraps it around her. Her clothes fall away by her own hands under it. He wraps a magenta cape around himself, and silently gestures to a high carved table. Trembling, she quickly climbs up to sit on the table and watches the figure of Luíz loom before her in the magenta cape ...

... Luíz stands above her holding a leather belt stretched taut between both hands. She feels the screams rising inside her, but years of practice of holding them back trap them in her throat ... her lover kisses her gently, holding each breast ... his hand moves up to her throat ... soon it will be over ... The belt slashes down across her thighs and she watches red welts rise ... Luíz pulls the yellow cape down around her and buckles the leather tight under her breasts. She watches him cover them with moving fingers and changing rhythms, hears him sucking first one nipple then the other, but all she can feel is the blood burning in her thighs, which excites her more now ... at his command she reaches inside his matador's cape, to mount him, master his wideness, master his mind, but his eyes cruelly laugh at her, pushing her back, and the belt slashes again. She knows her lover has trapped her, but she can only submit ...

... Luíz grips her inner thighs near her groin and stretches her legs wide till she feels a pain that has become a delicious pleasure. She lies back on the cape and watches from a trance as he draws patterns between her thighs with the sharpened end of a white tapered paintbrush. The line between pain and pleasure disappears. When she cannot stand the pain, or is it the pleasure, she moves her lover's head down and he licks her wounds slower and slower, or is it faster and faster, till her pelvis jerks with unrecognizable rhythms from another dimension. He dips the paintbrush into her and uses her wetness to paint circular patterns at the top of her thighs, just stopping where the wounds had been. The paintbrush traces over each wound and moves up her body in patterns of stripes until she's sure she's passed the edge of madness. She throws her head back and stares through the cracked stars of the window and dares not look back as she feels the pointed end of the wand score down the center of her body, and the hot liquid of her own blood spreading in its wake. The feel of the warm blood covers her chest in new stripes, and her throat contracts with new expectations. She looks down, longing to see the red of the blood, but its her lover's whiteness on her chest instead . . .

. . . She sits on her cape, writhing and watching and laughing like a loon while her lover chooses broken jars of blues, lavenders, mauves and pinks that line the shelves. His hand moves down, spreading deep inside her while his other paints her body in formless patterns. Her own chorus of low-pitched sobs that come from a place deeper than she'd ever known before fill the room and she surrenders all of her will to Luíz . . . At his command, she strokes and sucks like a wild creature of the wood, and pulls and teases on her knees, and licks and growls in the dust, and whirls and keeps them both at their pitch of frenzy . . .

. . . She watches, hovering above her own body, as they crawl across the ancient floorboards, Luíz ahead, pulling her with him. When they reach the windows, he mounts her from behind, brutally jamming into her, and baying and grunting with sounds that don't sound human, and she underneath bays and cries even louder until he breaks her in an orgasm of his laughter that isn't laughter at all. Her head will break from this laughter. She snakes across the floor to it, in the dance of light coloring her body through the star-shattered panes above her . . . He holds the strap above her and she knows to become very quiet . . .

. . . Luíz pulls her from the floor, and leads her upstairs. Methodically he bathes her wounds and lays her in the Paisley bed where they sleep until the light changes to deep orange, and they have to prepare for the night's performance. She awakens and carefully buries today under her barrier of pain, saying nothing, for now her lover is tender again.

She wears her barrier of pain around her chest . . . she knows it protects her . . . in a way it is her guard . . . but if ever if faltered, that something else she dreads to know more than death would come through, that something from that other place even deeper inside her than she felt today, would find her screams in its darkness, and she wouldn't be able to stop them . . .

". . . Bethy . . . Bethy . . ." It was Carlos calling to me out of the present of his brightly lit studio.

The dark colors of the pictures in my mind began to be replaced by the sun off the Mediterranean and I realized I must have been standing there for some time.

"Bethy, este mañana cuando yo . . ."

I heard Carlos talking to me and saw him standing in front of me but I couldn't focus . . .

Behind him a couple danced in rain . . . two beautiful young ballet bodies, the girl in lavender chiffon, twirling above the man's head in a one-handed swan, lighter than air, higher still before falling weightless to his shoulders, long tapered legs slowly slithering down the man's back, skimming the floor for just a second in a perfect split before bounding back into the air, suspended again as if she were meant to fly, ecstatically diving into another dancer's arms, her Luíz, her lover, the miss, the fall, how quickly he abandoned her for other dancers who were whole, how she pretended that all was still beautiful.

"Why cry, Bethy?" Carlos was walking toward me. I watched him come into focus and the dancers vanished. "Bethy." Carlos's face was close to mine. The gray eyes were clouded over. He was wearing the black tee ... But he'd been naked ... No, he was fully dressed ...

My eyes became accustomed to the brightness of the studio ... something was different about the rhythm of his walk from before ... The stiff way the arms were at his sides, why were they like that? The raised tense shoulders looked hunched, they'd been sloping, the golden skin of before was pale ... his fingers, that ring, was he wearing it before, a black ring with a pentagram, abstract, but yes a pentagram, why hadn't I noticed it before?

He was almost to me. "Bethy, no cry." The ringed hand rose to my face.

"I must go," I screamed out to this stranger from the Ramblas. What was wrong with me? Why did I come here? Was I out of my mind? Who would know if something happened to me? Who knows what could happen?

"Pleeze ..." Carlos started to put his arms around me. His skin felt like ice.

"No!" And I ran from his studio of angles and light with feelings of danger and death pursuing me. I fled through the garden of lilacs to the courtyard and gate and squeezed through the tiny door into the streets of Barrio Gótico.

I walked and ran, twisting and tripping on my high heels through the cracked cobblestone alleys, until I came onto a big square with buildings and arcades with pillars, lined with the colors of benches and cafés and children chasing and feeding pigeons and I could see the port not far away with its tour boats surrounded by their miles of passengers on the promenade. I stayed at the harbor feeling safety in moving with the crowds, until the glowing orange clouds over the Mediterranean disappeared into the rust-colored mountains of the evening. I left with corners of pictures of Luíz's storeroom drying deep into my skin like the colors of a rotted painting under my polished clothes.

Five

I slept fitfully that night or not at all, afraid to move, yet afraid to lie in one place in the dark. At the first steel gray of dawn, I dared to get up, furtively, and sit at the round table by the window. Turning the brass lamp on low so as not to disturb the night, I wrote down the details of the days in Luíz's storeroom in my journal. I wrote every cruelty, minutely, furiously, allowing myself, making myself feel the pain of his strap, and the pain of Bethy's submission, always hoping against hope it would be the last time. I wrote in fear, spreading words over words, forming a barrier of words. I'd be safe this night, if only I could finish writing it all before morning. The Barcelona sun began to laser its way through the heavy folds of tapestry guarding the windows of my hotel room, lighting up my pages. A secret Pied Piper was calling to unfinished pictures in my mind, and I'd be lured too far to them in the night to turn back. I held the book shut to me before I hid it in the drawer of a carved commode, deep between folds of clothing.

What was happening to me? I couldn't let this happen to me. It was a mistake to come back. But I was here with a major film to produce. I couldn't leave now. Tomorrow I'd be starting my meetings with Studio Goya y Ximínez. I'd planned to spend the day at the Olympic site doing my preparation, analyzing the technical problems of the film. Work . . . my structure and alignment, the one place where I always felt everything was right.

Finally the morning arrived and my workday could begin. The hotel concierge arranged a car for me to the Olympic Stadium at Parque Montjuich. As I rode away from the Ramblas and out of the city, I tried to refocus. The crystal air as we approached Parque Montjuich was a blessing after the hot diesel-filled clamminess of the city. I began immediately to study everything, shots I would need as well as shots I wouldn't, the mountains behind, then a slow pan over the intricate old facade of the stadium entrance that had been completely restored to every detail of its 1920s ornate grandeur. A cut to the emptiness of the new streamlined interior waiting for the millions who would come from all over the world to watch the drama of an ancient spectacle. I made my notes in a different journal than this morning's, a yellow legal pad I filled with the production numbers of my profession. Numbers, a secure cloak I could wrap my mind in.

Seventy percent of my film would be shot at outdoor locations, all the studio shots in Madrid. This would mean enormous technical expenses, logistical problems, especially in a foreign country. In straight columns, in tiny figures, I wrote more numbers on the yellow pad, more calculations. Studio Goya y Ximínez had written me, "We promise you the most generous budget for this film. Our backers will spare no money that you should contract with us." Hadn't they read the reviews for *Firenze* last year that acknowledged me as "showing herself again as the master of shooting brilliant footage on a shoestring"? Didn't they know that my budget for the celebrated *Firenze* was so bare, it was amazing it was shot at all, let alone finished? I'd had to stop the editing in New York until I'd raised enough money through contacts in London to pay off the production bills we'd run up in Italy. But who remembers in the movie business, where fame brings instant money? How long would it take me to get used to the idea that it had happened to me?

I left the Olympic Stadium and went to explore the Palais San Jorge, a brand-new high-tech sports pavilion. An American film company was out front, setting up to shoot. Standing on the side watching, I was both curious as to what film they were shooting and amused at the grandeur with which the big American film companies always did their location shoots. Huge trucks with the latest equipment were parked end to end for the length of more than two city blocks.

The magic inside ring of the film shoot in front of Palais San Jorge was heavily guarded by sassy American production assistants wearing fashionably used blue jeans, throwing their weight around directing the massive lights, dollies, cameras and cherry pickers being hauled off the trucks. One very young woman in very old jeans was yelling instructions to a group of middle-aged Spanish workers unloading the wrong equipment, "No! No oooooo!" she yelled condescendingly for all to hear. "The video playback equipment stays in the video truck." She strutted away brandishing her walkie-talkie with the same bravado as the studio execs strolling by importantly in polo shirts. "Mmmm ... nooo ... ahaaaaa ... Stallone ... Thursday ... mnnnn," the execs were murmuring too low for anybody to hear their confidential deals.

"Get the number two light off," someone shouted. More production assistants marched by, bellowing through crackling walkie-talkies, clutching their clipboards as if they were Original Scripture. "How long is it gonna take you guys to get the fucking number two light off the fucking truck."

"Stand back please," the chief girl repeated condescendingly to the crowds that were gathering all around, some to watch, and some hoping to somehow get into the movie.

How completely different this scene before me was from my own location shoot for *Firenze*. Our crew was so small, nobody stopped to watch what was going on, or considered asking about it. And I, the maker of every important decision, was also in charge of shyly saying, "Please stand back" to the occasional passerby who, thankfully, was interested enough to get in the way.

But this time, with the budget I was being promised for the Olympic film, I'd spare nothing. My crew and my actors would have the same grand trucks and trailers as these Americans of Palais San Jorge. With *Firenze*, we'd had to headquarter our poor actors in the washroom of a sympathetic nearby bar that needed some extra lira. And a little piece of cracked sidewalk had served as my executive offices. Still, I'd stretched my budget to make sure my crew and actors always had the best lunches I could afford, and luckily in Italy the food was always good. But on the Olympic film, I could finally give a crew of my own the same long white-clothed lunch tables as these Americans had set up, with special catering trucks to keep all kinds of specially prepared dishes hot. I openly smiled with satisfaction. Some things are milestones for knowing how far you've come.

"Excuse us, señora." Two Spanish pickup crew members, an electrician and a gaffer on a lunch break, came out of the American entourage of film activity toward me. "We just talking," the gaffer struggled with his broken English. "Ah . . . please don't think we bold, pero . . . we think we know you."

This is crazy, I thought. I only have one commercially important film, and it only now opened in Spain. No, how could they know me?

"It was very long time ago." The gaffer eerily searched my face to make sure he was right.

"It was aquí, in Barcelona." He looked self-consciously to the other. "We work then on film American too. There was a girl working with us, an American, but she live here. Don't think we being familiar to you, but she was girl very nice, work hard, everybody like her."

I froze. "No! It wasn't me." They were probably wrong. It

was a different girl they meant. Other Americans had worked here too.

"Sorry to disturb you, señora." The gaffer pulled the other away with him, embarrassed. "See," he began to argue with his friend in Spanish. "I told you it wasn't her. The other girl was different, so thin, a dancer."

They went back to their group, but I could hear them. I could understand them.

"I tell you it's her. Look at the doe's eyes."

"There's more than one woman with doe's eyes in America. Why would she lie?"

"Don't you remember what happened with her? So terrible for her."

"No. What happened?" The gaffer sat down on the back of the film truck and opened the paper around his sandwich.

"The bullfighter . . . remember? The hotheaded Gypsy one, crazy for her? Crazy jealous of everybody! All the guys were afraid to go near her."

"Ah . . . yes . . . he was famous too." The gaffer thought for a while, "I remember now because the girls in production always gossiped about him, but she loved the other one, they say, the ballet guy, also a Gypsy, a real bastard to her, they always talked how he beat her, then he followed her all the time and she went back to him. Young people, they crazy."

"Remember that day? They both came to the set. The ballet guy said something to her, maybe about coming back again. So she stayed and talked to him, for just a minute, she's working, busy. But the bullfighter one went crazy about it, grabbed the ballet guy by the neck. Smashed him against a stone wall. So fast! The ballet guy, he's no match for the other. We tried to stop them but the bullfighter was too quick for us. He slammed the other's head into the floor. Blood was pouring from the side of his mouth, the head too, and gushing from the ears. By the time we got the bullfighter off, the ballet guy was like a rag doll."

"Ah, sí, I remember everybody was screaming and the ambulance didn't come. The girl was hysterical, we tried to calm her down, drag her away from his body. She crumpled up like a rag doll herself. She had his blood all over her arms. The police came. We all swore to the police that it wasn't her fault, everybody liked her. She had a kind of innocence."

"I wonder what happened to that ballet guy?"

"The ballet guy died before they got him to the hospital. Something when he hit his head. The bullfighter finally got off. Seems the other one had a knife, tried to stab him. None of us ever saw the knife, but it happened so fast."

"Who knows? He was a famous bullfighter, more popular than ballet dancers. Bigger promoters."

"They said the ballet guy had drugs in him too. Who knows? Wonder what happened to the girl."

"She never came back to work. Not even for her pay."

"She should have come for her pay. Good pay with Americans. And they liked her, it wasn't her fault, everyone knew that."

"She probably went home and married some American." The electrician looked over at me again, "I'll bet you that's her. Not too many people have those same eyes."

"Well, if she married some American," the gaffer said, "it had to be a rich one. She's dressed pretty good. The other one didn't have too much . . ."

The foreman of the American film crew mercifully came around to call his men back to the set, "C'mon hombres, let's work it, I mean, how long can ya take with a sandwich?" The two followed him back into the circle.

I started to rapidly walk away. It had taken me years to stop seeing that day Luíz died, and now it was threatening me again like a hideous creature rising in front of me. I'd hear my own screams, strange screams, child screams that had come to me that day from somewhere else. I'd see Luíz, and the blood pouring from his mouth. I'd put my hands there to try to stop it and the child screams would get louder. But nobody could hear me. I'd be on the floor screaming and screaming as they pulled me away.

"Hey, how're you doin'?" An assistant director ran up behind me, before I could find my way through the last throngs of people. "Remember me? I AD'd for you on that thing in the Grand Canyon two years ago."

"Yes," I said inaudibly, grasping for any thoughts that might push away Bethy's memory.

"I didn't know you were here," the assistant director continued. "Are you working on something?"

"I'm thinking of producing a film here." I started to walk fast again.

"I saw your *Firenze*." He followed a respectful few feet behind me trying to keep up a friendly conversation. "Great! Had everything. The violence was terrific. Bruce Willis is probably jealous."

I stopped. It was no use. The screams whirled in the air around me, and the smell of Luíz's blood began to whirl with it. Nausea made me shiver.

"Great style," the AD persisted. "And who did that neon blue lighting for you?"

"Paola Boninni . . ." Anything, I ordered myself, talk about anything, anything that might calm the panic.

"Real stylish stuff! I'm real surprised I never heard of her. You know, I do a lot of shoots in Italy, I should've run into her somewhere."

"I didn't know her before either. I was lucky." I allowed the assistant director's shoptalk to come through to me . . . verify the present. The filthy sight of Luíz's blood was becoming stronger. I hung on the AD's words, thankful for anything else to grasp.

"You know," the AD added with a wink, "none of us thought you had it in you to make that kind of sharp action film. You're really getting into the mainstream now, I mean, real good, sinister. But you always did those love things?"

"I guess they didn't work for me before . . ." Stay in control, talk about the present . . . Elizabeth.

"I'm glad this one did." He paused. "Say, if you need any help on your new film here, call. Here's my number, I've done a lot of work here and know my way around. Besides," he laughed, "I never refuse work in Spain."

"Thanks." I nodded and continued walking, this time conscious of every step, counting the cracks in the pavement for what may have been miles until I felt the panic fading.

I knew from my first years back in America of fighting to shut Bethy's screams away from me that they would always come back unless I gave myself the right of going back to finish that last day in Barcelona. I walked slowly along the road, allowing myself to see the ambulance taking Luíz away, and Bethy walking away from the film set . . .

. . . It was February, damp and cold. She wore a long brown overcoat with a hood that she could hide beneath. She walked for hours around the city, counting the lines of the pavement, sobbing out loud. She walked to the familiar places and sat studying every beloved cornice of each beloved building. She found a bench on the Ramblas opposite Teatro del Liceo and sat dancing over and over in her mind every step in every ballet she'd shared with Luíz. Every love duet and every practice session until it was etched in her mind.

It was well into the evening and very dark when the festive crowds began arriving at the lit-up old opera theater. Bethy left her bench and walked down the Ramblas to the darkened port and went from ship to ship asking for a job as a waitress on any one going to the States. She left late that night bundled into the shelter of her coat, carrying her smallest bag packed tightly. All her dance clothes and point shoes had to be left behind.

The trip to America seemed endless, but it didn't matter. Time and place were insignificant. When she got home again to America, something or nothing would happen. At night, Bethy lay in the bowels of the ship where the staff slept, breathing the hot chuffs of heat from the engine. She listened to the sea mice chase water beetles across the storage's black-spotted floors. During the day, the smell of the food she served to the passengers who frolicked above in the clean salt air made her sick, and she was thankful for the distractions the illness caused her. Her screams floated around her all the time. But she endured them. Soon they would go away like a terrible illness that must take it's course.

It was hours later when I reached the center of Barcelona. Bethy's screams had finally quieted, but the gnawing inside me would not. Tomorrow I had to be myself again. I stopped at an almost empty restaurant and ordered the kind of big Spanish meal and bottle of red wine that I knew would make me sleep for twelve hours. I ate and drank every bit, not even tasting it, filling myself up, safe drugs, swallowing smoothly. Tomorrow, I couldn't afford to show the personal distractions that I'd learned were deadly in the film business, or to feel any pain that would leave me vulnerable. That would be deadlier.

Six

The Hotel Colón room service knocked on the dot of ten, "Señora, café y las flores," an old man offered, wheeling in a freshly linened cart bearing a pot of life-giving Spanish coffee and three vases holding six dozen elongated black buds. I tipped gratefully, and was closing the door when I began to notice a spicy Eastern perfume. In the warmth of my hotel room the buds were rapidly changing into giant black blossoms. I carefully plucked the engraved note and one velvet bloom from its regiment, then burrowed back into bed to read:

Para Elizabeth,
Bienvenida a Barcelona.
I look forward with great pleasure to our first meeting today at noon at our offices on Paseo de Gracia. If you are free in the evening, I will be honored to have the most talented woman in Barcelona as my guest for dinner in the grand dining room of the Hotel Ritz.
Yours,
Jorge Ximínez, President,
Studio, Goya y Ximínez

I studied the too beautiful flowers in their too expensive vases and the too perfect card. My Hollywood dealings had taught me that no matter how seemingly ideal your film partnership, don't make a move or sometimes even a comment without processing the little things through several possible scenarios first. And my New York dealings had added: everybody's hiding something but it's never what you think.

I admired the tasteful calligraphy the invitation was written in. "Hmmm, Jorge, are you trying to catch me off guard?"

Your British-accented secretary had made a point of denying that you'd be at today's meeting. "Oh heavens no!" she'd clipped. "The meeting in Barcelona is strictly a preliminary for you to meet your creative group. Of course, he will not be there. Señor Ximínez never attends to preliminary matters. He's our senior financial officer and attends only to the larger financial matters. Señor will be in Athens all week at a board of directors meeting."

Bad taste, Jorge, to have her lie like that. But more importantly, what could you gain by it? Maybe to have her reestablish your power? Why would you need to?

Maybe I'd been too anxious to do this film, for my own artistic reasons, and the thought of working here again had drawn me too much, and I hadn't been as careful and meticulous as usual in checking out all the business facts.

No, I'd checked them thoroughly. Through a contact in the investment banking department of an international bank with a branch in Spain, I'd obtained the year-end report of Studio Goya y Ximínez and studied it. Jorge's personal finances were extremely sound as well. My New York staff's research on him had told me that he was also the chief financial officer of a huge worldwide holding company, the parent of his film company. Rethinking it, I could see that a man with these business credentials might have the grand style to send flowers as extraordinary as these black ones with the strange perfume as his business calling card. But still, they made me nervous.

Before leaving New York, I'd watched tapes of the maturely handsome Jorge giving speeches at the Harvard and Wharton business schools during a recent trip to the States. I couldn't help enjoying and being intrigued by the fine proud bearing, impeccable manners, patience and knowledge shown by this man whose enemies repute him to hold first place as supreme shark and most infamous corporate raider. His positions range from an oil and gas development company in the Middle East to a heavy equipment manufacturer in Germany, and a big slice of a French fashion house. A recent headline in a London financial journal read, "XIMINEZ RUMORED TO BE ACQUIRING STOCK OF FRENCH RETAILER" and later that day the company's stock soared on the international financial exchanges. Jorge had been jetting regularly from Madrid to Moscow long before the rest of the world even had a glimmer of how fast the walls of Eastern Europe would come tumbling down and new business opportunities would open up. It was rumored that even before that the astute Jorge X had somehow closed a deal for television advertising in the Soviet Union.

I replaced Jorge's card deep into his black blooms, and began thinking out loud. "Sorry to doubt such an impressive invitation to dinner, Jorge, and such a tiny contradiction of communications, but I've got good reason to be a little paranoid about my business these days. Since the success of *Firenze*, my fast growing company is eyed as a prize by the international film industry; a takeover specialist with your connections could buy up my company's considerable international bank debt, and own both the company and me, providing a perfect American base for your Studio Goya y Ximínez films.

"Or maybe on the other hand this beautiful bouquet is innocent of black business motives and simply the start of another intriguing episode in the life of a powerful male with many adoring female satellites who is obsessed by the conquest of just one more. Please stop here, Jorge, if that's the case. I've already had the firsthand pleasure of how powerful males pursue their females with the same precision, tenacity and guile they would going after a political or business coup, and when they succeed, how merrily they reorganize or discard the captured entity." I stopped speaking.

Games again, pain again. Does it ever stop? It was over six years ago that I finally broke off an almost catastrophic love affair with the French financier Yves Bolanieu, a rival of Jorge X. It's frightening how sometimes even now, thinking of Yves can almost become a sensual experience. Yves was the king of every young woman's older-man fantasies. I glided one of Jorge's black flowers over my breast and down between my thighs. The velvety petals stiffened and moved up into the center, then homed to my clitoris and closed around it. Yves's first kiss had been to my clitoris. But the next morning and always after, he made me earn his going down on me, and each time he made it harder. I was never disappointed with the ecstasy that followed.

Yves had much more than sexual power over me. He came into my life at a crucial point when I was working overtime as a line producer to earn money while simultaneously trying to produce something of my own. A run of bad weather had put me way behind schedule reshooting a difficult sequence on location in the Philippines for a large studio. We'd been going from location to location battered by storms in every one. Every day, the studio back in California would scream at me through our crackling connection, "When?" I could barely make out the voices. "The bills are killing us," they yelled. "The backers are threatening. Just tell us when you'll be finished." I'd hang up and trudge through the mud to alternately bully and beg my crew in their sodden tents in the jungle not to defect. I was miserably wet, mosquito-bitten and desperate along with them. The continued delay made me late, putting difficult financing and production details in place for my first fully independent film. There were other bidders for the rights I wanted, and there was only so much

I could do by fax thousands of miles away in Manila. I was frantic not to lose.

"Let me help you," my new expert businessman boyfriend Yves had offered long-distance. "I'll represent you with the bankers here, chérie," he assured me. "You concentrate on finishing your job there. You're ninety percent done already. We'll talk every day and I'll fax everything for your okay."

Yves was amazing. In no time, rights were secured, loans were taken care of, office space rented, and production staff hired. Accountants and lawyers appeared and met with Yves on taxes and contracts. He even put some of his own money into the film. "Everything is perfect, chérie," he promised me the minute I arrived at JFK. And everything was. "Now you need a well-deserved rest," he said during a romantic dinner the next night. "I have the best idea for you, we go to vacation at my house in Bermuda. There are important people from France coming I want you to meet. They could be very good for you to add more money to your film. I took the liberty of telling them all about it. Chérie, I hope that is well with you."

It was magnificent, in fact it was exactly what I needed. A few weeks later, when the film was under complete control thanks to Yves's incredible managerial abilities, he offered, "Chérie, an important friend's yacht is in Newport. You will love it, but if you have to get back for anything, we get off and take a plane quick from anywhere. If not, you read your new scripts on the boat where the sea is so quiet, I am sure you concentrate better. I wake you early for our sunrise and then I see that you go right to work." It was even better than Bermuda.

As time went by, I became so absorbed by the magical Yves who made everything so easy for me, that I hardly noticed how my hard-earned ego and new film company were being absorbed as well. Only at the last moment, a blessed inner voice pulled me back to reality. Or rather it was the luck of a quiet afternoon in my office. I'd decided to study the books even though Yves's accountants so graciously took care of everything, and it turned out that besides running a film company I was actually involved in some kind of money-laundering operation for Yves Bolanieu's international financial operations.

True, it had been "of extraordinary benefit" to my career as well, a perfectly logical Yves later tried to calm my shock, and maybe I should have been, as he put it, thankful for the artistic opportunities the arrangement had provided me and that I might not otherwise have had, and accepted that none of us were angels that just fell from heaven.

But that wasn't the point. And me of all people, the one whose supposedly unshakable shoulders had been cried on again and again with heartrending laments from my otherwise logical friends who'd blissfully denied to themselves that the men they adored were using them for their own means. Oh yes, and he was married too.

But I always bow my head in thanks and throw kisses to Yves for giving me that painful moment when the reality of what was happening became obvious, and I could then refocus on my film work with the same determination I had always shown in dancing. Discipline is a tool you can always take out, brush off and use to save yourself again. Ironically, this must have also been the moment when I shut the door to the last traces of Bethy.

After Yves, for the next six years my work became everything to me as I learned the craft of developing my own film scripts from my own film vision. I would stay in my loft day after day ordering food in, not allowing myself to be distracted by so much as shopping and cooking. Next I worked to translate my scripts into storyboards. One day a shot of the interior of a car, empty. Tomorrow, revised to a shot with one leg entering and the hands on the wheel, the face missing. I worked on until it was perfect.

I would make myself take Sunday off so as not to burn out, but I was impatient for Monday. There were occasional dates, yes, but only to wear borrowed ballgowns at premium-dollar-a-plate dinners where I could network with the people I'd need to raise enough money to shoot *Firenze*. As soon as I had the bare minimum I started production, which took me out of the insulated cocoon of my loft. Shooting in Italy, I couldn't help but meet attractive men, but if I sensed at any time that something could lead to romance, I quickly took control and discarded them. I couldn't afford the luxury of the pains of coupledom anymore. Six years is a long time for a young woman to not have any romances. But my first money and power earned from the success of *Firenze* was worth it all. And I'd become different. Sounds had become clearer to me, and my vision sharper. Where had my mind been before? And no one could say that I owed my success to some influential husband, boyfriend or otherwise male mentor. When I accepted my Oscar, I gleefully thanked only the Lord.

I shook myself from the past, and pushed the flowers away. Twelve noon was getting closer. For today's meeting I chose a loose, below-the-knee brown suit with a business beige blouse and a smooth leather portfolio for a touch of Wall Street. I jumped into the shower to strategize. Ideas always come to me in the shower, the best when I'm washing my hair.

Think it out carefully, I warned. The Olympic film is the success you need now to ensure your place in the industry, or you could quickly go back to being as unknown as you were before. . . . With this film, you're only interested in the creative elements, that's why you came . . . unless they're perfect, no amount of money can convince you to do it . . . You'll find it all out at today's creative meeting . . . Jorge X and his enormous black blooms are probably romantic ego play, and have nothing to do with anything.

"**Play, Play, Play,**"an inner low-pitched voice urged me. "**Isn't that what you really want? Remember me? Remember dancing? Remember how it felt to soar?**"

I wrapped myself in a plush towel, and took a few more sips of still hot Spanish coffee. On second thought, I decided, the shorter, swingy white linen suit would be a little more chic than the longer loose brown, but I stayed with the business blouse. Long strides carried me out of the Hotel Colón, up the traffic-choked Ramblas, around the grand park and fountains of Plaza de Cataluña, and on to Paseo de Gracia to the place where the blue mosaic sidewalk starts.

Just like walking on Madison or Park Avenue I thought, and felt the morning's anxiety subsiding as I passed familiar glass-facaded buildings that housed giant international banks. The same exorbitant French and Italian designer boutiques lined the avenue, as well as the requisite Benneton shop filled with trendy teens. As many new Mercedes-Benzes and BMWs rode the heavy traffic as the traditional Spanish Fiat and international Fords. Older, serious-looking businesspeople in somber colors walked with fit and trim yuppies wearing designer suspenders under Italian and English suits. Japanese and German tourists brandishing their cameras, and the ever present University of Barcelona students all paraded up and down Paseo de Gracia, in and out of streamlined marble entrances, and past the fantastically curled and spiraled buildings by the famous Barcelona architect Gaudí. Nobody noticed me here, or if they did they weren't taking the time to acknowledge it.

I stopped on the corner of the Grand Hotel Avenida Palace, the Barcelona address of Steven Brandon, and took his card with the telephone number written on it from my purse. What an unfortunate scene in the café yesterday. Should I go in, for just a moment, call up from the house phone, see if I can somehow pick up the pieces?

"Yeah, go ahead," Bethy would have decided without thinking twice. I pictured her walking down this same street on her way to rehearsal at Liceo, already a little late, looking desperately for coffee. She'd swing her dance bag stuffed with its leotards, leg warmers and point shoes, her hair would swing in a long blond braid. **"So you'll be a little late for your appointment,"** she'd reason slyly. **"Big deal. It's not as important as love. You know how you really want love. You could love Steven. He could love you. Remember love? Remember our sunshine?"** But this time, Elizabeth the Woman quickly walked on.

Paseo de Gracia featured a dozen new Barcelona cafeterias and bars with window displays of plates of Spanish tapas alongside pan pizza menus, and a new McDonald's serving wine and brandy. Food isn't expensive in Barcelona, and a good thing too, because the population seems to be always snacking on something or drinking coffee, brandy, soda, agua mineral, twenty-four hours a day. A few more blocks and I came to the quiet part of Paseo de Gracia where an extraordinary mixture of sleek high rises and old European residential architecture lined the boulevard. The most imposing townhouse on the block announced that this was the corporate headquarters of Studio Goya y Ximínez with the initials SGX on a discreet brass plaque.

Inside the entryway, I came face-to-face with one of those little filigree-gated European lifts I'd always feared as not airworthy for Americans. It stood ominously waiting for me, empty, with exposed heavy ropes hung from somewhere high above, and off to the side a carved mahogany banister spiraled up into a dark infinity. "Okay," I deferred to this antique alien vessel, "I'm intimidated. I'm an American who even gets nervous in our own high-tech steel elevators. So please, be gentle with me." The lift properly ejected me on the fourth floor into a salon that took me back several hundred years to the Spain of Velázquez. Four men rose in true courtly style, and with genteel scrutiny thoroughly looked me over. If only I'd stayed with the loose, below-the-knee brown.

Jorge Ximínez moved away from the others and glided toward me with the same dark-suit-and-handmade-shirt dazzle of

Yves Bolanieu. His amber eyes, perfectly straight nose and full mouth hadn't been done justice by the videos.

Jorge bowed with only his head moving, like a prince in a romantic ballet. Peasants always bowed with their whole torso.

I pulled myself together and coolly held out my hand for a firm business handshake.

Jorge X took my hand in his, held it for a moment cocked, in the European manner that a true gentleman displays when he takes the hand of a lady. He touched his lips to my palm, just a hint of moistness.

I replied by glowing my most disarming smile, with the utmost calculated spontaneity. "Señor Ximínez, mucho gusto," I said, warning myself not to say another word. There'd be enough time at dinner to find out all about Jorge. Or should I call Steven instead? Steven? Where did that come from? . . . **"You know how you really want love,"** that voice nagged. . . . **"You could love Steven . . . he could love you. . ."** I panicked, briefly, that they'd know what was going on inside, but they didn't seem to notice anything out of the ordinary. I calmly shook the hand of the next man.

"Elizabeth," Jorge X said, "I'm pleased to present to you, mi buen amigo, your director for the Olympic film, Barcelona's formidable José Alonzo."

Good. It was well know that José was gay. There'd be no further threat to my equanimity.

The director was friendly in this formal setting, wearing a short-sleeved checked shirt. "And this is Sven Jansen," he introduced his quiet, gaunt, and very respected Swedish cinematographer. Film insiders have accurately described this team as two separate halves of the same person, still joined. José is the brain and soul for all their brilliant film innovations, and Sven, the cold technical body that muscles the Brain's ideas. One is never seen without the other. If they are lovers, it would be a case of narcissism. "And this is Paco Cortazar." José went on to introduce the wunderkind screenwriter who'd recently joined them as their protégé. This was the group I'd come to meet today and I gave them my full attention.

"We've admired your work for many years," José was telling me in Spanish, speaking slowly so that I could understand. "Last week, we watched videos of *Tristesse* and of *El Pecado*. Formidable."

"Muchas gracias, señores." I was surprised at the two films he mentioned, early artistic successes but commercial flops that nobody could even find anymore. Even though I'd always been proud of them.

"Ciao," Jorge interrupted to say, gliding away from us toward the lift. "I leave you creative people now, as I have promised Elizabeth." The creases in Jorge X's trousers stayed sharply perfect in motion.

As soon as Jorge left, we began working in earnest. We distributed scripts, and brainstormed on and on and talked of the vision of our film through the serving of lunch, the clearing of plates, and the serving of espresso in delicate cups with tiny carved spoons. We were alive together, we could hardly wait to meet again, set a production schedule, scout locations and start the casting. At seven P.M. without anybody having taken the traditional afternoon siesta break, we decided to stop for the day.

"Elizabeth," José explained to me in his best English, "we modern Spanish taking our siesta after work now. No more in afternoon. We dine very late. Ten-thirty. We stay much later. True! We enjoying the nightlife in Barcelona."

We laughed and kissed goodbye on both cheeks. Friends already, in addition to being colleagues. We were sure the Olympic film would be the best of everyone's career. We all piled into the lift and descended to a still sunlit early evening.

My taxi crawled through bicycles, pedestrians and thick traffic exhaust back to the Hotel Colón, as the driver added to my recollection of the language with the choicest four-letter words.

Finally, we arrived. I was at the front desk in a flash. Messages? None from Steven? I opened the door to my suite, grabbed the phone and dialed his number.

"Hello, this is Steven Brandon," the familiar plane voice answered.

But at the sound of it, I was sure that anything I would say would be wrong.

"Hello, Hello? Is anyone there?"

I hung up as quickly, hardly believing I hadn't the nerve to speak, and busied myself rearranging Jorge's black bouquet.

Jose's "modern Spanish" siesta sounded right, but yesterday's events had brought up too much of the past in me too quickly. I couldn't take the chance of dreaming, especially with a dinner meeting scheduled with Jorge later on. I needed to take one of the emergency quick unwind pills I still carried with me but rarely used anymore. With a vodka and soda from room service on top of one, if I dreamt, I'd sleep so soundly that I'd never remember ...

... **Bethy is giggling ... Daddy makes another funny face and she squeals with laughter. Such a funny story about the tree outside her bedroom window so it wouldn't frighten her at night anymore ... "Come, my Bethy Dolly," he says and removes her white robe for the bath ... Marya is crying. Lately she always cries at bathtime. It used to be so much fun for the three of them.**

"Please don't cry, Marya," Bethy tries to console the delicate young woman, confused ... "Why are you crying, Marya?" Marya only puts her arms around the naked Bethy.

But Daddy won't let her. He pushes Marya into a corner of the bathroom. "Please don't do that, Daddy," Bethy pleads for her. Daddy is smiling and feeling the water, making sure it is just the right temperature for his little girls.

Bethy jumps into the bath, but Marya won't go. Daddy starts to yell at her in Russian.

This time, Marya dares to yell back at him, "Don't touch her, stop it . . . I die" . . . and then more, in Russian . . .

Daddy stands perfectly still, staring her more into the corner until she seems to go limp. He lowers his voice to her in Russian, still staring at her . . . she obeys him and walks to the bathtub. He's holding his crystal glass of brown liquid and dips his finger into it and puts some on Bethy's tongue . . . It burns her throat and makes her cough . . . She is coughing and laughing, and splashing in the warm bath . . . Beautiful classical music floats into the bathroom, and Marya is quiet next to Bethy in the water.

"My little girls," Daddy purrs to them both. His soapy hands smooth all over Bethy's body, her chest and stomach. "My special girl," he coos to her. His sudsy hands move down between her legs . . .

. . . Oooh, such warm sensations. "You're tickling me, Daddy," she shyly pulls away.

Marya becomes wild again and grabs Bethy away from Daddy. She slips through his long soapy fingers and hits her shoulder on the tub. Marya tries to get out of the bathtub and pull Bethy with her.

"Bitch, Bitch," Daddy yells at Marya and grabs her by the hair, forcing her back into the water. Daddy's face becomes redder and he pushes Marya's head under the water. She goes so easily. Somehow, she doesn't struggle anymore, the water is still.

"Please let her up, please please." Bethy is pulling on Daddy's arm. "She didn't mean it. She's sorry."

Bethy is begging him. "Let her up." Marya is too still. Oh please God, let her up.

Daddy lets her up, she is crying very low, and choking back her cries at the same time. She looks terrified. Bethy doesn't dare move.

"My little girls," Daddy begins to coo again and soap Bethy again between her legs as if Marya's outburst hadn't occurred. Bethy rubs soap on Marya's back to make her feel better . . .

. . . Daddy finishes drying Bethy and leads her to a table filled with little cakes he has bought especially for her. "Come my favorite girl, show Daddy how his little ballerina can split her legs so wide, and then you can have all the cakes you want."

Of course she would do her splits for Daddy, even without the cakes, but he loves her so much he wants her to have the cakes as well. She will make him proud. Bethy lies down on the bed and splits her legs wide while Daddy feeds her the delicious sweets . . . Oh how wide she can split. This night would be so wonderful if only Marya weren't so sad. Daddy is feeding her cakes now too. Maybe Bethy was mistaken about what happened in the bath . . . yes, that is it . . . she was mistaken . . . mistaken.

. . . Marya is crying again. "Why are you crying?" Bethy begs her.

But Daddy answers instead. "Because she is afraid that you will tell someone how much I love you, how I bathe you and touch you. You see, in Russia, it is different. Daddies don't love their little girls like I love you. Daddies only work, and can never play with their little girls. Marya is afraid they will find out in Russia if you tell. She is so frightened they will make her leave us and go back. Then they will punish her there. Please Bethy, promise me, you will never tell, for Marya's sake."

"No, no, Marya, I will never tell," Bethy weeps. "Don't leave us. I love you so much. No, I'll never tell, never, never . . . never . . . never, never."

But Marya cries more. Daddy is walking toward her. Marya is cringing.

"She thinks you will tell, Bethy."

"Never . . . never, I won't tell, Marya . . . I promise, I promise, I won't tell . . . never. I love you Marya. Never!"

Marya is quiet now . . . so still, she is hardly there . . . like a ghost . . . Daddy is brushing Marya's hair now, brushing it over her shoulders . . .

Seven

At nine thirty that evening I arrived at the door of the Ritz dining room to honor Jorge X's invitation to dinner. I'd decided to match the flamboyance of his black blooms calling card of this morning by going all out for it myself. I wore the Paris-bought black strapless fantasy, covered with its demure bolero jacket. "Madame, follow me please," the tuxedoed maître d' carefully averted his eyes from the spun silver rose at my hip, which drew the ruffles up to a side slit, exposing my outer left thigh between the silk when I walked. I wore almost no makeup but I'd swept my hair up to highlight the long diamond earrings Yves Bolanieu had presented me with at dinner at the Ritz in Paris. This time it'll turn out very differently, I chuckled to myself. Who knows? Maybe I can play the takeover game myself. Studio Goya y Ximínez would be an ideal European base for me. Yves Bolanieu will turn green.

We arrived at a table in a secluded corner. Jorge X had carefully planned his seating so that a clever theatrical backlighting erased every line in his face, and softly colored and lifted the slight sag of the jawline that comes with age. In this magical lighting there wasn't a hint of a crow's-foot or dark circle, just beautiful tight young skin. With his solid youthful body and agile movements, Jorge looked thirty-five instead of fifty-five, but he'd still kept the polish and dignity that takes fifty-five years of sophisticated living to acquire—the eye of this type of gentleman rests on the ankle, not the thigh.

Imagine how this Hollywood lighting is transforming me, I mused. In my mind's mirror, the years disappeared from my own face as well, and Bethy's pinky smooth one with the wide-spaced eyes took center stage, under the dancing chandeliers, wearing the lipstick color she called magenta, the face of a daring ingenue who would one day be a business star, tonight being showered with attention by the fabulous Prince of Business.

The Prince rose and took my arm, breaking into my thoughts with a slight British accent, "How beautiful you shine tonight, mi Elizabeta. Please, sit down. Allow me the joy of your company." One had to admit how appealing it was, the way he called me "Elizabeta."

Two handsome waiters meticulously adjusted my crimson velvet chair while two more stood at adoring attention. A fifth brought a fresh bottle of champagne.

Yes, I was definitely in Jorge's territory. The whole room reflected him ... brilliant, mature ... irresistible. Jorge beamed and toasted me, "To the most beautiful and talented woman in Barcelona. Please, grant me my one desire that we become good friends."

I raised my glass to his, copying a bit of his flourish myself, "Mi buen amigo, salud, amor y pesetas y tiempo para gustarlos," My good friend, health, love and money and time to enjoy them.

Jorge drank down his vintage Mumm's too quickly. Was I making him nervous?

The langostinos were brought in surrounded by an intricate ice sculpture. I took a tiny sip of my champagne, then cracked open one of the pink-shelled creatures on my plate and put a delicate piece of white flesh into my mouth. Jorge followed my lead. Eye-to-eye we rolled the luscious morsels around in closed mouths, without moving a muscle ... studying each other ...

Jorge X drank a more controlled sip before he spoke. "I am a great fan of your work. Such inner energy, a thoroughbred heart, but I like the quiet ones the best. For me they are like the quiet engine of a collector Rolls-Royce speeding on an open road. The movie audience becomes spellbound."

"What an unusual and beautiful compliment, Jorge. Thank you very much." We sat eye-to-eye for another moment. When I raised my glass again, I was surprised to see I'd drunk more champagne than I remembered. I put down the glass. "I'm a great admirer of your work too, Jorge. I recently saw a tape of your lecture to the Harvard graduates. I remembered it. Your audience was spellbound too."

Although our setting looked distinctly like romance, our conversation stayed strictly on business, with Jorge doing most of the talking. He actually knew very little about the day-to-day of filmmaking. He had great appreciation of it, but his other interests had kept him away and he insisted that Juan Goya was the force and talent behind Studio Goya y Ximínez. Jorge and Juan were friends from boyhood, and Jorge had put up new financing for Juan's company two years ago as a favor. Juan had made many excellent films for years, but they'd been on a smaller scale. When he'd acquired the rights for this one, Jorge had suggested from a business point of view that they ask me to work on it with him. Juan had been extremely enthusiastic from his artistic point of view. Now everybody was sure it would be a great success. "Actually," Jorge admitted, "I know very little about the script except that Juan says it is excellent and perfect for you." Jorge's British schooling was obvious on the word "actually," and it fit him beautifully. This Jorge was dynamite.

With this out of the way Jorge X proceeded to give me a complete rundown of his own industrial businesses, where his expertise was. They were certainly fascinating, but why was he going out of his way to give me his résumé like this? . . . Well, people do talk about what they do . . . and the extraordinary flowers this morning did say romance . . . maybe it was his way of impressing me . . . I was impressed. At least he wasn't interested in my film company, he hadn't asked a question, or really known what questions to ask. I had to be careful, but I was beginning to like him.

Our first course lasted almost an hour. Finally the last of the langostinos were removed and the pheasant consommé was served with another wine by a corps of waiters in svelte black tails. I watched Jorge X sip the hot soup. He blew on it in the exact way Yves did. His lips looked soft, and the cleft in his strong mature chin looked even sexier. Did they go to some same international business hunk finishing school?

Jorge moved closer to me. It was only by a decorous hair, and his enthusiasm permitted it. "Elizabeta, I have a wonderful idea, next week I must go to Paris on some business—for only a few days—and after, why not we meet there? I have a superb apartment on Avenue Foch, that is never used. You would be most comfortable there. Then we go to Athens, and I show you Athens like you've never seen Athens."

Now you never know how these things are offered but I took the most obvious, that the nitty-gritty of romance had started. "I . . . don't think I can," I answered.

"Oh come come. Greece is more beautiful than you can imagine this time of year, the countryside and the little villages, you cannot imagine. The streets are so narrow that you put out your arms in the middle and you touch the buildings side to side. And the people, so warm, so wonderful, they invite you into their homes for foods like you never had. But before that we meet in Paris and enjoy its charisma a little too, before it gets too hot and too many tourists come there. We visit the opera and the designers in Rue Faubourg St. Honoré. You shop, it is not a problem, I have accounts, my gift for the film's success with you."

"It all sounds wonderful, Jorge. And believe me, I love Paris, and thank you for your generosity, but I'm afraid I don't have an extra minute to interrupt this project, because I'll have to return to the U.S. in a few short weeks. To be honest, if you want to make money on your investment in this film, it's far more important for you that I get right to work."

"I already have money." Jorge said it very slowly and all enthusiasm left him with the words. "Money never makes any man happy. People find love so much easier without it. 'One' is the loneliest word for a rich man, even should it mean one hundred million, if he cannot share his beautiful things with a beautiful woman . . . especially one I've waited too long to meet." He sat back and ordered another bottle of wine. His eyes showed a surprising longing.

Had he meant woman, generically, or was it specifically me he'd wanted to meet? Almost on cue, the corps of waiters, together, looked to Jorge as though promising as loyal male consorts that they would go the limit to help him win his lady to France and Greece.

Jorge continued, seeming to gather some strength from them. "I'd so hoped you'd say yes, Elizabeta. I too watched tapes of your interviews, as you saw mine. We both were interested without meeting each other. There was something that made us watch again. I know I should not confess this, but already yesterday I canceled meetings in New York and flew here when Juan said you were coming today. I do not watch often."

It was hard to believe that Jorge Ximínez could cancel any meetings anywhere after that complicated geographic list of his businesses, but still I was beginning to feel flattered by it.

"Elizabeta, do you not want to go to Paris with me because you don't feel right about being with a man who is still married?"

Almond eyes were telling me with all their manhood that they wanted me to say, "Yes, yes, that's it, of course. What other reason could there possibly be?"

I said nothing.

Jorge looked more despondent. "In Spain, you know, we cannot divorce so easily as you. We are a Catholic country. The marriage will stay for name and family only. My wife and I both understand and respect this. I know it is hard for you American women to understand this, and you become suspicious."

I don't know why I felt I had to protect Jorge's ego from my rejection, but I did, I guess women always feel that way about a man's ego, especially a proud man, so I said, "But, Jorge, I wouldn't like to fall in love with a married man, and with you that could be a real danger."

Jorge looked easier. His ego was safe. It was only morality in the way. I felt less guilty. The endive salad was placed before us. The ceremony of its dressing and saucing smoothed the moment.

"You surprise me a little, Elizabeta. Meeting you in person, you are so much more soft, simpática, than in the television interviews. There you seem only to talk about work. Work, work, all the time work."

"Is that why you talked about work before, Jorge?"

"Yes, it is. I wanted you to be comfortable."

"I didn't mean to give a stern impression, but you know how you've got to be careful in those interviews. If you say anything personal, they edit it to all come out differently."

"There was one question though that you are very clever to never answer," Jorge said, "and I think that probably every man in the world cannot help but wonder. Why is it you never married? I am sure there have been many opportunities."

"It depends what you call opportunities."

"Bolanieu?"

The way he'd said Bolanieu had an air of insult in it for all Frenchmen. So Yves made him lose his manners too. We had that in common. "Especially not Bolanieu," I answered, and perversely enjoying the jealousy Jorge couldn't help displaying in the almond eyes, added, "Although it can't be denied that Yves Bolanieu is one of the world's great lovers."

A triangular procession of tuxedo-tailed pages wheeled in the chateaubriand armed with all sorts of silver servers and flaming braziers and placed it before us. We sat regally as three waiters with white gloves carved and flamed and sauced and served, then left us to enjoy our feast of tastes, smells, beauty and each other. Jorge robustly addressed his chateaubriand and I became equally involved in mine. For a while we almost forgot about each other in the savor of the meal. When the last tidbits were being pushed around on our plates, our attention turned again to the room and each other. Like two sated fat cats, who have found the best seats in the house, we lazily sank into our crimson thrones. The Armagnac was poured.

Jorge X studied me again before he spoke. "I have a dear friend who has been such for a long time, also a very successful woman. You remind me of her."

"In what way?"

"She holds herself very much like you. She is a fine worldrenowned dancer."

"What kind of a dancer?"

Jorge immediately caught my interest in the word "dancer." "Mercedes is one of the most famous flamenco dancers, fiery, talented, intelligent, exquisite . . . She grew up with Gypsies in Sevilla, and studied with the great dance masters in Madrid. Her flamenco technique and sensuality are renowned in all of Spain among all the aficionados. I would like for you to meet each other."

"I would like to meet her."

"Mercedes and her husband are both influential and interesting people in every way, and proud people. Of course they are married, but her husband, Rodolfo Ceballos, is bisexual. And

Mercedes? She is the finite creature of the artistry you see in her dancing. Neither is limited by the conventional."

"But they are married? That is conventional."

"Mercedes and Rodolfo are soul mates who will always come back to each other to dance and choreograph for their company. They have been married for fifteen years. Still it is yet another kind of love. They had a child, a boy, but he died of meningitis. He would have been ten years old. Rodolfo and Mercedes were profoundly sad for a long time. Rodolfo told me she'd never be the same, but then it changed. They opened a small flamenco nightclub to distract themselves from the tragedy, and formed their own flamenco ballet as well. She became an even greater artist. You can see I know her well. Tonight I will take you to her club, Las Cuevas, to see them dance. Las Cuevas is just outside of Barcelona."

"I'd love to see them dance."

"And Mercedes would love to meet you very much too, and to know about your work. I know that. Another woman of great talent as independent as herself with no need to crawl into her space. She hates people who try to crawl into her space. She is like a cat that way."

"You make her sound a little ominous."

"No, she is very kind and very respected by all in Barcelona for her generosity as well as her artistry. She will offer to help you with many things of the film you might otherwise have trouble with, and she can. That is how Mercedes is."

I couldn't help thinking how suspicious of Jorge my New York friends would be. That city makes you distrust everything. Just last week at our girls' night out in New York, there were all kinds of confirmed stories of trickery. "Puleeze!" the Beautiful Mateless Supergirls would've warned me here, "these elegant Continental guys love a ménage. They're always trying for it." But if Jorge's thoughts were running ahead to two women delicately sucking each other's nipples in all kinds of positions, nothing of it was displayed in his face. Jorge had proven himself to be considerate and intelligent and intriguing.

And there wasn't any danger of my falling in love with him, at least not anymore. I admit intense sexuality flared from him, romance too, but not the true love I craved. It would be only a battle of wills. Jorge sipped his Armagnac, and as if in answer, gently brushed aside my Yves Bolanieu diamond earrings. His hand rested on the back of my neck. I was reminded of a lion and lioness I'd once seen mating on a shoot in Africa. When they were finished, the powerful male ever so gently bit the back of his lady's neck.

The check came and Jorge grasped my hand as we left the Ritz dining room. Yes, I'd stayed just long enough at this party and it was time to leave before things became less smooth. Jorge saw my mood change and rushed to pick up the moment, gallantly gliding me to the door where his silver Rolls-Royce awaited in true princely mode. The feel of the soft Barcelona night was all around us. "I must go," I said. "But what have I done?" he asked. "It is still early and I thought that you do want to see Mercedes dance, do you not?"

"Yes." I had to agree to that. "I'd love to see them dance. But perhaps not tonight."

"Ahh, Las Cuevas is beautiful and her flamenco company is magnificent. They are the most artistic in all of Spain. And they leave for tour soon. Once your work starts for you, you may not have the chance again."

That was true. If I came in two hours later tonight, it would be all right, but later it would be disastrous.

Limo doors were opened, we settled in, and the fountains of Plaza de Cataluña receded behind us.

"Unaccountability," Bethy's voice whispered in the rush of their waters.

Close to Jorge in the enclosed darkness of the limousine, the aura of raw maleness beneath his mature cover of stature intensified. It would have been hard for any woman to resist him. He wrapped me in his arms, and the way the man kissed was an experience in itself.

"You are my prize, my flame," Jorge X whispered as he began to undo the zipper of my dress. For now, this master of seduction techniques had won, the most innocent places became the most erotic under the slow hands of this more experienced lover. It was obvious why so many famous women were mad for him.

"Unaccountability," Bethy's voice inside urged closer, and my light silk dress became a weight too heavy to bear. I leaned back halfway on a huge Oriental cushion and put my leg through the slit. **"Yes!"** She approved the move she recognized as her own.

But after a half hour of passionate kissing and moving of hands over bodies under the softness of both silk and finely woven trousers, Jorge X moved away from me, and sat quietly, looking composed and handsome in the light from the little limousine bar. For all his display, the truth was that Jorge X hadn't been able to raise an erection.

Was it the alcohol, or could it be that Jorge was really sexually impotent, as many powerful middle-aged men can be, those same men who always arrive in public view with the most beautiful women on their arms, preferably two and very young, besides being married to some other seemingly content beauty who is at home with his beautiful children of several years ago. Bethy was often one of the girls on the arm, enjoying the nightlife and restaurants, and courting compliments. What do these men feel beneath their show of sexuality? What must it be like for them to admit nature's cruel trick of aging to themselves, when their whole male being seems to be tied up with showing the world their conquests of women? It makes the other men fear them more.

But Jorge wasn't upset. In fact, he seemed quite pleased with himself, his fantasy and image were his climax and satisfaction. Triumph was his. After all, didn't he have one more famous woman passionately wanting him to make love to her?

"Cariña," Jorge was saying, softly, "I will show you the true meaning of love in so many other ways. You see how I am the man you must love." Sitting more proudly straight than before, he leaned back against the plush leather of the car.

We rode through the night shadows of the trees watching giant stars that never changed their position in the sky. The wines were clouding my senses, and I laid my head on his chest. I don't know how long it was before I felt Jorge lovingly brushing my hair over my shoulders. "Elizabeta," he lowered his voice to me as if the night itself might overhear, "you cannot know how long it is since I have known these real feelings I have for you. My only desire is that you should love me. Only with you can I be a whole man again. Please, come with me to Paris."

The car turned into a pitch black road. I sat perfectly still, not knowing how to console the churning of opposite feelings that I could feel unlocking in the man beside me in the darkness, not daring to move lest I tip their balance.

The gravel of the parking lot of Las Cuevas began to crunch under the wheels of the silver Rolls-Royce and we heard the distant sounds of flamenco guitars and castanets. Jorge directed the driver and straightened his tie. The churning stopped. He poured himself a scotch and drank it quickly with another on top. His Ritz dining room confidence returned, edged with an arrogance now. "Cariña," he said to me, "I cannot wait to introduce you to my extraordinary Mercedes and for you to see her dance tonight. You see for yourself how beautiful she is. Once we make love together with the Argentine actress María del Cardo. They both have supple bodies of angels that stretch to all positions."

"And you?"

"Formidable," he boasted.

I forgave his boasting.

We entered Las Cuevas just in time to see Mercedes's arched profile silhouetted on stage, in a dramatic dim light, hat to hip, blazing ruffled skirts falling to the floor around her. Nothing could be heard except the two flamenco guitarists seated in a dark corner of the stage, softly playing their rhythms and chanting their mournful notes.

I thought Mercedes saw us in the back of the club as she began speaking to the audience slowly in Spanish, "I dedicate this piece, *Tangos*, to my friend and lover and husband, a consummate artist of the world whose work is joyful and inspiring."

Everybody cheered in dedication to Rodolfo and we looked for a seat in the dark.

Mercedes swept across the stage, back arched, skirts trailing behind, dark eyes slyly looking out from under the hat's brim, the rhythms of her castanets tantalizing the audience to come along with her to the heights or depths of her passion. Immediately, the flamenco guitars were accompanied by the audience's staccato clapping, which built in wild unison as the lights came up and Mercedes took control of their collective emotions. Body and skirts and tasseled shawl swirled. Her castanets seduced them with perfect rhythms. Then everything ceased to stillness until her razor-sharp execution of intricate heelwork made her audience gasp. Artist and audience became one.

"Bravísima, Bravísima." The audience went wild, rising and cheering as Mercedes swept the stage again, the arched male dancers in black pursuing with long strides on their knees behind her. Her strength fired the stage, and the men rose to fire back at her, slapping their thighs with their hats. They stood in a line, hands to their waists as she circled each. Eye-to-eye, her castanets talked of love and her body talked of desire.

The guitars changed to clear high notes, pulling Mercedes away from the men to bend and dip along the front of the stage, her fluid arms dancing a dance of their own.

Fire again! Hats over eyes, the men stomped in a chorus from the side of the stage, answering each challenge of Mercedes's heel rhythms with their own, until her head threw back and she finished *Tangos*, spent, on her knees, covered by her tasseled shawl.

"Bravísima!" The audience exploded again with applause. I remained in my seat, ecstatic to be seeing this perfect dancer before me.

After the performance, Jorge and I visited Mercedes backstage. I was amazed at what a petite and bubbly person she was. On stage, she'd appeared very tall, intense, a giant. She'd worn a classic chignon hairpiece and arched flamenco posture, but now she had a short cropped haircut with shiny black spit curls that punctuated her dark eyes and elfish high cheekbones, and she had a young easy way about her. Only in one small section of the performance had I seen the playfulness and warmth of the real Mercedes I was seeing now.

"Mercedes Ceballos," she introduced herself, holding out her hand and eagerly wanting to know everything about my film and my trip here. "I wish you such good luck in our Spain," she told me in a throaty voice with the most charming occasional crack. "If you need anything at all that I and my husband, Rodolfo, can give and help with, please, please ask. Shoot here at Las Cuevas. We make everything available for you. We will dance in your film. No pay! We don't care. We dance our flamenco for love."

Shortly afterward we left. "Jorge," I told him during the ride back to the city, "your stories about Mercedes and María del Cardo are admirable fantasies. But you shouldn't involve her."

He raised his glass to me and didn't answer.

*E*ight

Jorge flew to Paris that week, alone. This time a small bouquet of lilacs informed me of his departure with a calligraphic note declaring, "Elizabeta, live romance with me." Poor Jorge, he made me sad, that split between his feelings and actions.

Those of us in Barcelona couldn't wait to start working on our film. Our whole group now included José, Sven, Paco, me, and Jorge's partner, the quiet intellectual filmmaker, Juan Goya. Juan and I had already had many transatlantic conversations. We carefully went over the production needs we'd discussed, and the budget we'd have. It was glorious. Finally, I would have my own project with a big enough budget to do everything right.

José, as director, was as excited as I when he called to set up our location scouting. I told him, "We can start immediately" and immediately he showed up, wearing orange and yellow striped bermudas, a bright blue polo and well-worn sandals. The tall, gaunt and silent Sven followed at his side in old faded jeans and a blackish tie-died shirt. It was Sunday and off we went to an ancient Spanish square where José and I danced the sardana with the local people while our perfectionist Sven never stopped studying camera angles. Then back to the beautiful red-clay heights of Parque Montjuich, where we took our Polaroids of the restoration of the original facade. Arm in arm, José and I almost skipped through the gardens of Costa i Llobera and around the fountain planning the shots we would take at night when it was illuminated. Sven walked behind us, silent, documenting everything we considered with still more Polaroids.

We drove to Tibidabo, five hundred feet above sea level, and looked out to the Pyrenees, the sea, and the distant island of Mallorca. Lush blue and green surrounded us. "Elizabeth," José said, "we'll have to shoot in Mallorca."

"Fine, fine," I agreed.

"And," José continued, "Sven will want to work with Fernando Colidos, the lighting director, to make sure it is right. Also more expensive but worth it."

"I think we can manage it," I approved confidently.

"Also there is art director and a costumer who I want you to see work of. Expensive, but . . . formidable! If we could?"

"We could," I readily answered, I was beyond happy.

Toward evening we left for Sitges, a nearby seaside resort where Sven and José had a house. The plan was for Paco, our young screenwriter who hadn't come location scouting with us, to meet us at the house and we'd all stay for a few days to do more development. As we drove up the driveway, two magnificent white collies bounded down toward us to greet their masters with paws on shoulders, little whines of happiness and giant licks. Paco walked behind them, wearing thick glasses, dressed in light beige chinos and loafers without socks.

"Ah, look how Paco look so serious as usual," José nudged the quiet Sven.

José and I had already jumped out of the car and were playing with the dogs in our mutual excitement. "Don't look so serious, Paco," José said. "This film will be the best of all our careers."

"But against the odds." Paco wouldn't cheer up.

"So young to be a pessimist already." José laughed, and gave his protégé a hearty hug.

Paco pulled away and started talking too rapidly in Spanish for me to follow. When he finished, José looked deflated, turning to me with his head down and translating that it seemed that Jorge Ximínez had lied to all of us. He had neither the financial backing for the film nor the ownership rights he'd claimed, even though he'd presented contracts.

We were in shock as the dinner guests José and Sven had invited to meet me arrived. Today's rumors about Jorge fired through the cocktail banter and snatches of conversations spread from group to group . . . Jorge was overextended in his real estate holdings . . . he owed millions . . . the political disruptions in the Middle East had destroyed his oil interests there . . . the man of the hour was barely holding his own . . . his position was deteriorating rapidly. And to complicate matters, it seemed a French banking syndicate owned half the rights to the Olympic film. They were threatening to sue Jorge for his half of the rights if he defaulted on his half of the money. They'd had an offer for the full rights from a new bidder who seemed determined to win it away from Jorge at any price. No, the dinner guests didn't know who the new bidder was, only that he was an old customer of that bank in Paris.

Jorge's black bouquet and all his romancing became suddenly, painfully clear. I remembered his soft eyes as he said, "Elizabeta, next week, I go to Paris. Come with me." Jorge was using me, using my new fame and my American company to front his financing for the film with his French bankers. "Then we go to Athens." He'd had the nerve to say, "I show you Athens like you've never seen Athens." Sure Jorge, sure! And now, what nerve, this new love note, "Elizabeta, live romance with me." To think, I'd felt sorry for him. I should've remembered how sneaky guys can get when they're impotent. So much for "Play, play, play," Bethy.

Well at least it was interesting that he'd been that sure he could use my name to secure his financing for a film this big that he'd presented contracts to us. I'd amused myself with the thought that I could finance it myself, but really hadn't taken the prospect that seriously. What he had done gave me confidence, and I felt that old energy of the fight.

José and Paco urged me on. "We have to do it anyway," they said. "It's too good not to. What was money to this opportunity?" José began to get excited. "We are artists, are we not? This is love, is it not? If we are committed, the money for the film will come."

It seemed my new colleagues were as crazy as me. We vowed to hold tight and continue our preproduction until we knew for sure what Jorge's situation was. It could all be just a rumor. At the same time, I would begin to investigate the actual situation at the French bank, figure out how much financing I'd need to outbid their French bidder, and where it might come from. Would they lend it to me? If not, where else could I get it? Maybe another banking syndicate? If that were possible, I would become the sole producer of the film, taking my chances, for failure or success. José, Sven and Paco would take limited chances by working for only a small percentage of profits when, and if, we had them. We would have to use a minimum crew, and do all the design work ourselves. "Just like *Firenze*," we agreed. After all, it wasn't any different for any of us, we were used to it . . . and, if we were successful . . .

"We go to Mallorca to look for locations anyway." José had another idea. "We will not change that, we take a boat, is not too expensive, and we stay at the house of a good friend of mine there, an actor, it doesn't cost us anything, we go first thing tomorrow morning."

We said goodbye to the last guest and sat down to finish cementing our plan around a leftover cornucopia of food and wine. We were becoming giddy from being up since early dawn, when Mercedes telephoned. I hardly recognized her voice, it sounded so different. The throatiness and its occasional crack were gone and a higher pitch was in its place. Mercedes had transformed herself again.

"Elizabeth, you must be the guest of Rodolfo and me for our most magic night in Barcelona," she almost sang. "It is the five-year anniversary of our Club las Cuevas."

"I'd love to be there, thank you for thinking of me, but I don't think we'll be back from Mallorca in time. We're leaving tomorrow, but we'll have a lot of work to do there."

"Please you must come, oh please," she pursuaded as tenderly as one might a shy child. "Please do not refuse. This is the most important night for Rodolfo and me."

"Thank you so much but I don't know. We'll try our best," was all I could promise.

"All the celebrities of Spain will be there, the bullfighters, the artists, the aristocracy. I will introduce you to everybody, and we will have an especial paella, and drink the finest Riojas."

"I—"

"Please say yes," she cut me off.

"I wish I could," I assured her, "but I can't promise."

"If you come, I will dance my new solo that Rodolfo has specially choreographed for this night," she bribed me. "If you come, I dedicate it to you. I call it *La Gitana*."

At the end of her description of the extravagant festivities, she added, "I wish I could give you all some of my good luck. I am so sorry to have heard the rumors today that the Olympic film may be canceled before it begin. So sorry I am for my dear friend Jorge, for his bad luck, and for you, my new friend, Elizabeth."

"You've heard wrong," I assured her. "The Olympic film is more on than ever or we wouldn't be going tomorrow."

"Well maybe, you will make it back from Mallorca anyhow, some way. I will send you a special gift to remind you. A pair of antique hand-painted castanets. I will send them with the invitation."

"How kind of you, but really you shouldn't."

"No, I want you to have these, even if you do not come to Las Cuevas. They have been used by many famous dancers. They bring you luck."

"Thank you, you are very generous." She understood how I must be feeling, she'd had her problems too. And she was being a soul sister to me, as dancers are to each other ... maybe we could get back in time ... "I appreciate this so much, Mercedes. We'll try our best to be there to wish you luck too."

Later that evening, still in my optimistic mood, I tried to call Steven Brandon. Perhaps enough time had passed since the awful day in the café that we could start again somehow. I'd invite him as my escort to Mercedes's fiesta. There'd be hundreds of people there, so neither of us would be uncomfortable while we passed over the hump of how we'd both acted in the café. Maybe he wouldn't mention it. I certainly wouldn't.

A desk clerk was handling Steven's calls. "Mr. Brandon is not here tonight," he told me very politely, "but I expect him to call for messages soon."

Before we went to bed, I tried again. "Yes," the same clerk confirmed. "Mr. Brandon called right after you. Yes, he received your message, but I'll tell him you called again."

Well, maybe Steven wouldn't call back, maybe he would. If not, what could I do, that was that.

It was late and the high-spirited José whooshed me away to spend my night sleeping in, as he described it, "the best room in the house, designed by the fabulous Pierre Moreau, who you meet tonight at the dinner."

"Country French." I appreciatively surveyed the artful flower-bedecked wallpaper and curtains.

"And for our American Princess, we give French lace too."

He opened an antique fruitwood trunk at the foot of the bed and took out a mass of lacy coverlets, shaking them and presenting them for my inspection.

"Thank you José. Tú eres muy simpático, How nice you are. These are beautiful."

"De nada, mi amiga. Enjoy! Buenas noches, Elizabeth, I go to confirm with my friend in Mallorca. Sleep well and tomorrow we work."

When he left I burrowed into the down and the four-poster bed, and drew the lacy coverlets over me. I must sleep, I thought, but my eyes were wide awake in spite of the exhausting day we'd had, and my excitement was turning into a jittery feeling . . .

. . . too much adrenaline . . . that's what it must be . . . pumping, that's all . . . I'm overtired. I concentrated on trying to relax, but the jitteriness was becoming stronger. I was starting to feel frightened, paranoid, my throat tightened as if it was holding something back. A scream, I thought, . . . How ridiculous! What am I thinking? . . . I closed my eyes, and pictures danced past. I opened them and sat up pulling the lace coverlets around me . . . What was I doing, nobody was there, I really was exhausted . . . Maybe if I left the table light on . . . maybe it would make me feel easier . . . only some anxiety . . . of course . . . after these last few days . . .

It was some time later when I woke up drowsy enough to want to turn out the light. But when I looked at the night table, its antique vaselike lamp had turned into an urn with snakes crawling in and out of it. Instantly, I was wide awake with horror before I realized I'd seen this before . . . Oh no! Not this! Not this again! Yes, this same thing had happened once before. It was in New Orleans, when someone had put something in my drink in the French Quarter. I'd had this same wide-awake but tired feeling, the same paranoia . . . and the same snakes had crawled out of an urn on a big heavy commode. I saw it vividly. I ran to put a light on in the hallway and the bathroom the way I had then. Yes it had to be those two men in the espresso bar this afternoon who'd tried so hard to pick me up while I was waiting for José to finish a telephone call. I'd left my coffee on the counter and went to the ladies' room. That's when they did it. Why do people think that is funny? If I put all the lights on again like last time, it would help . . . just relax . . . another light, the radio, soft music, it'll go away . . . jittery, jumpy . . . that's what it was . . . those two men in the coffee bar . . . if I can relax . . . fall asleep, it'll pass. Why do people do these things?

But no matter how I tried, the same sequence of pictures pressed into my forehead, the same indelible dream colors, almost their scent, I remembered them exactly . . .

. . . a steep hill on a tree-lined city street . . . spidery cracks in the pavement . . . A little girl is walking down the hill . . . Another hill. She wears black ballet tights and slippers and skips a jumping little dancer skip . . . at the bottom, a park, trees, lawns and a highway along the river in back of them. New Jersey is on the other side, sketchy, only parts of the skyline sit on the river in the fog . . . she turns the corner into another street with grand apartment houses . . . but one gray stone building on the end of the block is grimy, decrepit . . . the stones are cracking with big veins running through them, the building might fall down. She looks up. The tall windows haven't any glass in them. Some are boarded up . . . surely no one lives here anymore . . . Her soft ballet slippers pick their way carefully up the sharp edges of the broken stone steps . . . unsure, you might fall in if you step in the wrong place . . . careful . . . careful . . .

. . . At the top of the steps is a stoop in front of a gaping hole that had once been a door. The little girl walks through it, everything is red and brown. From somewhere around a corner comes . . . faint music, high-pitched laughing . . .

In a pinpoint of light, she follows a brown rug around a curve until she comes to where the noise is coming from. She is laughing too. Her voice is high, very young, much younger than ten? The pinpoint of light widens and she can see where the noise is coming from ... an apartment without a door ... again that same gaping hole ...

Men in suits and ladies in high heels are on the other side of the threshold, laughing and holding glasses. The faces fall into place ... the musicians from Daddy's orchestra, and Marya's black-haired friend from the ballet who speaks Russian with her. They all see the little girl at the door ... "She is here, she is here," they come to greet her, holding open their arms. "Our Bethy Dolly is here for her tenth birthday party."

Marya comes to her from the middle of the crowd. She is smiling and happy, wearing her flowing green dress with its yellow wildflowers ... her blond hair is brushed out around her shoulders ... Her eyes are rimmed in blue eye shadow. She rushes to embrace Bethy ... singsong in English, "Oh yes, yes, my beloved daughter, my little spoon, is here for me."

"No, no, you are dead." Bethy runs from her to the gaping doorway. "I know! It can't be! Daddy told me."

"No, my baby, I am here." Marya tries to pull Bethy back through the doorway to her. Bethy cringes back, screaming, "You are dead! Pneumonia!"

"No she is not dead." Marya's black-haired friend from the ballet calmly takes Bethy's hand and tries to lead her back.

"I know she is dead," Bethy screams in a little-girl voice. "She died from pneumonia! Daddy told me."

"No, she committed suicide," the ballet friend explains in a musical voice as Marya twirls around the room—because you told—you told.

"No, no, I didn't. I didn't. It's not true! I never told, I never told."

Another ballet friend in a flowered dress joins them and takes Bethy's hand to reassure her. Her voice singsongs, "Marya chose to take her own life, so she has the choice to come back. See, she is alive, and she wants you. Go to her, Bethy. Go to your mother."

"Come to me, my dearest baby spoon. Come to me." Marya twirls back to Bethy. "Come see that I am no longer dead."

Bethy allows Marya to take her hand, but Marya begins to lead Bethy to a coffin in the middle of the room. It is surrounded by flowers, and people holding their drinks and looking in

"Nooo! You are dead," Bethy screams to Marya in her little-child voice. She tries to untangle from Marya's hand but the vise locks her.

"Look in the coffin and see that I am not there," Marya whispers. "See that I am alive."

Bethy looks into the coffin, and begins to scream, child screams, horrible screams. It is Bethy in the coffin.

"Come my baby," Marya coos, and lifts the coffined Bethy to her as if she is lifting her from a cradle.

Bethy cannot stop screaming. The head of the coffined Bethy in Marya'a arms begins to vibrate, banging against her shoulder. It has no mouth and only gaping holes where the eyes should be . . .

I shot up and ran across the room to the bathroom to wash my face. I lay down on the floor and pressed my face onto the cold tile. Please go away, I begged the images again and again until they subsided.

I tore off the pajamas José had given me and got dressed again. Drugs in coffee or not, I couldn't stay in this room another minute. What if the dream came again? . . . No, it won't. Last time, once the drugs had worn off, it was as if it was gone . . . You'd forgotten all about it the next day. It was years ago. Stop being stupid.

Still I couldn't stay there. If we left as soon as the dawn came, I would forget the dream once we were on the road, the way people always forget their dreams. I would suggest to José and Sven that if we were to accomplish anything besides talk, we needed to start before the traffic. I went downstairs to the kitchen. Everything was quiet. I made some coffee to make sure I wouldn't fall asleep later and busied myself cleaning up from the dinner party. When dawn came, caffeine-energized, I woke everybody and shooed them out and on the road, only letting them talk about work. If we were to do this all ourselves there were a million technical and logistical problems to solve, there'd be no time for anything else.

We'd been working in Mallorca for a few days before I realized that Steven had never called back.

Nine

"Por favor, please hurry," I pleaded with the taxi driver handing him five hundred pesetas, but he wouldn't drive any faster. "How much longer to Las Cuevas?" I called through the glass partition. No answer. The gift of sapphire earrings I'd bought for Mercedes in Mallorca sparkled at me in the dark.

We'd all wanted to go to the anniversary party for Las Cuevas, and as it turned out we were able to make it back to Barcelona that night. Earlier, at the hotel, I was hurriedly zipping into the favorite royal blue silk, the low V back I always wind up wearing when I don't have time to plan another outfit, when I couldn't help noticing how much younger I looked in it than I did the few short weeks ago in New York. I'd lost more weight, probably because of my excitement about the film, but it was spooky the way my face seemed to be taking off the years. I studied my face in the mirror. My skin looked tighter, and my cheeks had their pinky glow back. The eyes appeared more widely spaced, and the defined cheekbones and sharp jawline profile of Bethy's Teatro del Liceo ballet photos looked back at me from my mirror. Her magic ballet ability was long gone from my body, but somehow the look had returned. Staring at my reflection, I realized I missed dancing more than ever. I knew I would feel a loss watching the others perform tonight.

Especially Mercedes, with her fluid, athletic movements, her perfect line and impeccable technique. There was no start or stop in Mercedes's dancing. Every movement flowed, no matter how staccato the flamenco rhythms became. To me, Mercedes was living energy, a dancer's dancer. Jorge had caught my envy immediately that first night at Las Cuevas.

"Si, cariña," he'd looked knowingly at me when the lights came up after Mercedes's performance. "You still want to be dancing."

"What an enticing thought, Jorge." I'd felt instantly uncomfortable again, not with the truth of it, but with the way he could so easily see through to my feelings. "And what then? Will I have to go through the agony of injury again?"

"The agony for what you love more than life."

"Quite the opposite. I earn my living very nicely otherwise."

But Jorge knew he was right about me and dancing.

Now in the taxi, I couldn't wait to see Mercedes dance *La Gitana* tonight, and I was thrilled at the thought of her dedicating it to me.

"Here, take this," I called again to the driver's back, handing him another five hundred pesetas over his shoulder through the open glass. The driver had gotten what he wanted, and we arrived at Las Cuevas momentarily.

José, Sven and Paco were already there. "Did you get lost on the way?" they greeted me, then kisses, scrumptious foods, wines and introductions all around the simulated Gypsy cave that was the nightclub's main room. Mercedes and Rodolfo were busy embracing the filmmaker Almodóvar, the artist Tàpies, and José Greco, who arrived with his son and daughter, both noted flamenco dancers, and Mercedes was excitedly giving instructions to an army of waiters and chefs. I was sure she hadn't seen me.

At last the performing guest rock singer was replaced by the club's flamenco guitarists. It was time for Mercedes to enchant. We all sat down at our tables. As Mercedes entered from a side doorway in a dazzling red flamenco dress, we all turned, bewitched by her, the lights went down, and she stood perfectly profiled in arched silhouette, black hat to hip.

"Señoras y señores," she began in Spanish above the applause that preceded her to the stage, "I dedicate *La Gitana*, the Gypsy, to my new American friend, a great filmmaker who was once a great dancer. A dancer leads the voyaging life of a Gypsy, and understands the center of a Gypsy's heart, which is freedom."

Maybe it was the way her own voice understood that word "freedom" that carved out such an emptiness in me. My heart whispered to me, "Why should she be up there and not you? Go and feel what it's like to be in her body tonight. Go and feel again what it's like to be dancing under the lights. Go revisit your once joyful place where the outside world always disappeared for you, where only that special moment of the dance existed, when the music became the world, when everything was perfect." I listened, and slipped into the music and the magic. It was Bethy at twenty that I saw up there, dancing her first solo allegro variation at Teatro del Liceo. Bethy, covering the stage at breakneck speed with the Russian leaps she'd perfected under Madame Verosha. She rode the air in a perfect split with her back leg arched up behind to touch the back of her head, a perfect landing without a sound, the beats now crisp and high, with perfectly pointed feet she'd worked so hard for, her dazzling pirouette finish slowing down to a suspended balance, one arm gesturing to the audience, then blackness. And it was Bethy not Mercedes curtsying to the floor when the music finished and the lights came up again, Bethy's taut, long-legged ballet body costumed in a short sequined white tutu, accepting the roses and the thunder of applause.

"Bravísima, Bravísima," the audience screamed as Mercedes finished *La Gitana*, and flowers covered the stage. Mercedes accepted the flowers and adulation in a humble bow to the floor.

A half hour after the performance, an elegantly gowned Mercedes joined us at our table. Mercedes embraced me. I held her to me.

Mercedes sat down. "I am so glad you are able to be here tonight."

"We almost weren't." José spoke in Spanish also, smiling around the table to all of us in appreciation that we'd made it in time to see her performance.

"Hombres, you make Elizabeth work too hard," Mercedes flashed her black eyes and scolded José and the others. "Soon she will be back to New York, and will have not seen anything. Elizabeth, why you don't come with me to Pamplona for La Feria de San Fermín? The bulls will run through the street."

I looked around the table. Nobody really needed me for a few days. José and Sven would be busy finishing the edit on another project of theirs, and with much still unresolved on the Jorge matter, a few days wouldn't hurt. "Maybe I can?"

"Formidable." She took that as a yes. "We leave the day after tomorrow, July 7. Be ready at six A.M." And she was off to mingle with the other guests.

Mercedes made all the arrangements for our trip and called me the next day to share them. Everything sounded glorious and she had made it so easy for me. She picked me up promptly at six in a chauffeured car, which took us to the airport. A small airplane was waiting to fly us to Pamplona. We were like schoolgirls, in jeans and bright tank tops, skipping across the runway, jumping around in excitement, singing Spanish songs, holding hands and laughing. Pepe, our pilot, was in as festive a mood as we were. He sang and laughed as he made the last preparations for takeoff.

"Vamos para arriba," Mercedes called to Pepe over the engine's noise.

"Arriba," I shouted, trying to roll my Rs the way Mercedes did.

"Arrrriba," she coached me.

"Arriba," I tried again, improving a little, but not enough.

The little plane shot up into the blue, with me shouting "Arrriba" again and again until I finally mastered the Rs. What a ride the daredevil Pepe gave us, diving and bumping. In this small plane you could feel every turn and angle. When we arrived in Pamplona, I was dizzy, nauseous and ecstatic. Mercedes jumped out of the plane ahead of me, turning back to take my hand, but when I stopped for the dizziness, she let go. "Vámanos chica," she called, running ahead.

"Yo vengo," I answered, trying to keep up with her. When I finally caught up with her at the airport entrance, she was already at the wheel of a red sportscar with our luggage stashed in the trunk.

We'd be sharing a large sunny room with tall windows and a balcony, she told me happily, in a parador, an inn, on a street called Estafeta, in the center of town, near the ancient town square, where "how do you say it? All the action is." If we hurried we could get there in time to see el encierro, the running of the bulls, go right past. It starts at eight A.M. Would I like to drive? This car was fantástico. I really should try it out. Mercedes pulled over and I took the wheel.

"Muy bien, chica," Mercedes encouraged me as I navigated the lush green countryside of Navarra toward Pamplona. "You look beautiful in this car. Your hair flies with it. Red is your color. How do you manage to look so beautiful, so early in the morning?" Mercedes moved closer and hugged me tight. She kissed me on the cheek and I could feel the dew of her skin.

I took my hand from the wheel and hugged her back. "Qué simpática tú eres," how nice you are.

I'd barely put my suitcase down when Mercedes was already out on our balcony shouting to the noisy crowd running down the street. I ran out after her. Balconies all over were filled with people drinking from wineskins and shouting to the racing crowd below. The street was in dusty pandemonium. More and more men raced by. Men, women and children lined the sides of the street, hugging the walls behind wooden barricades, and clapping and screaming and passing wineskins and bottles to each other. When one man tripped, a bunch of the wall huggers jumped over the barriers into the street, and in a flash, pulled him back with them to the sidelines.

I couldn't believe it when six massive bulls came charging behind the racing crowd. After the bulls came the less brave runners, their shouts whipping the bulls into a frenzy. In minutes, they were all gone, except for a herd of men who'd piled up on top of each other in the dust. As they untangled themselves they sang and drank from the same wineskins that had already made the rounds in the crowds of spectators. I'll never figure out how that heap wasn't gored or at least trampled. I was breathless.

"Chica," Mercedes was aglow with excitement, "this running of the bulls is just a beginning. It happens every morning of the festival. It is the only time the bulls have the upper hand at Las San Fermines," she laughed. "Late this afternoon, we go to the bullfights, the Corrida de Toros. We have an invite to sit in the especial box of the famous bullfighter, mi buen amigo Manolo Arriegas. He will fight today as the feature."

"I was once in love with a bullfighter, the beautiful José de Malaga," I reminisced, smiling. "I always called him Joselito, after the famous bullfighter, in fact—"

"No facts please," Mercedes snapped off my words with an unmistakable flash of jealousy.

"Well . . . all right," I was surprised at the complete reversal of her mood and must have been looking at her differently.

"What I mean is . . ." she laughed at herself uncomfortably, seeing my look, ". . . is that we haven't the time. I am hungry. Ven, come, we go to the square and find a café."

What I remember most about the square was the fact that everybody was drunk at eight in the morning, and thousands of red scarves of San Fermín were worn or waved by people of every description in a mass of musical confusion. Roving brass bands and medieval windsong oboes were punctuated by cacophonic beatings by corner drummers of jazz and folk of every country. We weren't drinking. Who had to? Marijuana wafted all around us. Walking made us high. We settled into Café Rio where our fellow patrons were crowds of students from all over the world. One young man from Germany was sporting his slashed shirt and bragging how a bull's horns had grazed him during this morning's run. "Right here, right here," he pointed maniacally at his bare chest. "I felt the breath of the toro right here, right here." His friends cheered him and raised their glasses. When he came over to sit with Mercedes and me, they cheered him louder. "Here," he said, "share with me," and rolled us marijuana cigarettes in hotel stationery. Mercedes and I wolfed down a hearty breakfast because the sweetish grass made us feel doubly starved. Shortly after our breakfast, the café and the square began to empty, the all-night partyers were leaving to catch up on some sleep, and we decided to do the same.

When we returned to the parador, we weren't really that tired and thought that if we locked the sunlight out of our room we'd have a better chance of falling asleep. But no matter how we tried to close the heavy draperies, the sun found its way through some opening, drawing shiny yellow ribbons on the floor tiles. Still high, we jumped barefoot along the little islands of sunshine in a game of tag, then settled down to unpack and undress for our nap. We sat on opposite sides of the big double bed, back to back, digging into the canvas suitcases on the floor in front of us.

"Chica, you are a woman I admire." Mercedes turned to face my back. "I do not admire many. I would not invite any other with me here. Only you have the spirit of joy, the intelligence, and the beauty to make San Fermín alive for me."

I turned to thank her for the compliment, and sat staring as Mercedes stood up in a black pleated and lacy see-through teddy. She was tying it together in the middle, under full breasts, with a thin fuchsia crisscrossed ribbon. The sides of the teddy were cut high above her hips to fully display her dancer's legs, which were so long they seemed to start at her shoulders. Mercedes was one of those women who really comes into her own when she's undressed. When she turned around, her teddy was cut even higher in the back, displaying perfect high round buttocks. In spite of myself, I had the urge to touch them, just to see if they were as firm as they looked. My cheeks burned from it.

"Why you not get undressed?" Mercedes walked around the bed toward me. "Did you fall asleep sitting up?"

The combination of her high heavy breasts pushing through the black lace, and the black lace itself had a startling effect on me. It was the kind of sexy lingerie that always turned me on the minute I put it on for men. In fact, I always wore it more to please myself than them. Now, seeing it on another woman, I was too conscious of my nipples starting to rise. I sat still, trying to regain control, but at the same time relishing how out of control I felt.

"Chica, ven. Stop staring and take off your clothes. We must get some sleep. We have the biggest day ahead." Mercedes was joking with me in the most innocent offhand way, sitting down beside me and putting her arm across my shoulder. With her other hand she started to unbutton my blouse, so smoothly, so unlike all the men who'd bumbled with little buttons. "What skin you have, piel de rosas, skin of roses," Mercedes stroked my arms and neck. "I would kill for such skin." I sat there wondering if she could hear my heart beating as loudly as it seemed I could.

Mercedes undid my jeans, and pulled them down to expose my hips and belly. "You have a flat tummy like we dancers will always have. Nobody, nobody can ever appreciate our bodies like we ourselves. I am so happy for you that you never lose your body, even though you no more dance."

"I wish that were true, Mercedes."

"It is true," she assured me softly. "You are like every dancer, our bodies are never perfect enough for us. It is because we understand perfection like nobody else. Here, let me see your legs. I judge, not you." Mercedes grasped the waistline of my jeans at the sides and started pulling and tugging those tight jeans over my hips and away from me, as if she were pulling tight boots off me. When she'd finally tugged them off, the momentum pulled her backward to land against the far wall. She looked so funny flying across the room that way that the tension of the moment softened. We both released it with our laughing.

"Bailaremos, let's dance," Mercedes sang out, throwing her head back, beginning to clap softly and snap her fingers, luring me in flamenco rhythms. I followed along imitating everything she did, head high, back arched, stamping my bare feet, turning when she turned, and locking my eyes to hers at the end of each turn. Her arms raised as if the fingers held castanets. My arms raised to follow. When her invisible casta-nets followed the line of my body down, my invisible castanets followed the line of hers. We watched ourselves in the full-length mirror of the giant armoire, two almost naked women dancing the flamenco in spotlights of sunshine through the draperies. We looked different, me tall and blond, with small breasts, my movements soft and balletic no matter how I tried to make them look like flamenco movements. Mercedes, smaller with round muscles and full breasts above a tiny waist. Every move she made looked strong and fiery.

"See how beautiful you are, mi amiga." Mercedes curved and snapped her fingers so artfully to me. Her body had music inside. "Elizabeth, look what inside fuego, fire you show for flamenco. Why you choose ballet? You should chose flamenco." We passed each other in a paso doble, kicking forward as if through the ruffles of colorful flamenco dresses.

"No mi amiga, you should have chosen ballet." I put my hands on her shoulders and raised my leg behind me in a ballet arabesque. "We would have danced together at Teatro del Liceo." I lowered the leg to a ballet fifth position and extended my arms in a flowery port de bras to invite her to follow me in a partnered pas de deux, but instead she wrapped my arm around her waist and arched magnificently backward over it. Mercedes looked up at me with her elfish grin, then moved one shoulder toward me as if she would rise, but she bent even lower instead, till her head touched the floor. Her dancer's body was so strong, she barely needed my arm for support. I lifted her easily to a standing position.

Mercedes put her hands on my shoulders, and ever so lightly pressed me down to my knees. To my own amazement I began to caress her calves and kiss and suck between the top of her thighs, doing all the things that pleased me the most, in the exact way I'd always begged my male lovers to do them to me. The men would never do them exactly, whether from male stubborness or male superiority, or maybe just male misconception. I sucked and bit her lower lips, using my teeth in little nibbles, the way I'd always fantasized the perfect lover would. My tongue rolled and licked across her with a particular sideway movement. I held her buttocks in my hand, feeling her taut muscles and then reached up for the indentation of her waist, and further to the spots of excitement I knew on my own breasts. It was as if I was making love to myself the real way, without all my frustration at the male lovers who would always impose their will. I was my own fantasy lover, not having to accept their needs. This was woman's need, the natural, most precious needs. I almost forgot that Mercedes was there until she began the throbbings of orgasm and I tasted a woman's come for the first time. I was rocked back to reality with crashing feelings of guilt and confusion. I could almost hear my friends and colleagues in New York, already whispering, "Did you know Elizabeth was a lesbian?" What do these labels ever really mean.

"Come, chica, you need some rest." Mercedes could see what I was feeling and kneeled beside me, stroking my head and my face. She caressed my breasts with the side of her face and nudged them with her chin, making me smile again. "Preciosa, not to worry," she told me matter-of-factly. "A woman knows how to please another woman and should not hold that back. For you it is new, virgin. It happens. Only I know. Only you know. If we both do not tell, nobody else know. Besides, who else really cares, except Jorge? It would make his fantasy so happy. But we not tell Jorge either, just for fun."

She led me to the bed and we quietly lay down. I was relieved when Mercedes cuddled into a ball, far away from me on the other side of the double bed, and quietly fell deep asleep. Had she planned this?

I lay there reflecting how I'd never thought I'd be involved in a lesbian relationship, I'd never thought of it at all. Like most women, my focus was always on men or lack of men. I wanted to have a child, a little girl. I'd name her Maria. My daughter Maria would trust that my world is good, even perfect, and has always been. How could it not be, I'm her mother? When she grows up, she'll be like me. Why not? I wanted to grow up and be like Marya. And when I tell her all the stories a mother remembers for her daughter about how she was as a little girl herself, I'd be careful to only tell her up to age ten. When I'd hold Maria protected into me in our big bed on Saturday mornings, I'd tell her how happy Bethy Dolly was. I'd coo to Maria, like Marya cooed to Bethy in her Russian expressions. I'd say, "We are like two spoons in a drawer, my darling girl." I'd say, "I love you, my dearest baby spoon," just like my mother had.

*T*en

Mercedes and I didn't speak about what had happened when we woke at one o'clock. Instead we dressed quickly and went out sightseeing along the famous ancient Roman aqueduct of Pamplona.

After a full-course Spanish lunch that we didn't start until three, we followed the crowd to the Plaza de Toros, the bullring. When we were seated in our special box, in la sombra, the shade, Mercedes looked over to a flower-bedecked box that was even closer to the arena than ours. "See there," she pointed.

I saw the perfect-chiseled features and fully mature beauty of a woman in her early fifties. She was sitting proudly alone, wearing a classic Spanish red and black lace mantilla, pronged with a high red comb into dark, loose hair. Her skin was porcelain. She looked straight ahead, head high, dark eyes clearly refusing to communicate with anybody around her. She was an island of old Spain in this modern baseball stadium crowd. "Is she a famous actress?" I asked Mercedes.

"No, that is Doña Fernanda Rosa Alcázar, the mother of Manolo Arriegas, the matador you are about to see. They are the loves of each other's lives. Doña Fernanda is the only woman Manolo trusts, and his business manager."

"What about his wife?"

"Oh, there is no place in Manolo's life for another woman, even a wife. And Doña Fernanda, she is completely absorbed in her son. She makes sure no other woman can come near him."

"What about sex? Don't tell me they're lovers as well."

"I do not think that. Manolo always travels with a big-enough male entourage. These guard him from women in spite of all the passion he pretends to ... Except if should he want sex, then they become very resourceful." Mercedes was trying to sound casual, but it was obvious that she was warning me she would not like it if I was attracted to Manolo.

"Really," I commented, not displaying any emotion whatsoever.

Momentarily, the band played the fanfare and the procession began. Everybody who would participate in today's spectacle, the Corrida de Toros, entered and took a turn of the ring.

First came the matadors, each splendidly decked out in his traje de luz, his suit of lights, the sequined and jeweled short jacket and tight-fitting pants that is the romantic costume of this daring profession. Two of these bullfighters were very young, as my own Joselito had been, and one was dressed in lavender, the color José wore on the day I first watched him fight and fell in love.

"See, chica, that is Manolo Arriegas." Mercedes pointed to the chiseled-face matador in white who was older and more confident than the others, and clearly the crowd's favorite. "He will fight first."

Manolo walked stylishly around the ring, stopping to bow as he passed the president's box. When he passed our box, he looked up and smiled. If he was at all nervous for what was about to come, he didn't show it. We stood to acknowledge his gallant and very sexy attention.

"Do not be fooled by his smile," Mercedes warned me in a biting whisper. "Romance is only a play for him."

"So how is that different from other men or maybe women as well?" I bit back.

"Pobrecita." Her smile taunted me playfully. "You have had such bad people in your life. Maybe we change this now ... maybe?"

"Maybe, maybe not."

The picadors on horseback followed the bullfighters in their parade, carrying their long lances, wooden poles with heavy triangular steel-pointed wedges at the end. I'd always hated their brutal job in the bullfight, which is to stab the bull on the hump of his back each time he tries to charge and gore their horse from underneath. True, the horses wore heavy grayish-colored protective mattresses over their sides and everybody told you they wouldn't feel it, but I'd more than once seen a horse gored in his hind muscles from the rear when his rider didn't turn him fast enough. I was already feeling queasy at the thought of the barbaric spectacle I'd let myself in for.

Next, the brave banderilleros walked into the ring. These are the toreros' right-hand men. With daring dancelike moves, they place three sets of colorful paper-covered short poles with sharp blades on the end, called banderillas, into the shoulders of the bull as he charges so that the poor creature will be sufficiently weakened to allow the matador to perform his spectacular capework later with the muleta. The muleta is the shorter red cape he uses for his most dramatic passes before the finale, which is always the death. My Joselito always placed his banderillas himself. His young body was beyond beautiful, arms high above his head, feet planted firmly together on the ground, arching his body to sidestep the charging bull.

Mercedes broke into my Joselito thoughts. "You have such a look on your face. What do you see in that mind?"

"Oh, just more facts about a man I loved very much, Mercedes," I answered, perversely enjoying how aggravated she looked. "And what do you see in your mind?"

"Some new facts, chica, new facts, remember?" she yelled at me triumphantly above the brass band and the noisy crowd. The arena cleared except for the picador on his horse.

With more fanfare, the bullpen opened, and a huge black bull came charging in straight at the horse. The picador deftly moved his mount aside and the furious charger rammed his horns into a wooden barricade instead. The lesser toreros, helpers called peons, who'd been in the way, jumped over the barricades, then returned to wave their capes at the bull, turning him to charge the horse again. This time the picador turned his mount at the exact moment he leaned forward to stab his lance into the confused, charging creature's back. The strike must have been perfect because the crowd cheered wildly. I turned away and Mercedes laughed. "Watch," she commanded. "This part will be over in a second." And thank God it was. A few more well-placed brutal stabs and we were on to the next part of the drama.

At this point, an intermission from brutality, several toreros, including Manolo, took their turn executing the graceful verónicas captured on bullfight posters and postcards. The brave bull snorted, bleeding from his back wounds, and charged and danced with each matador, following the lead of his colorful cape. The matadors gracefully tried to exhaust the bull in this short virtuoso series of pas de deux.

The next part of this bullfight was breathtaking, making me almost forget what I was really watching. Manolo had decided to place the banderillas himself, and perfect placements they were. Each time he stood at a distance from the bull and stared him eye-to-eye. Then he spoke to him, encouraging him to charge.

The animal froze to photo stillness and not a sound could be heard in the stadium until the bull, having made his decision, ferociously pawed the earth and charged Manolo at high speed. At the same time Manolo ran head-on toward the bull, but deftly sidestepped just as they met, his compact matador's body rising up and leaning forward over the bull's horns. With each pass the whole arena was sure Manolo would be gored through the heart. But at each charge, he escaped untouched and another pair of colorful banderillas swayed from the bull. The crowd became crazed with joy and the band played faster to accompany the mass passion.

Nothing could go wrong for Manolo now. Mercedes and I sat squeezing each other's hands. We couldn't speak. We could hardly breathe for the tension. Manolo took the red muleta and his sword for his grand finale of verónicas. Now, the only sounds in the arena were the shouts of Olé following each brilliant pass. Manolo tested the bull with a few preliminary verónicas. "Olé, Olé," the crowd screamed until Manolo arrogantly went to his knees before the bull and raised his arms to the sky. While a united gasp for Manolo's reckless defiance of death rose from the stadium, he strode on his knees toward the bull, taunting him, daring him to charge, holding out the muleta draped and supported by his sword. The furious bull charged and Manolo, still on his knees, swept the cape over his head forcing the bull to miss his mark and retreat back. "Olé, Olé." The stadium was in ecstasy. The cool Manolo was so confident and daring that he stayed on his knees with his back to the bull. The bull pawed the earth in his fury and charged back with riveting speed, and again Manolo swept the muleta above his head, this time rising to his feet. The massive bull pawed and charged Manolo once more, and again Manolo turned his back to the bull, finishing with his signature pass, swirling his cape around his body, narrowly missing the horns. The bull's blood marked Manolo's white suit.

"The man must be crazy," I barely gasped to Mercedes.

"He is," she gasped back. "But look at Doña Fernanda. She is the most crazy."

Doña Fernanda sat placidly fanning herself with a little smile on her face, elegantly detached from the screaming humanity around her.

Finally, it was time for the kill. Manolo methodically squared off with the bull and sighted him over his extended sword. They stood staring at each other. The bull refused to charge this last time. Did he know? Manolo was patient, talking to him, urging him on. But the bull would not charge. Manolo threw his handkerchief to the ground. Still, the bull would not charge. The crowd held its collective breath. In a poster-perfect move, Manolo rose to his toes and charged forward until the animal charged back head-on to meet him. At the moment they met in the center of the arena, Manolo deftly placed his sword exactly in the place on the bull's back that he'd targeted. The tricked bull slowly staggered to his knees. Manolo raised his arms to the crowd. The crowd exploded! The bull rolled over tortuously, pitifully, until his legs waved in the air. I sat shaking in tears at the barbarism of this spectacle with its decadent beauty.

The next thing that happened was an homage to both bravery and barbarism. One of Manolo's banderilleros was instructed to cut both ears and the tail off the bull as a trophy to Manolo for his brilliant fight. Manolo paraded around the arena while the crowd threw flowers and gifts to him, wild with adoration. A team of horses entered and dragged off the dead animal. As Manolo passed our box, one of the banderilleros ran up and presented the ears and tail trophy to me. I felt bile rise in me at the sight of it. Mercedes pushed her elbow into my side. "Accept it, do not disgrace us, accept it." Somehow I found a smile to return to the presenter for this public honor, and he went back to the arena satisfied. As soon as the crowd's attention followed him back, I stood to leave. Mercedes did not move.

"Go settle your poor stomach," she laughed and teased after me. "I stay, and see you later. Remember, tonight we go to la fiesta, for the bullfighters. We are invited by Doña Fernanda."

Eleven

Mercedes and I arrived at the bullfighter's fiesta after midnight, having spent some time with the ecstatic crowds of San Fermín. Manolo was seated at the head of a long dais centered on a flower-decorated platform. At the other end of the dais, Doña Fernanda Rosa Alcázar sat porcelain perfect, looking down the table in adoration at her son. Flanked along both sides of the dais were their entourage of male protectors and hangers-on. Manolo studied his wineglass intently while all the others studied Doña Fernanda expectantly.

"Aha, tonight's ritual, she begin," Mercedes said under her breath with an air of suspense.

"What ritual?" I asked the ever-mischief-making Mercedes.

"See how they look to Doña Fernanda?

"Yes?"

"This mean she has had her dream about who will be Manolo's love for tonight. Now they all waiting for her instructions to fetch the coveted prize for her coveted prize, Manolo."

"That's ridiculous. Manolo is a national hero and a grown man. He must have a mind of his own about who he'll make love to?"

"Not ridiculous for Manolo and Doña Fernanda. She has given her life to her son. She guide his every single move outside the bullring, and some say inside too well. She has made him what he is, he honors her every wish. If she has no dream, he has no woman tonight."

"I don't believe it. How do you know this?"

"Because I know these things. If you do not believe me, watch closely what happens between them and you will know too."

At that moment, a man at the right of Doña Fernanda stood and walked toward us. Doña Fernanda watched him carefully through perfectly made-up dark eyes while the men around Manolo laughed and raised their glasses to him in approval.

"The choice, she has been made," Mercedes announced. "It is you."

"That's ridiculous! She couldn't have dreamt of me."

"Why not? What could be more fitting dream for a darkly handsome bullfighter than a beautiful American blonde?"

"I can see nothing has changed in Spain in all these years."

"Sí, you are still the Belle of the Bullfighter's Ball."

"I think a darkly gorgeous flamenco dancer would be a more fitting prize for Manolo. They've picked you, not me."

"But I've already been dreamt of," Mercedes slyly answered.

"And how was it?"

"Uneventful," she giggled.

"Señoras." Doña Fernanda's henchman approached us, smiling amiably through tobacco-stained teeth. "Pardon, I am Marcos Ramírez, in the service of the great bullfighter Manolo Arriegas. In the name of his honorable mother, Doña Fernanda Rosa Alcázar, who gives this party tonight to honor her son's great victory at the Corrida de Toros this afternoon, I invite you both to join us in our grande honor to Manolo."

"He makes it sound like Manolo's a deity," I whispered to Mercedes.

"Second only to Doña Fernanda," she whispered back.

"Señoras!" Marcos almost demanded. "Please come now to join us to honor Manolo Arriegas."

"We have to do as he asks." Mercedes began to lead me toward the table forcefully. "Doña Fernanda has been generous supporter of the arts in Barcelona, to which I am thankful and have benefited very much."

The men at the dais stood to greet our acceptance of the illustrious invitation. We didn't quite curtsy to Doña Fernanda, but the spirit of it was there. I stood demurely in back of my chair, while Mercedes went up to her to personally acknowledge our respect. Doña Fernanda looked very pleased to see Mercedes, and looked me over thoroughly at this new close distance. I waited for Mercedes to return before we sat down. The male entourage sat down after us. Manolo continued staring at the ruby wine in his glass and never looked our way.

"Mercedes," I told her under my breath, "I don't think Manolo is interested in dreaming with either one of us."

"It is not his choice," she told me through the side of her mouth. "Doña Fernanda has decided."

Manolo continued to gaze morosely at his glass until Doña Fernanda gave a sign to Marcos, whereby Marcos and two others left their seats and came to sit around us.

"Señora." Manolo finally spoke. "Quiere bailar?" Would you like to dance?

I stood to take his hand and go to the dance floor, with Mercedes's dark eyes flashing after me. Marcos claimed Mercedes and the four of us tangoed our way across the floor. Two other henchmen joined us with partners, and Manolo and I danced in a protective square. Outside our dancing block, the fiesta guests waved and congratulated Manolo as we passed them. Manolo held me tight for their approval, and I held him tightly back, enjoying Mercedes's agitation. After the dance she pulled me with her to the ladies' room.

"Chica, do not look so happy," she mocked me. "You are only their fat turkey in tonight's gilded cage. Tomorrow they will remember nothing of you."

"It's only for fun, Mercedes, and it's your doing, not mine. She contributes to your projects. Besides, we're here in Pamplona to enjoy ourselves."

We combed our hair, and then I left her to flirt around the room. Fun it was having Manolo and Mercedes following close behind, both with jealous eyes.

When we returned to the table, another woman stood beside Doña Fernanda. Her green eyes fringed with long black lashes stared us down with the spite of a younger woman determined to have her man. Without a care of respect for a famous flamenco dancer and a famous film producer, the beautiful eyes only expressed their twenty years of age passion for a famous bullfighter.

"It looks like Doña Fernanda has had a second dream," I whispered to Mercedes, who was happily pouring me another glass of wine.

"Quiere bailar?" Manolo lost no time addressing the new table guest with the long raven hair and dark red lips. She wore a skintight silver-sequined low-cut dress. Manolo seemed thrilled that she rose with him to dance, followed by the block of henchmen and their assorted dancing ladies.

"And who is that?" I cheerfully accepted the solace of ruby wine from my flamenco sister, as Manolo and silver sequins glided away.

"She is Sandra García, a new actress and noted nymphet."

"Aha, every man's dream. I can see why Doña Fernanda changed her own."

"She changed her dream because Manolo, he must have sex tonight to calm him after today's bull. Then the two lovers, they will stay together for three more days and no more after that, because Manolo must rest and practice for next bullfight. Doña

Fernanda cannot disturb his schedule for the complications she sees you and I bring. So she have different dream."

"And we'll never know who really was the lucky one, will we?" I turned to my left to accept some more wine from Marcos, whose new job appeared to be to keep us from Manolo.

He motioned for three other men to surround us, making sure we did not interrupt the mating chemistry of Manolo and Sandra.

"Chica," Mercedes pulled me up and through their flank, jubilant that Sandra had so fortuitously saved me from the charms of Manolo. "It is already after two, and we must catch the train to Barcelona at seven thirty. We must leave right now if we are even to get some hours tonight."

"Ahaa," came a collective sigh from the men. Their work was over and they were now free to party with ladies of their choosing.

"Muchas gracias, muchas gracias," we graciously acknowledged the path they made so that we might pay our respects to Doña Fernanda. She sat regally fanning herself, obviously pleased to be done with us.

As soon as we were out of earshot of the dais, we giggled ourselves through the door, into the red convertible, and back to our parador. By the time we arrived, we were laughing so hard we had to put each other's hand over each other's mouth in order not to wake the other guests, who probably weren't home yet from their parties anyway.

We slipped into the dark parador like two errant teenagers on some school trip. Once in our room, my own laughter took on such intensity I fell onto the bed, followed by Mercedes. Then, laughing more from my laughter, she rolled off the bed onto the floor, pulling me with her in a clump of bedspread, pillows and blanket. Her face was so close to mine, she had two noses and four eyes, and her mouth had disappeared . . .

Suddenly she was shouting, "Get up, Elizabeth, get up." Mercedes was bending over me, shaking me to stop.

But I couldn't stop the laughing, it had become something else now ... terrifying ...

"Stop it, Elizabeth! Get up!" Mercedes was slapping me, "Stop it! Get up!"

My head would break from this laughter ... but I couldn't make it stop ... The room was empty, and then Mercedes was back rubbing ice on my arms and face. I tasted the cold trickling into my mouth and watched the drops glistening on my arms in the light and laughed and laughed. Other people were coming into our room through the open door, all mouths above me ... telling me to lie down, pushing me down, "Sh sh" ... the ice glistened in its bucket ... my laughter wouldn't stop ... "Shh."

... A girl of twelve is laughing ... she lies in a bathtub in a bright room ... ice shines around her ... people looking down at her, faces in white, nurses and doctors ... she tries to get out, but they push her back ... "Sh sh, Bethy Dolly" ... they push her back again into the freezing ice ... She's going to drown ... She laughs and laughs ...

The girl becomes me.

... I'm naked under sheets in a hospital bed ... I try to get out but it has bars on the side ... my arms and legs are shackled to them ... leather straps scraping ... the faces in white look down ... "Sh sh, Elizabeth," they won't let me up ... I hear the bars lock into place ... the faces leave and the room is dark ... I'm alone in the iron crib ... I don't try anymore ... I'm going to die ... I laugh and laugh ...

The laughter had subsided, and the room of our parador was dark except for the slant of light under the door. Mercedes lay beside me in the bed. "You are good now?" she was asking me. And again, "You are good now?" Her voice was fearful.

"I don't know what happened," I said. "It felt like I was in a hospital. It was horrible. I've never been in a hospital. There were bars on the windows and the bed ... I ..."

"Please, Elizabeth, it was only a dream, not a fortune telling. Don't worry, por favor. You drank too much wine, that's all." She was trying to reassure me, but it was obvious she was anxious herself. "It must be six by now, if we miss our train, Rodolfo will surely kill me. Please, we must pack and pay the bill. I must perform this night at Las Cuevas. Ven chica, please, you must pull yourself together. You only had a bad dream."

"It was a terrible dream. I can't explain it."

"Do you want to tell me about it?" Her voice was kind through her anxiety.

"No, I've caused too much trouble already. And I want to forget it. It was horrible. It'll spoil everything for both of us if I talk about it."

Mercedes was obviously relieved. She got out of bed and opened the curtains to the soft light of morning. My body felt heavy when I tried to get up and she insisted I stay still. But I wouldn't. I hurried after her as best I could, stuffing things into my suitcase. "Are you okay?" she kept asking me.

"Yes, I'm okay," I answered, my voice sounding muffled to me, almost too low to hear. But I was afraid to raise it. What if the laughing started again?

While she finished packing, I somehow counted out enough pesetas to overpay our bill acceptably. Mercedes drove the red convertible to the train station, where she managed to get hot cups of black coffee for me from a closed concession. I sat drinking, clearing my head in the cool morning air for two hours until our delayed train finally made it to Pamplona.

"Quick quick, más rápido!" Mercedes pushed me up the steps of the train as if she could somehow make up its delay time to arrive in Barcelona on schedule.

I took my bag from her. I was feeling better, and she was

right, it wasn't a fortune telling. I'd drunk too much wine, ate spicy food I wasn't used to anymore. And that was last night and this was today, and I had important business to get back to in Barcelona. I'd never been in a hospital.

Twelve

Mercedes was already seated in our train compartment and digging through our bags for her tapes, but I lagged behind in the corridor.

"Ven chica," she called to me, "what is it you look at that is so interesting?" and came back outside to see for herself.

"That woman in there." I motioned for Mercedes to look in the next compartment. "Do you know her?" It was quite possible she did, since Mercedes seemed to know everybody interesting.

"Yes of course." She proved me right, glancing in at the dignified, full-bodied woman who sat looking out the window. "That is Madame María Oracio, a famous opera star. Well, she doesn't sing anymore. She's probably on her way to join her husband, who conducts the symphony at special appearances in Barcelona. He is our Toscanini." Mercedes whispered this with great respect, so as not to appear rude that we were talking and staring. "And you should have seen our Madame María when she did sing, the most powerful contralto. She was more famous than him."

"I must meet her," I pressed. "Please, you know her, please introduce me." I didn't know what it was exactly, but there was something about the way Madame Oracio was sitting, leaning her arm on the window. Exactly how my ballet teacher, Madame Verosha, used to sit in her chair at the side of her studio. From the back, I might have thought it was she, although when she turned to us her features were very different. But the curve of her body, the grayish black of her clothes, was the same texture as the long skirts my ballet teacher wore, a sense of smell without any odor. The similarity stunned me.

During the introductions Madame Oracio spoke in perfect English, but now and then, on some words, her speech had the heavy accented rhythms my ballet teacher's had. I stood as close as I could to her, careful not to appear rude, listening to her voice, feeling a familiar hum of humor spiced with a sardonic edge. She drew me. I had to hear more. I invited her to our compartment to share the excellent cognac we'd brought with us. Madame Oracio looked pleased at my invitation and said yes, she would join us presently. We knew we'd met a woman who said what she thought.

It was only a few minutes after the train pulled out of the station that Madame María Oracio came to us. She was surprisingly contemporary and casual with us despite her formal bearing and the fact that she was a world renowned artist. Here we were, three women together in a closed compartment traveling somewhere outside of Pamplona for these few hours of time out of our lives. Soon we were deep in conversation and with our second cognac; we began to share intimate feelings the way women can and men sometimes can't ever. We spoke of our sexuality in a world where it had always been defined by men.

"You will see my girls," Madame was instructing us from her perspective as an artist and woman who'd lived a much fuller life. "A woman's sexuality is far deeper than the male defined 'he in me' in bed. A woman's real sexuality is within her own body. It is given to us more with pregnancy, childbirth, nursing, or in the deepest expression of our heart's desire through other creation."

"Si, Madame, si," Mercedes's emotions rose, "this I know more now, though I have always known it before. It is my dancing that is sexual to me in the purest way. Always yes, I feel the rapturous joining with my beloved flamenco to produce that moment of creation that I love above all. My choreography itself, my glorious child of the joining, who will never leave me. Si! It is my dancing, your music, and for Elizabeth now her filmmaking. . . . Yes, we three have found our true life mates. The rest, they are all second."

I listened to Mercedes and made the required conversational motions of agreement, but I hardly heard her words. I was caught up with watching the response of the famous opera artist sitting opposite me, not actually the response itself, but the way Madame Oracio folded her hands, held her chest, sighed, breathed, a tilt of her head, a fleeting movement of the mouth, the same as my ballet teacher Madame Verosha, the only one who gave ten-year-old Bethy the love she needed to dance after Marya died. I fought to keep up my part of the conversation as it sped along the tracks of Spain, all the while seeing a thin child crowded into the back line of a Carnegie Hall studio with its wooden floorboards and bar for a classroom. Each day Bethy pushed her matchstick body to jump higher and faster than Madame Verosha's other pupils who stood in front of her. She succeeded for her teacher's hug. I searched the face of Madame María Oracio, needing her to acknowledge something of the deeper connection I was feeling to her. But there was nothing. Of course, I was mistaken.

We rode more miles and drank more cognac and with it our talk lightened and turned to how sexual a man's power can be to a woman. I had to laugh since I'd always been such a good example of falling into that syndrome. "Especially if they're good looking," I added. "But watch out guys, women are starting to understand the sexuality of their own power, their own success."

Mercedes toasted my comment.

But Madame Oracio didn't toast with her. There was a pause, "Now that I am too old to sing, I am afraid that I have lost my power." She confided, "I'm afraid my success is in the past."

I couldn't imagine that she, who'd been critically acclaimed worldwide for all those years, could ever come to terms with such a thing. She leaned closer to me and for an instant I saw a look of deep sadness.

I jumped back. Her look hung in time. I stared at Madame Oracio. Her eyes clouded over and the look dissolved back behind them. She quickly turned away from me toward Mercedes and continued speaking, "But my husband still conducts and has more power now than ever, which makes him more sexual to me than before, even at my age. I follow him from city to city. And I let him pay the checks too, though I have much more money than he. I was always paid more than he, but it makes me feel young to have him pay. When a woman becomes older, she pays her own. I want to be young."

Madame María Oracio's features were her own, that I couldn't deny, but I knew I'd seen that face before. It was the look Madame Verosha wore all those times Bethy lied to her about the bruises on her body. I needed to say words I'd never dared say to her then. In my silence I dared now. I let my thoughts reach out to the essence of her that this famous woman opposite me somehow carried. I needed to feel the love again that my ballet teacher had given me . . . Oh Madame Verosha, Bethy understood you never believed her. How she wanted to tell you what those bruises really were, but how terrified she was that you'd hate her, tear her from you. Each time she'd lie, you'd hug her to you and she'd swallow the words from coming out . . .

Could those words be spoken now, or were they too buried . . .
If only Mercedes weren't here.

"Do not expect the same loyalty and caring in a man that
you will find in a woman," Madame Oracio continued. "Everybody thinks women go through life looking for a man like their
father. But they really go through life looking for a man like their
mother. You will never find a mother's pure unconditional love
in a man. His love turns selfish." When Madame Oracio finished
speaking she seemed different, the magic was gone; these were
only the words of a sensitive older woman. Yes, I'd been mistaken.

Mercedes was refilling our glasses. She clicked each glass
and raised hers high. "Ah, you are right there, Madame Oracio."
Now she turned to me, "But tell me Elizabeth, how is it that no
matter how powerful the American woman becomes, it seems
she will still always do anything for love?"

"There's nothing wrong with a woman hoping to find love,
Mercedes," I explained, "that's not the issue here."

Mercedes laughed derisively at me, "Except that your poor
liberated American girls still sacrifice their hope for a good marriage to love. Somehow some man must bring them some myste-
rious thing called "in love" for them to marry, and then later,
never is good enough for them, never happy." With that she
decided she'd had enough talk and left the compartment for
some air.

With Mercedes gone, I dared to cross over and sit beside
Madame María Oracio. We stopped talking and sat side by side
in the compartment, listening to the train wheels and looking
out the window at red hills and little towns flying by us in the
fog. At length Madame Oracio spoke, "Music was always my true
love. My mother was an opera singer also. From the beginning she
taught me everything. I worshipped her. I know you understand
Elizabeth, the depth of a relationship like that."

There it was! The recognition! Madame Oracio somehow

knew that Marya had taught me and how much I'd worshipped her. Or was I mistaken and it was only a coincidence that she would say that. Being an artist I would understand such a relationship.

Madame Oracio lifted her arm from between us and wrapped it around my shoulders ... All sound blocked out in the cabin except my own breath ... I knew the feel of that arm ... It was the same arm my ballet teacher had put around Bethy the evening she'd stopped at her studio to say goodbye before she left her forever for her new European ballet company.

Madame Oracio pulled me to her bosom. It seemed right. My ear was pressed to her throat. How easily I could feel the timbre of her whisper. "Don't look backward, my daughter. I've known so many artists from terrible beginnings. They turn from their misery, and make their own beauty to survive. What good to look back? Why feel such pain again?"

I fought to hold myself together ... light-headed ... dizzy.

Madame rocked me in her arms. The timbre began in her throat again, "My beautiful girl, I've watched your window of glass. It was shattered, but now it is whole. Look forward, you will see. It is your time now. Everything will resolve for you." Madame María shifted my head to her shoulder and we rode forward in time again until the sounds in the cabin regained their normal volume.

After a while, Madame looked down at me and patted my arm. Her voice was as before, with it's full warm tones and edge of humor back, "Remember, Elizabeth, one does not always have to tell everything. In America, there they must tell the whole world, then dwell on it forever on TV shows."

Mercedes returned to see Madame still rocking me in her arms. "Elizabeth, our darling, what is the matter?" Mercedes asked in alarm.

I couldn't talk for fear of what I might say.

"I think maybe you are becoming very homesick," Mercedes

concluded. "When we return to Barcelona, you come to meet the dancers of my company, and we be your family here. Give you the love you need. When you come dance with us, you will see how good you feel." For Mercedes, her love of dancing was her cure for everything. How lucky she was.

Madame Oracio seemed exhausted. "I must go back to my own compartment to rest now," she excused herself. "Thank you very much, my girls, for your pleasant company, and much good luck with the financing of your film, Elizabeth."

I hadn't told her about that.

With our famous guest gone Mercedes could see that I wouldn't be good company. I was exhausted too. Mercedes left again.

I rode the rest of the way in the silence of my own mind, seeing a little girl of ten with her eyes shut clinging to her ballet barre ... being pulled away ... her hands losing their grip ... "Marya," she called out, "Marya." There wasn't any answer. Again, "Marya." Again silence. I'd always fought myself to turn away ... but this time I couldn't ...

... Bethy is waiting outside her school for Marya ... It's winter and the late New York City, upper West Side afternoon is slate gray. Darkness is coming fast ... Bethy runs home by herself and sits huddled alone on the brown couch in the big drop living room ... Where is Marya? ... The old radiator by the window bangs in the silence ... she is afraid to get up to put on the light ... she sits frozen into the couch until at last the lights go on from the timer ...

The downstairs buzzer sounds ... it must be Marya. Bethy runs out the apartment door and down the stairs ... It's a package for Marya'a birthday on Friday ... How silly she was. Marya must be out celebrating the birthday with her friends from the ballet. Bethy runs upstairs with the package and sits staring at it trying to guess what it is. It's six o'clock. Marya wouldn't mind if she opened it a little bit, she never minds anything Bethy does ... Bethy tears away the brown paper. Inside, such beautiful shiny purple paper ... a little peek, that's all ... Ahh a velvet box ... it must be something beautiful ... she can put it all back together after one tiny look. Ahh, shiny pearl opera glasses for Marya to use at the ballet ... No, it's not that, it's a little gun with a white pearl handle ... what kind of gift is this? It must really be perfume in a bottle that looks like a gun ... yes, an antique bottle for her collection ... that must be what it is, Daddy is so clever, maybe Bethy can smell the delicious perfume inside for just a little ... she lifts the gun from its velvet case and puts it near her nose ...

... Suddenly Marya is running across the living room and grabbing the perfume gun from Bethy.

"I'm sorry ... I didn't mean," Bethy is apologizing for opening Marya's gift.

But Marya isn't listening ... she is caressing the gun to her face, feeling the cold metal on her cheek, rubbing it along her lips as if she wants to taste it ... pressing the pearl handle against her forehead ... it shines in the light as she passes it over her temples and ears ... she is sighing ... But Bethy thinks for a moment that Marya is moaning, and is she crying? ... it couldn't be, she's wrong ... No! it couldn't be ... she's wrong ... she's wrong ... Bethy takes the box in her hand and looks inside for the gift card from Daddy, but instead there's a bill and it's made out to Marya. The store must have made a mistake, nobody pays for their own gift ... they lost the card, that's all, Daddy will give it to her himself when he returns from his concert in Cleveland on Wednesday ...

... But he came home instead on Tuesday ... His face ashen, "We have lost our Marya," he said. "Pneumonia."

Thirteen

Getting off the train, my small bag felt too heavy for me, and walking itself was an effort. Mercedes on the other hand was all energy and bustle as she ran to a car waiting to take her to Las Cuevas. She hugged me goodbye. I tried to hug her back, limp with despondency. "I very worried about you," she said, "but now my friend, I have not time, or Rodolfo, he will be crazy. Later, I call you and we talk."

I found a cab back to my hotel and arranged a meeting with José, Sven and Paco. I tried not to think about what had happened on the train and to keep my energy up, but I seemed to be too tired for anything more than a short meeting at Café de la Opera. Over an espresso that refused to take its effect on me, they told me that while I was away, Jorge had held a press conference somewhere in Paris and gone to great lengths to publicly deny the rumors of his financial failure.

But public denial wasn't enough for José and me, who'd both lost money in the film business through bad deals before. We decided we should all spend the next few days in Barcelona together drawing up plans for a second version of the film we could produce ourselves if Jorge defaulted. When Jorge returned from Paris we wanted to be prepared to act quickly if need be. I found myself verbally agreeing with all José's words and plans but my exhaustion kept me from feeling their optimism.

Over the next few days, Mercedes made a campaign of trying to cheer me up with her party atmosphere. She knew everybody and invited me to everything. But Marya's perfume gun wouldn't leave my mind. Its pearl-handled shine was everywhere, the way the sun hit a car's windshield, on the doorknob when I came home. I wanted to be alone to think, but I was afraid of what I'd discover. So I went to my meetings with José, Sven and Paco, letting them do the work, then followed Mercedes to Las Cuevas later, and drank until it was time to leave with her. Mercedes watched me from the stage not liking what she saw.

Finally, she was convinced that it was my problems with the film that had me so down and I let her believe that. "If you get back to dancing, Elizabeth, you see, the blood would start rolling again, the tension will release and you find your solution." She meant well, offering me her life's and love's cure. "Come to the flamenco studio with me today, Elizabeth," she telephoned early one morning. "I find you shoes, I find you castanets, I find you dress. You practice with my company. This time you can't say no."

"Dancing won't conjure up the money for the film," I tried to beg out, "but you're right that it might be fun. If, that is, I was in dancing condition. It's very kind of you, but you know I haven't danced in years."

"You be surprised," she insisted, "how it make you feel better, clearer, just for workout purpose, blood will flow in you. Today my old teacher from Madrid comes to teach class. You should meet him. I introduce you. Rafael is a great master. Formidable! If you be shy, you just watch from back of room. Is okay for him. He is so friendly. Or if you don't like, you leave."

She persuaded me to go with her to buy dance clothes.

I became excited.

When we arrived at the studio, the dancers were lounging around the barre, smoking cigarettes and laughing. They greeted me warmly and encouraged me to put on a flamenco skirt and practice with them. It felt so good to be in a studio with dancers again that I immediately felt less tired. In a high-spirited initiation ritual, they slipped the colorful ruffled skirt over my black leotards and tights, and wound a shawl around my shoulders. At their urging, I followed them through some simple moves, until I began to improvise my own. The dancers sat down on the floor in a circle around me clapping, enjoying my attempts. It was all good-natured and sparkling, I forgot my shyness and became absorbed in my performance, first turning, then stamping, then swinging my skirts. The dancers shouted "Olé" and parted the circle as I spun around the room.

I was at the doorway when Rafael entered. His coldness stopped me in my tracks. "Friendly," Mercedes had said.

"Rafael, Rafael," the dancers warned each other, and rose to take their places obediently facing the big mirrors in the front of the room. Rafael ignored me. The dancers took their beginning poses for the rehearsal. Not a sound could be heard from them.

I slipped out of the studio, feeling like the intruder I was, and quietly went to the barres in a corner of a practice alcove adjoining the main studio. Common sense told me I should leave, but being back in the atmosphere of a rehearsal studio, which had once been my life, lured me to remain. How could it hurt to stay for a little while? Hidden from their view, I quietly removed my flamenco skirt and began my ritual ballet barre from long ago to the accompanying orchestra of their castanets.

Demi-plié, two, three, four. Graaande plié, six, seven, eight. I stretched my toes, feeling my way again in the sacred exercise regimen of ballet that is always the same from the first time the beginning dancer enters the studio to the time before a performance when the accomplished ballerina warms up. In every country, the language of ballet is the same: tendu, plié, tendu, plié. A good dancer will experience an unbreakable bond with these barre movements she's done thousands of times, each day working to make them more perfect than the day before.

By the time I reached my ballet fifth position, two guitarists had set up and joined the dancers. Mercedes had been right, it felt so wonderful to dance again, even if it was only this little bit. I couldn't stop now. I finished the ronds de jambe and stretched sideways through a port de bras . . . to the barre . . . away . . . to the barre . . . away. The first drops of sweat fell to the floor. My body was loosening.

In front of the big studio on the other side of my alcove, the male dancers furiously stomped out heel rhythms for their grand master Rafael. Which of them would Rafael pick for the solo part they all coveted? I watched their drama of competition through my alcove mirrors, feeling the tension again that I'd felt many times in their position of rehearsal and audition. Imagine, here I was in the rehearsal studio again, and part of the sacred ceremony of the dancer. My body remembered poses of its other era. If only I could be part of the experience in the next room even for a few moments, but I was only a speck on their wall.

Completely hidden from their view, I dared to go back to Bethy's world of dance that would always live inside me. I left the alcove and went into the next rehearsal studio where all was quiet and closed the door. I extended my leg onto the barre and allowed my body to loosen more. I stretched the leg into a second position ballet pose and slid it along the barre. The floor of this studio had the same dirt- and sweat-stained golden wood of Madame Verosha's studio in Carnegie Hall. I imagined Madame Verosha's long foggy windows. And her pianist Lucia . . . Lucia would play on Saturday morning when the sun bounced off the pictures of dancers lining the walls . . .

. . . two bodies are bending and stretching to the legato rhythms of a taped piano concerto . . . slowly to the barre, slowly away . . . one is a young woman of twenty-six, she is tall

with shining blond hair parted in the middle, pulled back and tightly pinned at the base of a long willowy neck. Her legs taper down in smooth black tights, and she wears a black low-cut leotard with fine thin straps to secure it. A little girl of eight stands directly behind her wearing identical black, the pink of their ballet slipper ribbons crisscross around arched feet at exact angles ... The bare arms of both are colored pink-white by the twisting silk-covered arms of a chandelier ... The older dancer changes the position of her feet and the little dancer immediately rearranges her own. A small thin arm reaches up and small fingers arrange themselves anew to match the formation of the elegant long ones in front of her ... The young woman turns ... The little girl looks up to her, and I see the adoration in her face. It is Marya and Bethy. They dance together in their own ballet studio in a corner of the drop living room on Riverside Drive. A simple barre is attached to the wall ... Marya holds out her hand to steady Bethy's balance as she raises her leg high on the barre ... It doesn't quite reach yet ...

As I watched the two dancers in my mind, my throat began to spasm ... If I could somehow swallow them back into me. The sounds of a violin played loudly in my mind ... If I could make the violin stop.

... a man walks out of a shadow holding a violin to his shoulder ... the bow sways over it and sweet curving notes fill the air ... "Dance for me, little rose," he murmers, and the sweet violin notes play faster ... The man speaks to Marya but Bethy can't hear what he's said, his violin is too loud ... Marya runs from the living room and Bethy goes to the center of it as if to a stage, jumping and twirling with joy ... he scoops her into his arms ...

Rage and nausea rose suddenly in me. My bare arms wrapped around each other, the skin of the right rubbing against the skin of the left, feeling the textures of that day ... **dampness of a** rainy Sunday afternoon, the scratch of the weave of the brown couch, his mustache brushing her body, her heart screaming ... Bethy cries, "Marya, he's hurting me, Marya, don't go away ... Please, Marya ..."

In shock I heard myself repeating Bethy's words, "Come back, Marya. Please, Marya. He's hurting me, Marya. Don't go away." The words had come out in a whisper, but already old habits had chased me to the door of the studio, looking outside around corners to make sure that nobody heard.

I went back in and closed the door tight before I turned and looked across the rehearsal studio to see myself reflected in the mirrors. "Why didn't you come back, Marya? Why didn't you stop him? How could you betray me too?" I shouted the words out quickly. I started sobbing. "Why didn't you do something, Marya? You knew it was happening all along. There had to have been some way ... somebody you could have gone to ... There had to be some way ... You were my mother, I loved you more than anybody in the world. How could you leave me, Marya, when I needed you so much?"

I needed physical pain to ease the other I was feeling. Along the back wall of the empty rehearsal studio there was a section of unused cracked wooden barre. I raised my leg and extended it along its neglected splinters and shards. I folded my body down over it, stretching it more till I thought the leg would snap. I would not release myself. Tears flooded over my face, and cold sweat rolled off my body. Circular puddles formed all around me. Through the large window the sun caught the metal of a nearby rooftop's flashing, the shine of Marya's gun.

Who could she have told? I asked myself. He was too influential. Nobody would have believed her! She hadn't any adult friends outside of other Russian dancers. She was a scared young girl herself. Wasn't I still a scared young girl, even now? All these years, I'd failed to admit the past. I hadn't the courage. What courage had she had? I'd abandoned her too, hadn't I? How had she died of pneumonia so quickly? She was never ill. Didn't I, Elizabeth, always know that wasn't the truth?

In the next studio, the castanets had stopped and the dancers were taking their break. Girls in colorful skirts and men in tight black trousers dripping with sweat lit cigarettes and walked through the alcove into my empty rehearsal hall to practice and talk and joke with each other. "What a workout you must have had too," they laughed, surveying the wet floor around me.

"Sí," I quietly agreed, then slipped from the room, changed my clothes and left without saying goodbye.

When I returned to my hotel, it was hours before I could recover. When I did, I sent a note to Mercedes telling her I couldn't continue our relationship.

She was on the phone within the hour. "Why with all you've done, and at your age, you still do not have the courage to do as you want?"

"I have too many secrets already. I've become their slave. I hate myself for that. I can't have more. What happened between you and me would only make another."

"What happened was only love, Elizabeth. I lived with many secrets too once, and they also kept me a slave," Mercedes said softly. "I learned to take the risk. I be who I am, I dance who I am. And nothing happens except that I am free."

"I cannot do that," I told her. "Please don't ask me."

"It is your decision and maybe there is nothing more I can do . . . I feel very sad . . ." And that was the last thing she said.

I too said nothing more and after a while I heard a click and knew she'd hung up. How could I have told her what I was really feeling? I didn't trust anybody, at least not anymore. The telephone rang again. I automatically picked up.

"Hi! Elizabeth?"

". . . yes?"

"This is Steven, remember, Steven Brandon? From the plane."

I was too surprised to say anything.

"Don't tell me you've forgotten me already. How are you?"

"Oh yes," I answered, still frozen in my conversation with Mercedes.

"I'm calling from Córdoba. My daughter and I've been down here seeing the sights for a few days. It's been great, terrific, but I'm on my way back and I thought that maybe if you weren't too tied up, maybe we could meet for a drink or dinner or something somewhere. I'd love to see you." Steven's healthy outdoor cheerfulness came through.

"Maybe." I was too spent to say anything else.

"How's your schedule look on Thursday?"

"Thursday?"

"Yeah, Thursday, it's always been a terrific day, follows Wednesday, before Friday . . ."

"Well I . . ."

"Look, please, I hate rejection. Just say four o'clock's okay."

". . . all right, four o'clock." I hung up. Right now I needed the security of the conventional, and this was as conventional as I knew, a date with a famous man.

I studied my face in the mirror as Bethy had done the first day she'd arrived in Barcelona. "Never let the world know about you" she'd said, and tried on different smiles until she found the most carefree.

Only one person knows, I reminded myself. Why ruin your life now?

Fourteen

On Thursday afternoon at five fifteen, I sat in the lobby of the Hotel Avenida Palace admitting to myself that I had been stood up by Steven Brandon. I have a policy of giving people a half hour, I defended myself to my New York and L.A. image, so it's really not that bad that I've waited a little longer.

"Tell me, luv, you look a bit wired." The Australian accent came from a lanky Crocodile Dundee look-alike in jeans and fringed suede jacket who'd been circling the lobby like a corraled wild horse, his alligator boots pacing a hole in the plush rugs. "Is your luggage lost somewhere in the blue with mine?"

"No!" I snapped at the thought of my tension being obvious to a complete stranger. I'd thought I was at least doing a good job at looking casual. "It's only a man that's lost," I added flippantly. "If it were my luggage, you'd see me a lot more upset."

"Glad to hear the bloke's not that important. This luggage foul-up is the second time in a week for me. First time was between Melbourne and London. How's a man supposed to do his business?"

"Two times in one week?" Poor guy, I thought. At the same time I was glad to see someone else as agitated as I. It made me feel a little less off balance. "You look fine as you are," I assured him honestly, "but I don't know how you're supposed to look to do your business."

"Please" he said, "will you join me for tea in the lobby bar while I wait for my luggage? I'd appreciate it. All this traveling, and business gets grueling for a poor bloke like me."

"Well . . . maybe . . ." The tea would calm my nerves, and there was still a good chance that Steven would come in and see me with this intriguing Australian, and I'd be one up in this game of hard-to-get. As long as I'd been tricked into playing again, I wanted to be in the lead. The stranger smiled his thanks with white even teeth. "My name's Patrick."

We proceeded to the lobby bar. Patrick sipped his tea with precise manners, but I sensed a terrific wiredness beneath the politeness.

"I breed racehorses," Patrick was telling me over a little cucumber sandwich. "I'm here to look over some studs at a breeding ranch about three hours' drive from Barcelona. I leave tomorrow."

"Well then, your clothes are perfect for doing business, and the rest will catch up with you. Why so concerned?"

"Because, luv, we all got our deep dark secrets. And mine's to do with gambling. I need that tux in my suitcase, and pressed to wear tonight. I'm off to a private casino right out of town. The stakes there are rather high and the players are bloody multimillionaires."

"Couldn't you go another night?"

"My girl, I can see you don't know gambling. A gambler has got to go now. It's not a casual affair. Especially with me. I was two million ahead in Monte Carlo last month, but I bloody gave it back, and then some in Estoril this month."

I looked around for Steven. Still no sign. Well, his half hour and a lot more was up anyway. He'd had his chance. Onward! "I have a secret too," I joked, flashing my own white even teeth at

Patrick. "I never gamble with money, only with men, but now I've given up that gamble. I've lost too many times."

"You're too staid, my girl. Let me cure you, and show you how real winning feels. Come with me tonight to the casino. You can roll for me, be my Lady Luck. I can use it."

"What if I lose for you?"

"Don't worry, luv, I've lost before. It gives the win a keener edge, and it keeps me a free and humble man not to have too much. If it does get too bad, the casino has a killing room with padded walls. I'll go out quietly. No one will ever hear the shots. But we'll win, my Lady Luck, and I'll show you a giant of a night."

A bellhop came over to tell Patrick that his luggage had arrived.

"Say it's set then, luv." Patrick gave the bellhop a generous tip and signed the check. "Meet me here at eleven and I promise you love and riches."

"Well . . . since you promised," I answered. It would have been hard to refuse Patrick even if he'd promised me I'd lose. His hard-chested good looks were the stuff of romance novels. He probably looked great in the tux. I took another warm sip of excellent jerez and stood to leave. "See you later, Patrick. By the way, my name is Elizabeth, but why don't you call me Bethy."

"Bethy, my girl, whatever you say. You've made my day."

His Aussie, long iii sounds on the words, "say," "made" and "day" would have given the whole corps de ballet of Teatro del Liceo loving goosebumps.

Patrick decided to pick me up at my hotel instead, and as we walked out of the lobby at eleven to face the huge cathedral opposite, we looked the perfect travel ad for romantic adventures. Patrick was a devastating picture in his tux, tall, elegant, and smiling his gleaming smile. I was dressed in a clinging white silk strapless, floor-length dress, with my straight, shiny blond hair swinging around my shoulders. I'd even worn eye makeup and lipstick for this glamorous occasion.

Patrick's untamed nature showed in his long uneven strides, and it blazed out of his green eyes. Even the squint lines were irregular, different-crooked patterns on the right than on the left. Holding Patrick's arm I felt something dangerous was about to happen. He opened the door to a dark green Jaguar convertible, closed it behind me, and leaned in to lightly brush my neck with his mouth. For a crazy moment I thought he would bite me. He raced the motor and we drove away. I purposely didn't secure the safety lock on the door.

"Are you married?" I shouted into the wind as we drove at breakneck speed under the stars.

"Never been, and never will," he shouted back.

"How'd you miss it?"

"Same way as you."

"How'd you know about me?" I yelled.

"I always know one like me."

"I'm not like you." We laughed into the wind for the rest of the ride. Patrick's blondish hair was standing almost straight up and mine was flying in every direction.

When we arrived at the casino, I was surprised to see that it was a smallish castle, as castles go, with barely a light seen from the outside. We parked at the far end, and walked through manicured gardens of trees to a side entrance. Once inside, the room was warmly lit, and charged with the high tension of serious business, nothing like the huge shuffling halls of the Atlantic City and Vegas casinos I'd been to. In fact, there wasn't a slot machine in sight. Roulette, baccarat and craps were the only games here. We approached the roulette table, where the other players were Arabs, some dressed in the traditional long robes and others in conventional suits and ties with turbans. I was the only woman at this table.

"If you play," Patrick warned, "the Arabs will leave."

"That's okay," I replied. "It's too fast for me to follow anyway." And it was. Stacks of chips became mountains in minutes as the little black ball jumped and landed on the black or the red numbers of the madly spinning wheel. Patrick's stacks grew so tall they had to be split twice, then three times, and even four. I was starting to feel his gambling high, and had to hold my champagne glass in my left hand because my right was busy enjoying the delicious feel of black and brown chips.

"C'mon, my Bethy girl." Patrick wrapped his arm around me. "Let's go to the crap table and shoot some. We're overstaying our welcome here. The Arabs are losing and think it's your fault."

"I've played craps before," I told Patrick, "but it was a long time ago. It was a lot of fun. I didn't have my own money to lose then. So I always lost my date's money. What did I care?"

"Why don't I bankroll you to begin with?" Patrick suggested. "Then you'll see how you feel. Here's ten thousand dollars in chips. You can pay me back if you win. If not, don't worry. I've just won two hundred thousand."

At the crap table, men and women dressed in Parisian and Italian eveningwear were placing their bets in Japanese and Swedish alongside an English rock group dressed in the latest heavy metal.

"On the nine," I said, handing the croupier a bright stack of red chips.

"Nueve, nine," he confirmed.

"Give me ten the hard way," Patrick put a small stack of blacks on the table.

"Ten, diez," the croupier confirmed. Somebody tossed the dice. It was a winner. Stacks of chips began filling up all the numbers and spaces on the green felt table.

"Four the hard way, and the six and eight." I put down more little round stacks of colored chips.

"Dos, snake eyes, tres, three, cinco, five," the croupier called the next three rolls, working rapidly to change the stacks of chips on the table after each.

I held my breath. Please no seven.

"Cuatro, four hard, seis, six, ocho, eight," the croupier's voice sounded as sweet as an angel's as he confirmed the jumping and rolling dice of the next rolls.

Patrick and I slapped hands high with a "haaa," and backed up our bets in the seconds before the die were rolled again. The heavy metals and the Japanese turned to us and we slapped hands all around.

"Nina from Carolina," I shouted, urging a nine out of the dice as they bounced off the inside rim of the table all the way down the other end.

"Nine, nueve," the croupier announced. My bright stack of reds grew into a bigger bright stack of red.

"One more time," I shouted at the dice again. And nine it was.

We took our chips from the green felt and lined them up along the mahogany rim in our corner of the table. Colored discs spread in a long curving row in front of us. We took them from the rim in little stacks, shuffling them from hand to hand as we watched the action on the table. "Siete, seven," the croupier called, and the stickman cleared the chips of those who had pushed their luck too far.

We set out our bets again. "Yo!" Patrick and the others who had bet on the eleven yelled on the next throw. Eleven it was, and then a five. The table became a hive of activity, with betters calling out numbers and handing their little colored round stacks to the croupier, who placed them on the colorful squares all over the table.

Heavy metal was on a roll now. "Nina nine for me too, mate." His black mesh-covered arm shook the dice. Nine came up. And eight when the Parisian-dressed Japanese lady called it, and so with four the hard way, and on and on until the hated seven was thrown, and hooked sticks quickly cleared the table of all our dreams. I quickly counted up. I had eighty thousand in profit. I gave Patrick back his ten in chips, and was ready to go again. I looked at Patrick. His eyes were colorless now and his body looked almost rigid with fear. I could feel a vibration coming from him.

"I'm big ahead now, my Lady Luck," Patrick's voice was gravelly. "Let's hit it again."

We switched our drinks to scotch for this third round of betting. The heavy glass felt good in my hand, made me feel more powerful and in control than the dainty champagne glass had. We placed our chips on the pass line for Patrick's come-out roll. The die flew down the table. A five came up. "On the snake eyes," I shouted to the croupier and placed a brown stack in back of the pass line myself. The group of Arabs joined our table now that I was winning, and caught the euphoria, betting high.

Patrick added more colorful little stacks everywhere. "C'mon baby," he kissed the dice and threw them.

"Siete, seven," the croupier confirmed. Craps. We'd lost. The stickman cleared the table.

From then on, things went bad. What happened, I don't know, but we kept losing and losing till I was out of chips and had to go to the cashier to buy more. My American Express platinum card easily bought me two hundred thousand dollars' worth of assorted colored little discs to play with. Suddenly I realized that even if I lost these too, nothing in my life would change . . . Why hadn't I noticed before? . . . How long had I had this kind of money? I almost couldn't wait to lose the chips just to prove it to myself . . . If I lost this money, the future royalties from *Firenze* and the Olympic film would make it up. There'd been no reason for me to have taken that first ten thousand dollars of chips from Patrick. Why was I still thinking that only a man could bring me my wealth, or worse still, that he had to pay my way?

I walked around the crap tables and looked at the men playing. I'd automatically assumed that all these men had more money than I, knew more about money, had more right to money.

They were all losing now and looking worried and miserable, except Patrick who was also losing but looking as happy as I was.

"Don't look so happy, Patrick," I teased him. "I'm back to make you win again."

"Watch out if you're trying to make me a rich and respectable man, Bethy. It won't work." Patrick was serious.

"I'll make you a rich man, Patrick," I promised, rolling a seven on my come-out, "but respectable might be too big a job for me."

"If I'm rich, the world will make me become respectable. It'll give me a wife and kids and life insurance, and a portly belly to hold my beer."

"Eleven, once," the croupier shouted out. I could see the color leaving Patrick's eyes again, and the rigidity returning to his body. The man was in fear of wealth.

We changed tables and rolled dice and placed chips and won and lost, and won and lost and lost and lost and lost. When we finally tallied up I was a hundred thousand behind, Patrick three hundred thousand, we were very drunk, and hysterically happy, Patrick especially because he was in no danger of being presented with wife, kids and life insurance. We were both free, and any cost was worth it.

"Dinner we must have, my queen," Patrick insisted, slurring now.

"Dinner," I agreed. I was slurring a bit myself.

Another part of the castle housed a plush restaurant. A band played a tango on a platform above a shiny dance floor. We staggered to a table where the waiter informed us that dinner and champagne were on the house.

"How sporting," I said, delighted.

"How sporting," Patrick agreed.

"Here's to joy, Patrick my rogue." I offered my champagne flute to toast.

"Here's to Bethy, who is my joy." Patrick put up his glass.

"Call me Elizabeth, the Wealthy," I countered with mine.

"My joy, Elizabeth, the Wealthy." Patrick's glass and mine hit with such abandon that they both smashed in front of us, spilling champagne on the ivory Spanish lace setting and into the bread basket. We felt no embarrassment. After all, we'd paid $400,000 for the privilege.

"A dance, My Queen." Patrick staggered up from his chair and bowed.

"A dance, my rogue," I agreed, rising to meet him in a tango. We executed our tango with the greatest comedy, turning and dipping, and tossing our heads, and glaring at each other, and forgetting all about dinner, only returning to the table to refill our glasses. We finally staggered outside to the green Jaguar.

"Here, Bethy or Elizabeth or whoever you are, have some of this and we'll straighten up and fly right." Patrick handed me a vial of white powder from the glove compartment. I took a deep sniff, and in a moment we were at the beach.

I ran zigzag toward the water, Patrick weaving behind me. The white silk dress and the immaculate tux from the early evening's elegance were in sandy disarray and shoes were lost.

"Elizabeth, the Wealthy, come back," Patrick yelled after me, too drunk to go another step. "Elizabeth, the Wealthy, I want your cunt."

"You want my what?" I yelled back.

"Your cunt, your cunt."

"My what? My what?" His Australian pronunciation of the word was irresistible. I had to hear it again.

"Your cunt, your cunt," he complied.

"What?"

"Cunt."

"What?

"Cunt."

I couldn't stop laughing. Patrick collapsed on the sand, trying to take off his clothes. When he finally maneuvered through the shirt buttons and the cummerbund, he started on the trousers, but passed out in the middle. I took off what white silk was left of my dress and ran down to the ocean where I lay down on my belly and dug myself into the cool sand. The Mediterranean waves lapped over me.

After a while I turned over to face the blackness of the sky. Steven's face appeared above me. What was it about Steven that wouldn't stop haunting me?

"Kiss me and you'll see," Steven's suspended face answered.

"I'm on a date with another man, and we're going to make love in a minute," I said, sounding ridiculous in the blackness, but determined to play the jealous angle even if only in a fantasy.

"But you love me," Steven's all-American outdoor face persuaded.

"You're wrong. I hardly even know you," I disagreed rather primly.

"Your cunt, your cunt, my girl. Come give it to me," Patrick's Australian accent called from somewhere.

"Elizabeta, cariña, it's me you should choose." Jorge's dark almond eyes began to appear under the stars. "I will give you everything. Diamond earrings three times as big as the ones Bolanieu gave you. And too, I am the best lover. The whole world knows." Jorge's face began to kiss my breasts. I lay back in the wet sand.

"Kiss me, and you'll see who you love," Steven's face repeated, his mouth so close to mine I could taste his breathing. But our lips wouldn't meet. I jumped up waving my arms, and all the faces disappeared except Steven's, which was now joined to a body in a sleek racing bathing suit. We ran together into the ocean and dived into an oncoming breaker.

I swam out into the blackness for what seemed like miles, with Steven right behind me, until I couldn't go any further. When I looked back for the shore I couldn't see it and began to scream for help.

"Hold on to my shoulders and I will save you," Steven instructed. I laid myself vertically across Steven's broad back and held on to his shoulders. We swam back with Steven plowing through the waves with powerful, long, regular strokes. We reached the shore, and Steven ran ahead of me onto the beach.

"Come back," I yelled after him. "I love you, I love you." But Steven ran ahead sprinting along the shore until he was a pinpoint and then the shore was empty. "I love you. Come back, I love you." My own voice woke me. Over on the horizon, the sun was starting to come up.

I walked naked back to where I'd left Patrick and my clothes. "Good morning, Patrick." I stood above him and prodded him with my toes.

Patrick opened one eye and looked up at me. "Where am I, and how poor am I?"

"You're on the beach, and not very poor, only $300,000 poorer."

"I'll live with that. We'd better get going. I've got a lot of driving to get out to the ranch. Say, my girl, you look devastating without your clothes. Will you be here when I get back next week?"

"I'll be here, Patrick."

On the ride back to town, I told Patrick about my fantasy by the ocean. "It's a good thing I woke up when I did," he said when I'd finished. "That bloody do-good American bloke might have come sprinting back, and I'd have lost my best girl. What do you need him for anyway? You'll have more fun with an Aussie. I'll call you next week, when I'm finished with my business. We'll go to Mallorca, gamble all weekend. We've got to win it back, you know."

"I know, I know," I agreed, feeling the thrill of the crap tables again.

The dark green Jaguar dropped me at my hotel as the morning bustle of Barcelona was beginning. I kissed Patrick good-bye, promising to go gambling next week, even though I doubted I'd ever see him again. He met too many women in his travels, too many enticing mares romping in the sunshine, to think about one he met last week.

But, as it turned out, there wasn't much time for me to think about Patrick either, because I'd hardly removed my muddied, tattered dress when Juan Goya, Jorge's business partner, was on the phone telling me that the rumors about Jorge were true, and Goya y Ximínez films had filed for bankruptcy protection. If I could get ahold of the international edition of *The Wall Street Journal*, I could read the details. Poor Juan, his heart was breaking. He had invested hope in the Olympic film. "But there is nothing I can do now. I am so sorry, Elizabeth, for the time you have put in with us. Maybe we can work another time on another film. Please, it has been my honor to be associated with you." And that was that!

Maybe it was hearing Juan's grief or maybe it was the reality of the morning, but the hundred thousand dollars I'd been so elatedly hysterical about the night before now seemed a horrendous loss. I felt poor and wretched, with deep circles under my eyes from lack of sleep and my nerves frazzled from alcohol and cocaine. I worried about my film company. Would it crumble also? It had happened too many times to too many.

Fifteen

I woke up later that day with an awful head but feeling clear enough to appraise the situation in realistic terms. What credit did I actually have to raise the significant millions I needed to produce this film myself? The answer—one Oscar and a lot of company debt. Would that justify the money a lender syndicate would have to give me? I went through a list of alternatives:

A major studio in the states, a Disney or a Paramount, might be interested enough to back me if I gave them the distribution.

No! An Olympic film doesn't begin to fit their proven marketable genres like thriller, horror or adventure. Especially without major stars or even near major stars.

I'd go to the stars themselves? If I could promise them a successful video release, American and European?

No! It would take too long to convince them, and I couldn't honestly promise anybody commercial success.

I could produce it as a low-budget film, like *Firenze*, with no expensive union rules?

Yes—my only route left. I could set up a small temporary base in Barcelona. Once the film was started, I could return to New York to find a moneymaking project to balance it. I would fly back periodically until it was time to edit, then bring it back to New York for the final cut.

No, the film is too big, it needs an expensive full crew, and I'd have to be here with it, which means I couldn't do other business in New York. Financially impossible.

But what if I could convince an international bank to finance part of it. A past Oscar is worth a try.

I got on the phone, but my inquiries brought quick answers of "No!" flat out. And "No," not so flat out. There were a few noncommittals, "We have to be careful," which made clear what I already knew, new fame is not a good guarantee for large investments.

Finally, I had the answer. I still had the best director and cinematographer with me. It was time for a sure thing.

I decided to contact an old friend and lover, the wealthy Count from Marbella. He'd been a generous patron of the ballet at Teatro del Liceo, and an always cheerful protector of its young artists, although some accused him of being an opportunist at the expense of young girls. Though the Count might parade the night as an aristocratically foppish bon vivant, during the day there wasn't anybody who didn't respect him as the shrewdest of businessmen, with intricate family connections. Some referred to these connections as a network of crooked cousins, and even doubted they were cousins at all. I called.

An overjoyed Count returned my call, "Sí, yes, mais oui, of course I remember you. My own Bethy, mi bellissima, how could I forget one so beautiful, young and devious."

I traveled to Marbella for our meeting, and waited for the Count in an opulent Riviera style hotel lobby. Dressed to the nines like everybody else, I'd chosen to wear my favorite black Valentino evening suit. While I waited, and waited—the man was late, of course, he'd always been—I became engrossed in the same thing every other pair of eyes in the lobby were watching. A young couple was standing at the concierge desk, making plans with a daring verve for life and sexuality that was becoming more open by the minute. This girl had the same rakish look I'd had that first year in TriBeCa when I'd put all thoughts of the ballet behind me and took any work I could in the film business, including hauling film cans. I'd cut my long hair off to a shiny, platinum blond, short, boy's cut. She wore an outfit I would have worn, a short tight antelope jacket, a black leather, tight, tight, micro-mini, black tights and high platform sandals.

We all watched this girl lick her lips and move her hands up her boyfriend's thighs . . . almost there, almost there. Her slim hips moved in rhythm to an obvious fantasy, while the boyfriend, a little more reserved under his trendy slouch of a hat, moved his hands rhythmically on her ass. Every man in the lobby openly envied him. The girl stopped her hands at the very top of his thighs, tantalizingly.

The older guests, of course, tried not to look, but the couple was oblivious either way. They were too caught up in their own moment as only the young and improprietous can be. I watched her swing her shoulder bag so carelessly, she couldn't possibly have had any money in it . . . I never had money in mine.

I couldn't take my eyes off this sexy couple. For a crazy moment I considered asking the girl to change outfits, to see how it would feel to be in those clothes again. She'd no doubt look charming in my black Valentino evening suit but I'd feel ridiculous in hers now, and look more so. I wonder how I would have chosen if at that moment the devil had offered me the mythical eternal youth in exchange for all I'd accomplished. Somehow in the face of youth, success can pale fast. Love has the same effect, or maybe the two become wound up together as one grows older . . . Elizabeth, I reminded myself, you're a successful film producer, here to raise financing for a film.

The couple was gone for barely ten minutes, when there was a bustle of confusion and a frantic checking for missing purses and wallets. Puzzled murmurings in the lobby crowd grew to a commotion and police strung their way through, taking down information and reports. "Lolita. Sí, Lolita," buzzed on the lips of police and patrons.

"Yup," a fellow American, who'd been relieved of a wad of pesetas while watching the couple, informed me, "what it all translates to is 'Lolita Decoy.' "

"What do you mean?" I asked the man.

"This cop guy there just gave me the whole story. That cute chick and her boyfriend are professional decoys for a pickpocket ring. They have different looks and different wigs. Sometimes she wears big round glasses and does a whole different bit, but it's her all right. While you fantasize about her, your pocket gets picked. They're doing a hell of business in distraction in the area. You have to hand it to her!"

"How much did you hand to her?"

"Enough." And he moped away.

Thank God I'm from New York, I thought, and always keep my bag in front and tight to me.

In the middle of this agitated milling crowd, a short slim man smoothed through the huge glass tourist lobby doors wearing an elegant old-world burgundy damask dinner jacket with satin lapels, and shiny black patent evening shoes. The elegant cane he carried was too short to be of service to his slight limp. It was more like a riding crop. His whole manner spoke of castles and yachts and polo matches.

With an aristocratic tilt of his head he demanded the hotel staff's attention. He stood waiting for a moment till he was sure he had it. He then elegantly removed one stainless white glove and flicked his riding crop cane. Satisfied that he had been properly acknowledged, he allowed all to go back to the former commotion while he stood smoothing his perfectly pointed mustache. Then he turned to me.

"Ahaa, my darling Bethy, heh?" he said.

"Monsieur." I smiled with only the corners of my mouth turning up. I couldn't be sure what would come next.

"But now it is Elizabeth?" His eyes bore into me. "How chic, how elegant, my Bethy has become. Heh? Valentino, is it not?"

What did he expect? An older version of that blond girl in the miniskirt?

We were quiet for a long moment while we searched each other out, and then we were in each other's arms in an embrace of thanks and mutual respect for having both survived all the hellfires and personal wars since the many years we'd been at play together in this city of Marbella. Once again my Count's eyes gleamed for trouble.

I couldn't get over it. We'd become equals. The Count was only a normal breathing man, in spite of his dress and his mannerisms, he was only rich, and after all, very nice about it too. But then again didn't I once think that all men dressed in dark expensive suits had some unattainable power?

"I've seen your *Firenze*," the Count said to me a little later when I was enjoying my cocktail in the warm breezes of the deck of his yacht. An attendant was pouring Pellegrino for him into an exquisitely cut glass. "I've had to give up my affair with the Dom Perignon, my dear, but please, you go ahead."

"When did you see my work?" I was pleased that he had.

"It was at a private screening. What a party they make after! What an occasion they make of it! Even with everything, the photo, I never relate then it was from my Bethy. Although, not so different you look, still as beautiful, but so different you become from my little Bethy who love so much to play. But so unlucky, that girl. Pobrecita rubia, always being left by some man."

"That bad?" I asked.

"No, not bad. A charming enough girl, but hardly you."

"And you, sir?"

"What parts we must play in this life." he looked at me as if I'd understand now that I was older. "And how easily the young believe us. But that is that. Heh?"

We drank and chatted about nothing in particular, together with old times, getting to know each other again while we cruised the soft Mediterranean night.

"Remember the night we ate the lobsters?" I reminisced.

"Sí, I remember it very well. Maybe you did not know it, but I needed company that night, not specifically yours, but company in general, and you gave me special joy, watching you pick out the most giant one from the tank."

"That huge one stared at me from the tank, a prehistoric lobster, and you kept telling me, 'Pick him, pick him.' "

"You looked awed, so cute, in your little suede jacket and the hot pants. I had to buy him for you."

"You looked so extraordinarily elegant to me in your dark suit. You paid for that meal in two hundred, American, and dollars seemed to be worth millions then. It took my breath away."

"I remember my Bethy eating the lobster, it kept coming, in different courses, and you kept eating it. Where was it going? And the amount of wine."

"Orchids and lilies all over . . . and there was an assistant, a kind of lobster-eating assistant."

"Sí, he cracked for you, you ate, he cracked . . ."

"I ate, he cracked, I ate. It was wild. He kept cracking and I kept eating."

"And I kept watching you, and loving you that moment, and knowing you would never love me who was old and ugly next to the beautiful young Luíz who gave you such heartache. Heh?"

"I thought he loved me."

"My sweet Bethy, everybody knew but you. You gave him success beyond his dreams, and he repaid you with the injuries from his ballets. Heh?"

"That's true, but that was another life. The beautiful young Luíz is dead, and your lobster eater is another person."

"But I am still here, my Bethy . . . Elizabeth. And still admiring your, as you Americans describe, heart. No matter what, you were determined to keep going and be a happy one."

"I needed to be happy more than most young women. And you helped me. I treasured that."

"Maybe now, I collect my marker, heh?" The ever-business-minded Count began to close in on what might be an opportunity. "You new film is very interesting to me. You know, a man loses his life being only rich, although the young girls never notice, heh?"

With that, I moved our conversation onto the nitty-gritty of raising the money for the film.

The Count made a list for me . . . "You my dear should start immediately to call upon . . ." And he explained how his poor aristocratic cousins would be robbed of their last money by a jealous government's taxes, without my worthy cause to contribute to. "We will make a limited film partnership with them." And with one of these royal cousins on the board of the French bank that had originally loaned Jorge the money to produce the film, and now held complete rights because Jorge defaulted, maybe it was possible that we could make some deal there too.

"Is it final that Jorge defaulted?" I wanted to be sure.

"Yes! My connection with this bank is very close. And I think they will lend to me to buy it off their hands. They have no interest to be in the film business. So you and I can draw papers as partners, as producing partners."

I wasn't sure I wanted to do it this way. "But if Jorge defaulted, why wouldn't the bank automatically sell the rights to that other bidder who's been trying so hard to get the film away from him? Especially if the other bidder is willing to pay as much as everybody says."

"Pah." The Count coughed a laugh. "This other bidder, I think he will soon pull out too."

"Why?"

"Because he is not interested in making this film so much. He is interested in Jorge's ruin. These two never stop with each other, Jorge and Bolanieu. Heh?"

"Bolanieu? Yves Bolanieu?"

"Sí, Yves Bolanieu! The one who gives French men the worst name to the ladies, but the best to the banks. Didn't you know that Bolanieu was the other bidder?"

The blood rushed to my head. How could I resist this? I would have my film and . . . "Are you sure Yves will pull out now that Jorge's out?"

"Who can be sure? Bolanieu has been moving into making films these last years, and has had some success. But maybe. Heh? Just maybe, there is something we can do to persuade him that it would be best if he changes his mind on this one. Heh?" The Count's eyes gleamed for trouble.

"I'm listening," I said breathlessly.

The Count raised his glass of Pellegrino, and I raised mine of vodka. We were ready to play our tricks again.

Sixteen

This is how the Count and I won the Olympic film:

We decided to keep my name out of everything publicly, in case either Jorge or Yves would try to block us. This meant we had to persuade the French bankers to temporarily enter the Count's name as a front for my private money bid against the Yves/Jorge rivalry. The extra interest points the Count was willing to pay for confidentiality helped considerably even though he insisted it was his royal lineage and not his money that still talked a strong language in Europe. The bulk of the money would be raised from the Count's list of notable relatives. The Count would put up a token bit of his own money, and the bank would lend us the rest as a partnership.

To back it up that I was out of the picture, I began to float some fast rumors that I was flying to L.A. for the collaboration of a lifetime with Paramount. To ensure it, everybody I met also heard my story of dissatisfaction with the on-again, off-again Olympic film. Inside, the gloating that I'd win it away from both Yves and Jorge kept threatening to escape from my throat in yelps and whelps.

The Count learned through Lady Marie Claire, his "prettiest

and most precious cousin," and an astute Brussels businesswoman, that although our indomitable Jorge X had problems in Spain, his credit in Belgium was still good. It seemed that Marie Claire knew Jorge in more than passing, as her apartment's lease was once in his name. A little more research through her sister, Lady Genevieve, who seemed to have had some little thing with Yves, turned up another rumor. Yves Bolanieu's food-exporting business in Belgium, Immolaire Ltd., was having a very bad year and his shareholders were more than furious with his film investments made with their money, and were ready to dump him unceremoniously. The Count's cousin, Jean Paul from Paris, confirmed this.

I immediately called Jorge X by telephone. The poor fellow acted besieged with guilt that I'd come all this way from New York to work with him, and "due to circumstances beyond his control," things were going so badly.

"No, no, I'm not upset," I assured him. "No hard feelings whatsoever. These things happen in our business every day. It's part of the risk we all take."

"I'm not sure you take it so philosophically," a skeptical Jorge answered.

"Jorge, truly, how can I be angry with you when everything's happened for the best for me? Had I been tied up with the Olympic film now, I couldn't have gone with Paramount . . . I'm very happy, please don't worry."

"Cariña, I must say, your luck in timing exceeds anything that has come my way."

"Look, I'm leaving anyday for New York, and I wanted to say goodbye to you and wish you the best."

"Mi Elizabeta, you show me the grace of a queen."

"I'm not a person who likes to argue, and it's not good business either. Why close doors that might be helpful to both of us in the future? Who can tell? Look, if you can make it, I'd love to see you before I leave. How about Friday?"

"Friday is impossible." He was definite.

I let out a sigh, appealing to his manhood. "What a shame, I feel terrible. Another night maybe? Please say you can find some time for me ..." And then I held my breath ...

"... Ah Sunday, the night could be possible. Where shall I invite you to dine? I send the limousine."

"Oh no please! This is my celebration. But I'm leaving Sunday. Maybe we could do it tonight? Only a drink to say goodbye. Ten perhaps?"

"Tonight I can't stay long. Such problems tomorrow."

"For a little while ... please? One drink? And let's do it American style, Club Chicago?"

"Ah ... the new one ..." He was interested. "But I will be late."

"No problem, I'll wait for you. The music is terrific there so if you're a little late, it'll be fine."

"I ..."

"Please say it's set. I'd love to see you."

"All right, I come there for mi Elizabeta."

"Wonderful! Hasta luego."

"Hasta luego."

I waited for Jorge on a stool at the end of the bar of Club Chicago, the latest in place, an almost authentic replica of a Chicago blues club. Dim lighting, the sculptured white stucco swells of simulated basement walls and a pocked and worn wooden bar had been installed for this new club's opening.

Ten was really too early for the place to swing, and very few patrons sat at the tables, mostly American couples and young Germans, dining on the same burgers, fries and buffalo wings as me. The Spanish, French and Italians were still in the finer restaurants dining leisurely with their wines and multicourse meals. Up at the stage, a giant mural of a keyboard waited in stunning black and white contrast for tonight's group of seven musicians, billed as the "Hottest Horns from Chicago."

I looked around the club and an unusual-looking woman sitting at the dark side bar along the wall caught my eye. At first I thought she was a patron because the waiters treated her as such, but she was dressed so oddly, in a long beige wool coat and a ski cap. This person is freezing on this stifling night, I thought. I watched her. She bent into her wool garments, camouflaging herself in them ... A homeless woman, I realized, who'd come in for refuge ...

I was surprised how the waiter respectfully brought the woman her cup of hot coffee. She held it tight in her hands feeling its warmth, then bent her head to drink, rather than bringing it up to her lips. She moved the cup along her bent forehead, feeling the warmth there. The woman lit a cigarette and smoked, bending her head to it in the same way. I watched her touch her face and arms over and again, as if feeling to make sure she was still there. Her face was intelligent, well-cut cheekbones. What could she have been? She caught me looking at her, and bent deeper into the colorless coat and hat. Manufacturing her own shelter.

Would I have the courage to go talk to her? One never approaches such people. There's that danger of discovering something you'd best not know. Emotions of theirs or yours?

Oh, those homeless people that approach you on the street, hustling for money every day, make it easy for you ... you would never, no matter what, do what those homeless do. They're easy to disdain ... but what of the homeless that somehow got trapped. . . . or for some other sadness live their lives this way? Did they choose it? Should you help them? How can you? I stood and went to the woman in the colorless long coat.

"Hello," I said.

She looked at me blankly ... I'm not here, she silently told me. I don't hear you. She went deeper into the shelter of her coat. I could see the bend of the body ... a mourning for something.

"How are you tonight?" I said simply in Spanish.

"Why are you talking to me? I don't want to talk to you." She bent away from me without answering. Then she rose from the barstool and walked around the space of the bar, proving she was not mad, but perfectly able to choose . . . to walk . . . to sit, like any other patron of the bar who came for the music. The horns had started playing, but she didn't seem to notice.

I went back to my seat at the end of the bar, and put money in an envelope . . . I gave it to the waiter who had brought the woman her coffee. "Give this to her please. And ask her to also order some food from the menu, and put it on my bill."

"She'll refuse from you." He nodded his head as if I should know.

"Then tell her the house is buying," I persuaded him.

"She'll know."

When I turned around the woman was gone.

The club was filling up fast now as the Hottest Horns from Chicago took the stage. A guest clarinet and a featured saxophone were starting a musical duel to the background rhythms of an energetic set of drums, electric guitar, bass and keyboard. Jorge arrived with the after-dinner crowd, as the trumpets joined in with the other horns. It was all too loud to hear any greetings. Jorge and I had to settle for kisses on both cheeks. I could smell a faintness of Dior pour Homme. "I can stay but one half hour," I managed to decipher over the horns.

The Hot Horns swung and blared louder with the solid appreciation of the crowd. I don't know what I said exactly. It didn't matter. Who could hear? But I chose my key words decisively and quickly.

"Yves," was my first word in the din.

Jorge sat to attention. He could hear the name of that nemesis in a nuclear attack. "Bolanieu?" he screamed back to make sure.

"Yes, Yves Bolanieu." Now his receptors were on alert. Over a drum solo, my story came out, quietly at first. "Poor Yves, he's had even worse breaks this year than you."

"What, what?"

"Terrible, terrible." I shook my head.

"What do you say?" The keyboards and four horns were back again with the drums. "What do you say?" he shouted.

"Immolaire Ltd., Yves's food exporter," I shouted back.

"In Belgique?"

"Yes, in Belgique."

"Did you say yes?"

"Yes! I said yes!"

"Yes?"

"Yes!"

"The food exporter?"

A moment of clarinet mellowness began. "That is Bolanieu's company." Jorge looked suspicious.

"Almost bankrupt." I looked saddened.

"How do you know?" He was very suspicious now.

"You know how close we once were, there is still a deep feeling in me."

Now jealousy fanned Jorge's obsession to undo Yves. "When do the stockholders meet?" he demanded over the drums.

"I don't know."

It didn't matter what I said anymore, Jorge was too smart to believe me. He could find out all the details himself. I was only a clue. And if there was any chance of pulling Yves down, any chance at all, I could rely on Jorge to act fast. I borrowed my next line from Mercedes. "I wish I could give you both some of my good fortune."

It worked. Gunner that he was, Jorge flew to Belgium the next morning to attack Yves in the corporate trenches of food exporting before Yves could get to the stockholders himself. Jorge zeroed in on his mark immediately, raising the money for a takeover of Yves's bankrupt company through Yves's own Belgium bankers.

Yves got wind of it and had to mobilize quickly to thwart

Jorge's commando tactics. He pulled his francs out of his Olympic film bid against us in Paris and jetted off with them to the battle-fields of Belgium.

The Count flew after them inconspicuously on TWA's cabin class. His task—to keep them both away from France and our film deal. The next day he faxed me:

July 4

Happy Independence Day ma petite from Bruxelles. It is such delight to be in this beautiful city once more. Do you know how lovely Brussels is, but to save you fax paper, I'll go directly to "what's happening," as you Americans are so fond of saying. I'm sitting in Restaurant du Chaton, a quaint little bistro you would love, and your illustrious Yves sits a few tables away, hasn't touched a morsel on his plate and I must say hasn't aged as well as our Jorge. Of course, he is on his second bottle of wine. Those French!

Aahh, I think on closer look here, that your Yves has had some cosmetic surgery. Something around the eyes to be sure, and maybe around the mouth a little too. Such vanity.

Oh . . . our Yves is leaving already . . . and you'll never guess in what, a long, longer than anything I've ever seen before in white sports cars. What is this? Maybe a Bugatti? And you wouldn't believe the chrome. Anyway, let him enjoy himself now, for tomorrow he deals with our cougar from Barcelona.

On July 6, at eleven P.M., the Count began faxing me again:

My Dear,

This just over the TV. You wouldn't believe this, our Jorge X was stopped for speeding tonight on the outskirts of Brussels. Why a man who never drives without a driver in a limo, would be at the wheel of a truck, I don't know, and why the police would search it is a further mystery, but it seems they found a huge cache of illegal weapons. I know he had money problems, but our Jorge, an arms runner? I don't believe it. Yves must have somehow set him up. Or maybe Jorge always had this little business on the side we didn't know about . . . aah, such greed. But here it comes now from the radio too.

July 7, at eight A.M.:

> My dear,
> I just got off the telly with a high official of the Bureau of Police (courtesy of my dear cousin Detective Armand). It seems that the police are instructed to hold Jorge without bail until this whole sordid matter is cleared up. The newspapers are blaring the story.

July 8, at six P.M.

> My dear,
> I think our mission is done. Jorge and Yves will both be here in magnificent Brussels for a while with their respective businesses. And I, I plan to fly to Paris this evening. I have spoken before with the bank there. These poor bankers, after all, are not moguls of films, and with Yves stretched out here to put his food company on its feet again, and our unlucky Jorge definitely out of everything for the moment, my dear, our time is right to buy the rights. Enclosed, all papers. Please check and fax me back.
> Oh, my dear, one more thing, please don't expect me right away in Barcelona, because I must stay in Paris to visit a little bit with my prettiest and most precious cousin, Suzanne. And you must, yes you must, promise me that upon my return from Paris you will be available to celebrate our new partnership. Adieu, ma petite.

Seventeen

A jovial Count telephoned me three days later, "Meet me at the jazz club El Dragón, the Dragon, tonight at ten, mi rubia. Remember, you promised me our celebration?"

"Sí." It was time to celebrate, and I was sure the Count hadn't lost his edge. I found him seated at a table for two along a wall at the side of the band where the amplified speakers threatened to deafen us permanently. Out on the dance floor, the international crowds gyrated back-to-back and belly-to-belly looking like a rush-hour New York subway gone wild. The surly bartender sloshed beers to the six-deep bar. "If ya wanna reservation, call the airlines," he roared over the noise to a phone caller.

"One drink and we leave," the count kissed me in greeting. "I have a special very original party for us tonight. It is at the studio of a very trendy artist, a most unusual fellow with the most unusual work, and into the most unusual things, devil worship."

"Devil worship?" I was a little alarmed.

"Oh come on, it's not really serious with them. It's for play. Not dangerous at all. And actually, Satanism is quite an interesting religion. You'll be intrigued, I promise. Much more so than here or any club on a crowded Saturday night in Barcelona during Olympics, heh?"

He was right, everything would be overcrowded and hot. Besides, I'm always interested in new things. What filmmaker isn't? Who knows, such a scene might come in handy for a future film.

"It's decided then? Heh!"

"It's decided."

We left the Count's car parked halfway up the sidewalk on a narrow street lined with stone buildings, deep in the heart of Barrio Gótico, and made the rest of our journey of intrigue on foot. We walked through a familiar maze of dark cobblestone alleys lit only by the full moon.

"You won't believe the lovely lilac garden on the other side of this doorway," the Count said as once again I faced Alice's narrow rabbit hole carved out of a wall of stone buildings.

"Oh I bet I will." I slid sideways through it. I was once again in Carlos's studio. I should have known.

A black-tee-clad Carlos met us at the door. His studio was ablaze with black candles throwing moving shadows up the walls of his paintings, and playing along the jutted angles of the balcony. The full moon through the skylight seemed to be actually in the room.

Carlos bowed to the Count. "Ah, the Count from Marbella. Your cousin Miguel Antonio told me you might be here tonight, you are welcome!" Then Carlos led the way without showing the slightest recognition of me. I kept quiet. He showed us to a circle of black-clad celebrants seated under the skylight.

I gasped. In the middle of the circle, under the moon, two young women who appeared to be twins were lying naked, end to end on a marble slab.

"That is the altar," the Count whispered to me. "In Satanism, a woman is used for the altar because women are believed to be natural receptors, passive."

The celebrants stood as Carlos approached the altar wearing a magenta cape. He rang a loud clanging bell, while turning in a circle. "Hail Satan," he chanted with the celebrants. "Hail Satan. Come Abaddon, Moloch, Nergal, Pan, Dembala, Bili."

"They are calling up their devils," the Count translated for me.

"Oh my God."

"Shh, don't say that here!" the Count warned, delighted at the dark divertissement before us. "They are only calling up some devil chaps to join their party."

"Hail Satan," the voices grew loud with emotion. "Open wide the gates of hell of lurkers of the darkness. Oh Princes of Hell, move and appear. Come Lucifer, Belial, Leviantha. Hail Satan."

"Oh my God," escaped from my throat again.

"Shh, don't say that here." The Count placed his hand over my mouth. "Don't worry so much. See, nothing is moving or appearing."

The chanters removed amulets from around their necks and threw them into the circle. The women removed their black robes revealing their nakedness. All sat chanting to themselves in a language I couldn't understand. "Nopeai babajehi ds berina val ooaoner, vouuple canisa."

"What are they saying?" I whispered to the Count.

"That is Enochian, an ancient language for this kind of thing, my dear. This chant will give them more sexuality, which in turn emits a greater discharge of the biochemical energy they will need to meet and accept Satan."

"How do you know all this?"

"My dear, I know! Satanism merely advocates greed, pride, envy, anger, gluttony, malice and unbridled lust. Not so unusual, heh? Except that one must give up one's guilt of other religions, not so terrible if one can stay careful of one's natural instincts? Heh?"

"Oh," I said, always impressed with the Count's knowledge of the dark side.

"Carlos is the high priest of this ceremony. You will see now, watch him."

At the altar, Carlos was uncovering two large canvases that had been placed on the floor at each end. His subjectless pastels mixed with the moonlight until the translucent lavenders and blues seemed to run like water down the canvases. Suddenly the altar burst into motion, and the glassy-eyed prone twins began to writhe on their marble platform. The high priest held a silver chalice over them both and poured a red liquid onto their chests. I felt sick as I smelled the blood. The celebrants rose from the circle and surrounded the altar. The Count and I stood away from the black-robed men and naked women as they each took a turn dipping their hands into the chalice of blood and painting stripes on the chests and thighs of the writhing twins.

"I think you should get this on film," the Count suggested seriously.

"I think I've already had that chance, and luckily, I passed," I answered as seriously. The moon through the skylight was flaming.

The celebrants unbound the legs of both twins and the glazed young women used their toes to excite the genitals of each painter as he or she kneeled to dip into the chalice of blood. When the celebrants finished painting, both twins were solidly in a trance, perfectly still. The painters put on their robes again and returned to the circle whereupon Carlos placed a black-wrapped bundle in the middle of the altar, under the moon. A man rose and took a long sword from a jeweled case and plunged it into the bundle. Something inside exploded. "Hail Satan, Hail Satan," all the voices rose to the moon.

"Hail Satan!" the Count joined in, nudging me to do as well.

I suppressed another "Oh my God."

High Priest Carlos looked huge in a black cape now, standing at the altar, reading from scraps of paper that had been placed in a wooden vessel at the side.

The Count whispered to me, "These are requests from the members of the circle. The High Priest is their medium to Satan to hear and grant their requests."

"Please, I think we'd better go now," I pleaded. "We've had enough of this."

"Oh no." The Count looked so disappointed in me. "It's almost over, we've got to hear their requests."

"My enemy, kill him," was repeated from paper to crumpled paper. "Kill her, torture, kill, destroy."

"I'd say there was a commonality of theme," the Count mirthfully observed.

"How horrible, please let's go." I was begging.

Someone struck a gong, and a naked male entered the circle to draw two crescents, a pentagram and a circle on the canvas under the moon. Then a woman approached the altar and Carlos handed her a jewel-encrusted box from which she extracted several long thin needles.

"Hail to Lilith and Hecate," she chanted as she kneeled before the twins.

The whole congregation was in ecstasy as she plunged the needles into the flesh of the tranced young women, through their cheekbones, and through their arms.

"Oh my God, this is horrible," I burst out above the chanting and stood to stop her.

"Don't be hysterical." The Count gripped me back down. "It's only an ancient form of acupuncture. These girls will remember nothing when they go back to their regular jobs tomorrow. These people are quite normal during the day, and this man Carlos is very respected, a fine artist.

"These drugged girls are being used as human dolls, and she's placing pins in them to avenge the enemies on those pieces of paper."

I jumped up again and started forward.

Just then there was a crash. Something heavy had fallen in the darkness from the balcony at its narrowest part. All eyes went up to that moon-illuminated spot in time to hear a piercing shriek and see a black-clad figure dive through a glass wall. Glass shattered to the ground outside.

"That's it!" I pulled the Count up. "I'm leaving. No more!"

"Don't be silly," he entreated behind me. "My dear, it is a little astral flight for all of us. That's all. Heh?"

"Right, a woman sticks pins in human dolls, and someone commits suicide by jumping through a glass wall. If I need an astral flight I'll film one." I didn't stop until I reached the garden of lilacs where I dared to turn around and confront the broken bleeding body I knew would be on the ground. But there was none, and the glassed wall of the building was perfectly intact. Not a sound came from inside the angled structure under the moon. Had it all been a series of illusions?

Eighteen

Our immediate money troubles were out of the way, but we had a much smaller budget to work with. "There isn't a moment to spare," I told my crew. "We need the shots of the Olympic preparation going on right now, because it'll cost a fortune to duplicate them later on a studio set in Madrid." All my candy visions of the giant film trucks of equipment parked on location vanished from my imagination, and I replaced them with just me, José, Sven, Paco and a few key crew members shooting with minimal camera, sound and lighting equipment in the best natural lighting we could find. Still, I was excited to have won my film and sure I could make it work. After all, the Count was right, who knew more about low-budget films than I? We settled into a tiny plain office on La Rambla de las Floras and started to roll.

We spent our first week feverishly shooting a montage of hurdlers, gymnasts, discus throwers, bicyclists, swimmers and the new Olympic Coliseum. José and Sven became particularly entranced with a young girl, a Scandinavian runner, and wanted extra footage of her. She ran every morning as the sun came up on the beach with her coach, her father, pacing beside her in a jeep. They contacted the father and he agreed we could have those special shots. By the end of our week we had a mountain of film cans. What we had seen with our eyes had been so memorable, we hardly dared to look at the film. It was Saturday night before we met at a screening room to look at our work.

Sven put up the reel of the Scandinavian girl runner on the beach first, and even his quietly unexcitable face registered surprise. José jumped up and down voicing it for him. "Formidable, Sven. Formidable! Look, Elizabeth, how the sunrise light changes on her. Una angelita lit by other angels. Her hair is almost white, and the colors coming up from the sky behind her. Sven my genius," he embraced him.

"Sí, Sven, you're a genius." I hugged the placid Sven myself as the long-legged girl ran by on the screen in front of us. Sven's camera began to move in to detail the blisters of sweat building on her arms and chest, then down to her feet kicking up the surf. Sven's slow-motion detail of the flying white ocean foam was in itself art.

"Watch this pullback," José called. The camera returned to normal speed and the girl began to sprint, her long translucent legs reaching out. "Look how this girl runs with God in her." José hugged both Sven and himself. "Soon here we will have a close-up."

The close-up came and we all stared in disbelief at the look on the young girl's face. This girl ran from terror not God. The shot widened out to include her father chasing in the jeep beside her and I felt her terror transfer to my own face. "Stop it," I screamed out, crying, shocking José and Sven. "Stop it, stop it." Sven immediately stopped the film, and turned on the lights.

"Elizabeth, but what is the matter?" José asked, as completely unprepared for my sudden hysteria as I was. "You know we can cut out her close-up in the editing. She does not look so pretty when she is concentrating so much. Is not unusual. Athletes can look like that. We don't use the close-up, that's all. Is nothing to be upset about."

But I was already shaking as the picture of the girl's terror broke open my memory. José and Sven stared at me . . . Careful, Elizabeth, I steeled myself, or the world will find out about you . . . What are you doing? . . . It is only a girl running on the beach that you see. Only a girl running on the beach. Only a girl running on the beach. I steeled myself again and reached into my repertoire of smiles, gripping my hands behind my back . . . Laugh at the tears, laugh . . . "I'm sorry, José, I must be exhausted." I half smiled, half laughed my apology. "Please, let's take a break and then look at the rest of the footage."

"Sí, Elizabeth." José still looked startled. "Seguro, you are tired. We will go to dinner and allow you to rest." José stood to leave and Sven quietly followed behind.

As soon as the men left I jumped up to rewind the footage to the runner's close-up. I froze the frame and studied it. It wasn't the terror I'd seen before, but as José had said, the face of an athlete agonizing to push her young body past perfection, bursting her heart toward her sixty seconds of glory. I let the film advance to the wide shot of her father, her coach, pacing her in the jeep. Their intensity was perfectly normal, even beautiful, an incredible athlete and her trusted coach, how could I have read my own agony into it.

I tried to move on. But it was too late. What I had promised not to think about was flooding my mind.

. . . my father's room is dark . . . black . . . I can only make out the angle of the half-open door . . . I feel his weight . . . I try to wriggle down and away like a wretched unearthed worm desperate to get back into my earth before my life is taken from me . . . I feel his sweat pressing me down . . . suffocation . . . searing . . . my screams escape into the blackness . . . I gasp to pull them back, but they go on . . . no, no, please don't scream, it will be longer . . . I'm going to die, yes, wish for death . . . please let me die, please let me die . . . And then my sweet miracle happens . . . I run away to my secret place in my mind, my beautiful pastel lights . . . my enchanted castle lights up behind me, lavender and pink. I'm grown, a famous ballerina dancing the role of Aurora in *Sleeping Beauty*. . . the music for the Rose Adagio begins . . . I'm dressed in my stiff white tutu, taking a rose from each of my three princely suitors and holding it aloft perfectly balanced on point each time . . . I know my last arabesque balance must last forever . . . I must concentrate . . . concentrate . . . because only these exquisite seconds of perfect balance can justify my existence for one more night, and I will wake up in my own bed in the morning and everything else will be a dream . . . If I fail to keep the balance I'll be plunged back to my death under his panting and my screams, and it will last and last . . .

"Elizabeth," I begged myself out loud, hearing a child's scream echo in the empty screening room. "You must let go of the past, of Bethy, because she is gone. You are a grown woman, your life is now. Your fulfillment is now with this film. *Firenze* took you by surprise. Nobody expected its success. But you've carefully won this Olympic film. It is who you are now. It is yours. It's José's and Sven's and Paco's. The past belongs to the past. You can't change what happened then. Are you going to ruin the present by grieving for the past? Look how good your Olympic film can be."

I sat freezing and shaking and waited for my hands to be steady enough to put up a different can of footage. Then I went to the back of the theater and watched my work. Olympic runners walked in slow motion across the screen on the very same track where they would soon give everything they had for that one moment they had dreamed of during the loneliness of their training. I watched bicyclists slanting at almost ninety degrees around turns, little girls flying through the air on uneven bars, yellow trucks carrying hurdles to the track for racers of all nations, runners with muscles straining like race horses coming around the bend through an early morning fog, and pole vaulters clearing the bar by fractions of an inch, praying they would do it once more for their country at that crucial moment. I looked at the footage we'd shot in the Olympic Village of the marathon runners. They ran through the streets with children running their play practices by their sides, little Olympic brothers and sisters waving flags and playing Olympic torches. I laughed along with the pranks of the American swimmers we'd shot later in the evening, young proud athletes sharing euphoria.

José and Sven returned from their dinner and were relieved to see that I was myself again, their colleague in control. I'd just been tired from the stress of the week ... Women, you know, I'd let them believe. We continued to roll our week's film.

"Look," I froze a particularly good frame, "there's my favorite, that decathlon fellow, the one that always lands on his feet with such a smile on his face."

"And look there," José pointed to the left of the screen as it rolled on. "Isn't that your American television broadcaster, the skier who did the commentary on the winter games in France?"

"So it is, so it is." My eyes picked Steven Brandon out of a crowd that was watching the practice we'd filmed at the pool yesterday. "The intriguing Steven Brandon."

"So you know him well?" José turned to me.

"We've met."

"Funny he's in the crowd watching the swimming practice, but look, he watches something else over right instead."

"He's an odd one."

"Still watching the right side, not the swimmers." José's trained eyes followed Steven as the shots of the crowd played out on the screen. "Elizabeth, isn't that where you were standing?"

"Probably not," I tossed it off. "But I assure you there were probably several other women there. Pool ... bathing suits ...

you know." I was trying to joke away my interest in Steven, which they'd already picked up. I'd weathered enough storms today and was in no mood for the seething I still felt from being stood up by him at the Avenida Palace.

"He's still watching over right." José wouldn't let it go. "Elizabeth, I'm sure that is where you were standing."

"I'm sure I was not standing where he was watching! How ridiculous, he happened to be in the crowd and was watching something over right."

José froze the frame. "But what does he look at that makes such expression of love?"

This was going too far. Steven hadn't even bothered to say hello to me. "José, you'd see anything as love," I snapped.

"Verdad, love makes me happy," he gloated.

"But in the end," I cut him off, "even for you it can be humiliating."

Nineteen

On Monday morning we were back at the pool to shoot another diving practice. A crowd had gathered to watch, and there on the edge, I spotted Steven Brandon. What was he still doing in Barcelona? I tried not to see him ... tanned, healthy good looks, blue eyes, crooked smile. As usual, I wanted the man who was the most elusive. No, not this time. How could I? Especially Steven, especially him, successful, an excellent athlete, the American prototype husband every American girl is brought up to long for. That alone was disgusting. "Relationship," he'd said on the plane, and three hours later he was in a café with that German girl ... a not quite, whatever she was ... the telephone messages he never returned, and standing me up that afternoon at the Avenida ...

"Hello, Elizabeth, how are you?" Steven's nonregional TV journalist's voice caught me from behind.

"Oh it's you," I answered, keeping my eyes on the film action. "I'd thought you'd left for L.A."

"You know," he smiled, "I thought I'd be gone by now too, but I got caught up in this so I took an assignment, and I'll be here for at least another week. But what about you, I'm surprised to see you. I'd heard your film was off, and I thought you'd be heading back."

"My film is on, and I'm here."

"I'm very glad to see that you are, because—"

"What happened at the Avenida Palace?" I got right to the point.

"Oh, that day! I was really sorry about that. I left you a message, didn't you get it? Well, let me tell you, you never want to be on a dusty road in Spain without a spare tire. We walked for miles! Thank God we came across a farmer with a pickup truck, he schlepped us to what he called a town, where some guy sold us a tire for more than I paid to rent the car. That wasn't bad . . . I would've paid more for the ride back if we could've got it! We rolled the tire all the way back!"

I'd never gotten such a message. I didn't bother to mention my unreturned calls.

"I can see you're busy, and I don't want to bother you while you're working. Look . . . would it be all right if I called you later?"

Wasn't he acting polite. "Call if you'd like."

"Great! It's really been nice to see you. Talk to you later!"

"Goodbye." I knew he'd never call.

"A picnic on Montserrat," Steven invited later by telephone. "The green serrated mountains, the magnificent architecture of the Benedictine monastery, the unique Black Madonna. Did you know that Wagner set his opera *Parsifal* there? It would be a beautiful drive and it would hardly take any time at all. It would be the perfect short break to ease the long workday. I know how early you film people start, you know we TV news guys start pretty early ourselves. Look, I'll pick you up and have you back before you know it."

"A picnic there would be very nice," I had to agree. I could do it. I'd see Steven this once, play it out as they say, probably put the whole thing to rest.

"Done deal, tomorrow at three," Steven said with the certainty of someone who knew you would have the time of your life. "And I'll bring the food. You only have to bring yourself."

"Tomorrow at three," I said, "and I'll bring the wine."

"Fantastic," he finished. "I'm looking forward to this."

The day was gorgeous as we drove up the steep peaks of Montserrat in a little Fiat. Steven looked straight ahead maneuvering the winding road. I looked straight ahead studying his profile out of the corner of my eye. As the intensity of the climb absorbed his attention, the earlier Rhett Butler bravado began to slip away.

"You were right, this is wonderful," I said looking around at magnificent green everywhere.

As soon as I spoke, it was as if I called him to some kind of bodily attention, and he donned Paul Newman this time, too casually dropping a hand from the wheel and leaning back in the seat. . . . he became a man who usually drove race cars at breakneck speed, totally in control on much worse tracks, only being a little careful here for my sake. "Trust me," he said.

The climb opened on to a grassy plateau. We stopped the car along the side of the road and left it to look at the exquisiteness of the sharp serrated peaks all around us, and the vista of the city and port below . . . funny how quickly the people disappear when you look down from a height. After a while we started to make conversation.

"Everybody was talking about you yesterday in the news room," Steven began, "how you bought out the film rights and took right over. Tough stuff, girl. Your art of filmmaking sounds like the action of Wall Street."

"Same riches to rags, plus the commitment it takes to become an Olympic skier."

"For most skiers, I guess that would be true. But for me, well, it wasn't quite the same thing, even though the results turned out the same. I was just some kind of kid who was some kind of rebel with no commitment to anything but freedom."

"So what made you work so hard at skiing?"

"I didn't. Skiing was a natural thing for me. I grew up in Colorado, and we skied every day. But I wasn't competitive about it like the other guys were. Believe it or not, I was more of a poet, more interested in being on top of the mountains, in the sky, with my snow, than in the skiing itself. It made me feel free to be up there. I loved that."

"You couldn't have made the American Olympic ski team on freedom and poetry. Something must have changed for you."

"You're right there, something sure did. I turned sixteen, and my father told me I had to grow up and get down to planning my business career."

"You didn't agree?"

"No way! My dad was a banker, and a powerful man. The more he pushed me toward Harvard and summer banking jobs, the more I rebelled. It was the sixties and everybody was singing about freedom, and the thought of being locked up with him in a bank my whole life scared the hell out of me. I spent more time on the slopes, and made my grades go down so I wouldn't be accepted to his schools."

"Was Harvard that bad?"

"It was for me! It represented his world, and I would have done anything to get away from that. I felt like I was choking, but he wouldn't let me loose. I had to do more than excel to get away. Making the Olympic team was my only way to freedom. Finally he was satisfied that I was Young Master Citizen, and kind of left me alone."

"What happened to the poet?"

"Oh, he's still here. Much later, after my father died, I got some of the poems I'd written on my mountain published. Funny how being a skier got me published. I think of all those writers who don't get published and how lucky I was, and ..." Steven stopped. ". . . I don't know why I'm telling you all this. It's strange, but somehow I kind of feel like I should . . . like there's some kind of understanding between us."

Here we go again, I thought, realizing how involved I was becoming in his story. Here comes that old "we met somewhere before in eternity" line. Give me a break.

"It's like we know each other better than we do," he continued according to script. "Even on the plane, there was something. Somewhere?" He turned to me.

"Mmmmmmmm," was all I could answer. Really, these guys! But then again, he lives in California. I looked for a way to excuse what sounded like a line. They're more open about their feelings, and more into cosmic connections in California, I tried to justify.

"Enough about me." Steven looked honestly embarrassed about his openness. "How'd you get into filmmaking?"

"Actually I was a ballet dancer. It was my own way to freedom. I loved it more than anything, but by the time I turned twenty-five, my body was failing me. Injuries. I tried so hard to recover, but I couldn't. I had to do something else, and I was lucky too."

"I should have known you were a dancer. You have a dancer's walk, and long legs, like those beautiful *Swan* girls I fell in love with when my junior high class went to the ballet. Do you know, I fantasized about those swans for years."

"Does that mean that you'd have returned my phone calls if you'd known I'd once been a swan?"

"What phone calls?"

"Steven, you're not going to tell me you didn't get my phone messages."

"No, and my daughter picked up our messages every day, no matter where we were traveling. Did you really call, Elizabeth? I specifically asked her if there were any messages from you."

"Yes, I called a couple of times."

"I can't believe she'd keep messages from me. Poor Jenn, she can be a little possessive but you've got to understand her. My wife died when she was little."

"Oh, I'm sorry to hear that."

"Yeah, and Jenn's such a sweet kid really, but she's been a lonely kid, and I guess I've been too indulgent a father. I spoiled her. It's my fault."

"Where is she now?"

"I'm still spoiling her. I sent her to Paris with a schoolfriend and her family. Of course it meant a new wardrobe for her, and lots of shoes. These kids love shoes. But what the heck, I'm trying to get her more involved with kids her own age. If they like shoes, she'll have shoes."

"Try tennis camp. I have girlfriends who keep complaining that their daughters are obsessed with their Florida tennis camp in the summer, and in the winter, it's only their New York teammates and Andre Agassi. But they're busy."

"I guess some kids can be sporty like that, but not Jenn. Maybe if my wife were here, she would've wanted Jenn to play tennis."

"Was she a player?"

"She did everything. She was a swimmer at school, besides being a skier. We made the Olympic team together. We were soul buddies discovering the world. It was more that than a romance. We were very young and got married. Then later Toni was killed flying a small plane in Hallstatt. They told me she was alone when it happened. I was a mess and . . ." Steven stopped again. "I really don't know why I'm telling you all this. I'm sorry, it's not exactly the best conversation for a guy who's invited a girl on a picnic."

"Oh please, please, I really like hearing about you." And despite myself, I really did. Maybe it was true about him not getting my messages. Maybe it was true about missing me at the

Avenida Palace because of a flat tire. At any rate, it was a beautiful day, and I was already here, a lovely peaceful interlude from the crazy pace of the film. We sat down on the grass with the spectacular jagged rocks all around us.

Steven produced a large picnic basket and blanket from the trunk of the Fiat. "Wait till you taste these mussels. I bought them fresh at the Boquería on the Ramblas this morning and had the hotel prepare them for us. Here," he said, opening the basket to display the wonderful aroma. "We also have a creamy montaña cheese with just a touch of pepper, a magnificent french bread with a nice hard crust, the reddest red apples you've ever seen, and these strawberries are the sweetest, most delicious strawberries you'll ever taste. I love that market. I almost bought everything."

I watched Steven lay out the food on a bright green tablecloth as if he were displaying jewels, he was so delighted with his market treasures. Was this one of those practiced male steps in the direction of that old lunch and lust routine? Or did he care this much?

"Here's the wine," I said, a little embarrassed at the unspecial bottle I pulled from a brown paper bag.

"It's perfect, Elizabeth. Let me put it on the dry ice."

"You've gone to such trouble. How nice of you."

"I told you on the plane," Steven kidded, "you could turn out to be the love of my life."

Why was he still giving me soap opera lines? Really! "From what I hear and read about you famous bachelors, there are too many loves of your lives."

"All media hype fiction." Steven laughed. Then the smile faded. "I can only say it one more time. I'm a person with real feelings."

No! This was too perfect, too pat, he looked too good in the sunshine. A staged romance out of Bethy's dreams. The ones that always turned into sexual encounters instead. I couldn't let myself in for it again, even if everything he said was absolutely true. "Ah yes," I sidestepped jokingly, "the seduction continues."

Was it my imagination, or did Steven really look disappointed at my remark? He took the wine bottle and started unscrewing the cork. When he finished, he looked up again. "How's the movie going?" His tone was different, impersonal.

"Great, a few more weeks, and I can return to New York to start editing," I answered cheerfully.

After that, Steven talked only about work, and I avoided anything that could possibly lead to the subject of romance. We played the parts of two Americans working in a foreign country enjoying some surface chatter. Soon, it was six, and we both had to return to the city for our late-day meetings.

The road looked even steeper on the way down.

"Don't worry, I've had a lot of practice on downhill runs," Steven laughingly assured my nervous look as he squeezed the car around a sharp descending curve. "And the Pacific Coast Highway too." He maneuvered with one hand on the wheel. "Have you ever driven that road? Winds all the way."

"No. I always take planes when I'm in California. I've never had time for that drive, though I've always wanted to do it."

"You should. It gives you an incredible feeling. Goes right along the ocean. Pacific lapping at your wheels, white lime-washed cliffs of rock jutting out of the water. Pure California. Next time you're there, call me, and I'll be your guide. We'll stop for lunch in Carmel and dessert in Monterey."

"Sounds good," I agreed in that casual way you answer invitations you know won't be followed up on.

"Listen, why wait that long?" Steven careened around a turn with barely a finger on the wheel. "I'll be finished with my work here on Friday and I was planning to drive up the Costa Brava, the Wild Coast. The scenery there is magnificent, and I've got a great idea. Why don't you come drive it with me? My plane leaves

Sunday, so you'll definitely be back in time to get a good night's sleep and be ready for work on Monday."

I didn't know what to say.

"We'll stay in separate rooms at night," he added quickly. "C'mon, you'll have a great time!"

"All right," I agreed, promising myself I wouldn't make love to him under any circumstances. Maybe he was telling the truth about all his romances with all those women being only media hype. Who knows? A lot of these desirable men are really attached to only one woman. Maybe he had no one. After all, when it came down to it, I didn't either.

"Friday for sure?" Steven asked again.

"Sure, why not," I answered. Nothing to lose.

Twenty

Once away from Steven, I went back to having second thoughts . . . A reputed womanizer! . . . But he didn't seem that way . . . I should know better than anyone about media hype . . . when I work this hard at home, I never have a social life and look what they say about me . . . You'd think . . .

Finally, on Friday afternoon, in the name of maintaining a social life and in defiance of my back-home image as a workaholic supergirl, I left before the workday was over, and dashed back to my hotel to put together some things to take to Costa Brava. With not much time to prepare, my weekend wardrobe consisted of cutoff jeans, a tank top, sneakers and the baseball cap I'd been wearing to shoot in the hot sun since early morning, a pair of jeans for the cooler evenings, a few clean polos and an off-one-shoulder snug lavender tee.

Steven arrived on time wearing a crisp button-down white shirt with light blue stripes, neatly rolled up to the elbows, newly laundered, pressed faded blue jeans and ginger-colored moccasins. He sported an irresistible smile. I threw my skimpy backpack into the rear of the shiny yellow jeep, and climbed in next to him.

"You look terrific," he said. "Except your cap should say LA, not Mets. I'll get you a Dodgers hat for next time . . . You look gorgeous . . . I'm glad you could make it."

"Thanks for the compliments. I'm glad I could make it too. I wasn't sure I would. This week was the craziest yet." The truth of that was evident in my voice.

"Things don't always go as smoothly here as we're used to." He laughed like somebody who'd also spent the week shooting footage in a foreign country.

"It was something every day," I admitted. "We had to rewrite the script because the elements we'd ordered never showed, sets weren't available that were supposed to be, and sometimes key people, technicians and even actors, didn't come to work. But somehow, the dailies turned out terrific. Spontaneous! Everybody who was there did a great job, and I'm glad it's over!"

"Sounds exactly like my week. My stuff looked great, and I'm glad it's over."

We laughed together. Steven had a knack for making me feel as if I knew him better than I could in the short time we'd spent together. "You know," I said, relaxing, "I lived in Barcelona for years, and never went to Costa Brava."

"I didn't know you lived here. I almost lived here myself, a long time ago. I've always thought Spain was fantastic. When was it that you lived here?"

"When I was dancing. I'd joined a touring European ballet company. When we finished playing here in Barcelona, the company went to Paris. But I stayed on, and joined a company here playing at the Opera. I was very young, nineteen."

"You must have loved it here to bypass Paris. What was it like when you were dancing here? Must have been some exciting experience for a young girl. What did you do?"

"I'd tell you if I wasn't so tired," I sidestepped. Why did I bring that up? It's exactly what I didn't want to talk about. What if he knew about Bethy? . . . All her lovers . . . How many were there? . . . What if he knew about the sexual acrobatics she learned in Barcelona . . . no, that's not true . . . I always knew them . . . I was taught well, before . . .

"Please, you don't have to talk for my sake. Lean back, relax. We've got plenty of time to talk this weekend."

"Well, It's just that I've been talking all week, that's all." Steven must have been skiing in America when I was here . . . He was with his young wife . . . healthy loving couple . . . shining American youth . . .

"The Costa Brava is a lot different now than it was when you were here," Steven was pointing out. "It's so crowded with hotels and people, you could be at almost any beach resort. But I'm going to take you to my own places where the cliffs are too rocky to build hotels, and the beaches are too rough for the tourists. The only things around are ruins of an old Moorish fortress or two, and a few old castles on top of some cliff here and there."

"That deserted?"

"Well . . . there might be a four-star golf resort that somehow sneaked in at the bottom around the corner from a fishing village, in case someone needs a sign of a modern civilization."

"Sounds great," I smiled. "I've always loved the outdoors, but I only have the opportunity on shoots these days. I've been a victim of the great New York indoors."

We kept driving north, through the cliffs of Costa Brava. Around us the dense white hotels and bikini-clad strollers, ubiquitous pan pizza waterfront cafés and tee shirt shops faded into a vista of sparkling blue-green sea. The cliffs were covered with a blue-green vegetation so thick that it followed down to the water's edge, casting a diagonal greenish shadow across the smooth golden sand. Steven snapped away all the flaps of our jeep and we were riding out in the glorious open.

"Hold on," Steven cautioned. "The road may become a little bumpy and dangerous here. I don't want to lose you."

I noticed he had both hands on the wheel now, so I figured

he must be serious and held on in time for a jolt that might have knocked me out of the jeep.

He laughed. "I know it may seem that I'm always taking you on crazy roads, but trust me, I'm not trying to kill you."

"You're sure?"

We laughed and bumped like two people in those little cars they have in the amusement parks. Our road had been blasted out of a slated stone moonscape of cliffs whose tops were hidden by ghostly moving clouds. We looked straight down to pointed white coral cliffs jutting out of waters of many changing colors.

"It's eerie," I said. "I'll have to remember this place if I ever shoot a science-fiction movie."

"No problem, let me take some pictures for you right now, and you'll have them if it ever comes up. I have a new Nikon in the back that's been waiting for an opportunity like this one." Steven stopped the jeep and we admired a grove of silvery green olive trees in the distance. Beyond, the low afternoon sun lit up a tiny Moorish village, making it look like a city of gold.

"A sunset cocktail for two?" Steven pulled the jeep well off the road after he photographed the area.

"Steven, how nice! I'm beginning to think you're one of the world's great hosts."

He dipped into a cooler in the back and pulled out two icy glasses and a bottle of Absolut Citron. He came around to help me out of the jeep. "Now," he said, "all we need is a nice flat rock."

We set up on a rock, and watched the colors of the sunset in awe. Indian turquoise and burnt orange seamed together in the blue vastness over the sea, and melted into mystical beams of light. The moonscape cliffs rising from the sea became red-hued dragons to protect the lone ships till the light of morning came again.

"We'd better go before the sun goes down completely." Steven picked up our glasses. "I've seen it sink into the horizon pretty fast up here, and it goes pitch black right away. Also, I'm getting hungry. How about you?"

"I'm starved."

"We're only a few more curves away from the lighthouse. There's a great Basque restaurant right there. You'll love it!"

"Perfect! How do you know your way around up here this well?"

"I'm very good with mountains," he laughed. "I've got ways with them."

"I guess you do."

"Let's go?"

"Let's go!"

Soon we were being seated by a jovial, aproned proprietor whose establishment was too far from the tourist hotels not to be a labor of love. There was only one other table occupied in the restaurant. A mellow red wine was uncorked, and a platter of fresh mariscos and a crusty bread was placed before us. We were surrounded by the heavenly aroma of garlic.

"Mi especial bouillabaisse?" the proprietor suggested.

"We'd love it," we agreed.

"But, I must warn, it will take some more time to prepare," the man said tentatively. "I know you Americans are always . . . hurry, hurry."

"Not this American," Steven assured him. "I live in California. Ask my friend from New York."

"Not this weekend," I assured him.

"Then will be okay."

"Absolutamente." Steven raised both arms to emphasize our double agreement.

"Formidable." The proprietor was pleased that we would have his special wine-laced glory of the sea.

I hadn't been this relaxed in weeks. I leaned back appreciating Steven's good manners—and good looks too. "Please tell me more about your skiing, Steven."

"I will if you'll tell me about your dancing in Barcelona."

"I'll make you a deal," I evaded. "If you'll tell me about your skiing today, I'll tell you about my dancing tomorrow." I have to be careful, I thought . . . He makes me feel too comfortable . . . Things I don't mean to come out, might . . . "We have plenty of time," I finished. "Besides, you promised to do the talking."

"Okay, I'll go first," Steven agreed sportingly, as the happy proprietor poured us more wine, cleared the crumbs from the checkered tablecloth, and brought us his own fresh paté to sample while his bouillabaisse perfected itself.

"Did you ever ski, Elizabeth?" Steven's face was glowing.

"No, but I'd like to."

"Maybe you can understand though what skiing was to me. Skiing was my freedom. I was completely without fear when I skied. When I was a kid, it was as if God had given me a magic mountain just for myself. I still get that feeling sometimes."

I was surprised at the emotion he was sharing with me. Steven had stopped talking and was looking at me, deciding whether to continue or not.

"Please go on," I urged him.

He thought for a moment, then let out his breath and continued. "I guess a lot of guys who grew up in the same type of environment I did, in strict churchgoing families, with fathers who worked for major corporations, or big banks like my dad . . . I guess we saw dads as tyrants. Well, till about thirteen, I was always scared and nervous and kind of skinny. At home it was terrible. I lived in fear of my father all the time. He was some kind of bear, that man. I don't know if girls can ever understand what goes on between boys and fathers. From the very first you're supposed to be just like them. Do you have brothers, Elizabeth?"

"No and I didn't know too many boys when I was little."

"My father's displeasure with me was obvious. He didn't have to tell me. I was a dreamer who loved nature and wrote poems about trees and grass and skies. He was set on having a son who was Harvard or Wharton business material. Or at least a college athlete like he'd been. But early on I even failed miserably as an athlete. Being near him made me feel smaller, insignificant, invisible, and I always thought he enjoyed making me feel that way. The only time I could be free of the feeling was when I could run to the mountain. I'd roll laughing down my mountain, every day, in my snow, knowing I'd tricked him.

"Soon I began to ski, and my mountain became the most important place in the world to me. If I wasn't there, I was thinking about it. As I got older, I put on weight and became stronger, and as people noticed my skiing ability, I became more acceptable to him. But by then I didn't care about his approval so much anymore. Thanks to him, I'd found what freedom was all about . . . and that was all that mattered to me. I began to crave higher mountains. I wanted to ski where nobody else could go. I played a game with myself . . . only if I could ski the higher mountain in better time could I be free. Soon, it was only going down the mountain at sixty miles an hour that could set me free . . . I don't know why, but I never thought of death or disaster. Soon it became jumping off cliffs. I was free . . . flying . . .

"Then I got a ski scholarship to college, and I never had to attend classes. Coaches primed me with the answers for exams in the locker room so I could make the grades to continue on their team. Finally, I made the Olympic squad and won the silver. It was the thrill of a lifetime for me, but it was a private experience. I was so free of fear when I skied that the competition itself didn't give me the edge it gave to the others, but winning did. The journalists loved me because I always gave them fun interviews that made their job easier. They wrote about my style, built it up into a personality thing. I became known as an all-around devil-may-care kind of guy. It wasn't true at first, but you know how people begin to fit into their roles."

Steven stopped talking as the proprietor appeared and placed a steaming red cornucopia of bouillabaisse in front of us, and scooped an intoxicating mixture of shellfish, garlic, basil and wine into thick ceramic bowls.

"Please, please, go on," I urged, truly caught up in the mood of the man opposite me. "What happened when the Olympics were over?"

"My wife and I spent a few years just following the snow, making a living giving ski lessons to stars and politicians, dragging Jenn with us around the world. We were ski bums, and real sixties people. Then Toni was killed in the plane crash, and I went berserk for a while. My mom in Colorado took Jenn for me, and I went back to living my life of freedom around the world, skiing the highest mountains, finding my perfect snow. I'd go anywhere and never stayed long. I went into cliff jumping and was paid great for exhibitions, but I would have done them for free. It was only because of Jenn that I wanted the money. I wanted her to have everything. I endorsed special bindings, new equipment. And women began to follow me everywhere. What more could a young guy want? I hurled myself through rocks, water, sky, twisting, jumping into space, back somersaults, jumping further. I never knew what I was going to do once I left the ground. It was unbelievable! Boulders and trees told me where to land. I never got tired of the snow swirling and blowing below me."

Steven and I sat staring at each other. He had a new look in his eyes. He'd touched some deeper feelings inside himself, and we both knew it.

I broke our silence. "I understand how you felt about freedom. It meant the most to me too. I don't know what to say except, please forgive me. After the Avenida Palace, I misjudged you very badly."

"The story of my life," he said. "Sooner or later, they find out I'm not such a bad guy. But to tell the truth, Elizabeth, I've never talked to anyone about skiing that way. People are usually more interested in hearing about the blood and guts of the competition . . . the hard work . . . you know, the winning . . . how I won the silver, what I thought of the other skiers. Trust me, I never thought about the other skiers until I became a commentator. It felt great just now to tell you how I really felt."

We sat, not having to rush, not having to impress, not having to talk anymore, not having to silently plan what might or might not happen later in the night, as men and women on first dates do. He'd wanted to tell me these things and I'd wanted to listen. It was a new, natural feeling of ease and friendship that I'd never felt before with a man. There had always been some deep battle, the pull, opposition, theirs, mine, dangers, compulsions . . . the high-pitched excitement of sexual buildup had always been at the center of all my relationships with men before. Orgasms were easy for me, simply technical achievements I could do again and again . . . to win. But what and why was I winning? I had no desire to win over Steven, only to stay in this new kind of happiness.

The proprietor brought the check.

"Please let me pay." I grabbed it.

"No, no, I invited you."

"But I've enjoyed this meal so much and your story of skiing . . ."

"Good, now we'll have to do it again," and he reached to take it out of the hand I held high away from him.

"Try Pensíon Vista del Mar. It's only top of this road and a la derecha, to the right." The happy proprietor gave us one more suggestion. "And you and your wife come back, I make you an especial rabbit dish from my country, very spicy, but for Americans, I make it mild. The Americans always ask for mild."

We said our good nights, and took his advice, checking into separate freshly painted rooms overlooking the sea at Vista del Mar. I went to bed immediately, hoping it would make the morning come quicker.

Saturday morning was sparkling as we met at sunrise on the balcony that adjoined our rooms. "How about some bicycling?" Steven asked. "I saw some bicycles downstairs last night. It might be a little hard going up some of these hills, but think of the good it does the legs."

"If you're up for it, I am," I accepted the challenge. The thought of bicycling through the crystal freshness around me made me feel even more exhilarated.

"Tell me, is this heaven?" I sang out to no one in particular as we pedaled through forests of oak and pine.

"Close enough," Steven answered for them all. "There's a golf resort hidden away about fifteen miles from here. Want to try for it?"

"Let's go." I pedaled furiously up a hill, determined to make it, but Steven's bike horn tooted at me from behind with such a froglike noise I had to stop halfway from laughing.

About two miles from our destination, we left the bikes and hiked up a cliff, beating a new path in front of us as we went. At the top, we shouted out to the sea.

A Western accent began to come through Steven's TV anchor's voice, "That's how I used tuh sound in 'em mountains a Colorado, but yuh cain't twang on the TV evenin' news."

"Did you like Western music then?"

We sat singing Western songs to the sky and the sea and forgot about bicycling to the golf course.

After a while, we climbed down through the rocks, and slowly inched ourselves around a long stretch of narrow rocky ledge. Foot in front of foot we curved down to a white sand cove sandwiched between the wild cliffs.

"It's wide enough here for both of us. We don't have to stand in the same spot anymore," I joked when we were finally standing, with both of our feet firmly planted on the beach.

"We're glued, Elizabeth, joined . . . there's some kind of connection . . . It feels . . . I felt it the moment I sat next to you on the plane. That's why we—"

I ran ahead of Steven, afraid he'd say more. How many times had they said more? And then it would happen . . . the way it always did . . . the irreversible compulsion to be the obedient sex object I always wound up being. Did I realize how easily I'd always accepted whatever they demanded of me, down deep hating myself, hating them, until I couldn't stand that hate. I didn't want that anymore. I dared not risk anything that might bring it back. I dared not say . . . I dared not touch. I felt too new.

Steven caught up with me on the shore, and took off his shirt and dove into the waves. I dove after, letting the coolness wash away my thoughts.

"You'll dry off fast when the sun hits high noon," Steven assured me as huge waves threatened to drown us both. Exhausted, with water in ears and nose, we went back to the beach and sat watching the waves.

"Will you tell me about dancing in Barcelona now?" Steven cheerfully asked.

"I would if the sun wasn't blazing hot like this. We're going to fry if we sit here another minute."

We climbed back up the now steaming rocks and found refuge in the thick trees where we'd left the bicycles. We mounted them and pedaled to explore the broken stone remains of a deserted castle.

"Tomorrow, I'll be back at my desk in Studio City," Steven said. "Seems like another planet from here."

"It is." I already felt the loss of saying goodbye to him . . . Careful, I warned myself . . . you don't know about his life in L.A. really . . . What if he does have a woman he truly loves there? . . .

That's why he's been only friendly, polite, even chivalrous about the separate rooms . . . you're two good friends in similar professions, enjoying a casual weekend together, far from home . . . "L.A. is another planet," I repeated his comment in a spirited voice. "And what time does your spaceship leave tomorrow?"

He was looking at me, with a wholesome good friend's look, nothing more. "Three o'clock," he said in an upbeat impersonal way, "with a direct flight from Barcelona. If I figure right, I'll make the plane easily, and you'll get back to where you have to be in plenty of time."

I pulled ahead on my bicycle, and looked back at him . . . no hands on the handlebars, ducking under branches . . . "We better get back," he shouted. "I've got some calls to make."

We arrived back at the pensión, made our calls and had enough time to secure a motorboat for a spin around the canyons of the coastline. Later we boated to a restaurant on the dock and dined on fresh fried shrimp from the sea á la Valenciana.

"Well are you finally going to tell me about dancing in Barcelona?" Steven asked after we'd devoured our first round of shrimp and ordered another. "I'm beginning to think you don't want to tell me anything about your life, remain a woman of mystery."

I panicked again. Why was he pushing me like this? . . . Did he sense? . . . Stop it! You promised yourself you'd stop it . . . You have a new life . . . a new career . . . Everything that happened . . . happened before . . . He's only interested as a friend . . . Why wouldn't he be interested in dancing? . . . Talk . . . go ahead . . . talk . . .

"Well, it was a long time ago," I began, "and I was very different. Like you, I lived in the air. Now, I live very much on the ground, but then, I was a girl who could only live in the air. I could turn and spin there, I was fearless. Everybody said I was a natural turner and had an incredible talent for jumping, but really it was only that I wasn't afraid. Now, in the movie business,

I have to be afraid. You have to look around every turn twice, your ideas are stolen easily, along with your money."

"What made you start dancing?" Steven asked.

"My mother was a ballet dancer. She took me to Madame Verosha, a famous teacher, to see if she would accept me for her class. I stayed with her for years. She taught me everything in the Russian method. After that, it didn't matter who coached me, I already knew my center and how to use my inner energy and concentration, which are the most important things for a dancer. A year after my mother brought me to Madame Verosha, she died. From then on, all I did was dance."

"So you were always your own person, even when you were a kid?"

"No, as a dancer, I was always somebody else's instrument, the choreographer's, the audience's. It may have looked otherwise to people outside, but I was never my own person. I always did everything exactly as I was told. I took direction."

"That doesn't sound like you."

"Well, I didn't know who the person that was me was till much later. My job as a dancer was only to do everything perfectly. I never questioned anything. I made sure I took class enough, sweated enough, three hours a day of class, six of rehearsal, and performances. I had no other thoughts. It was my life. But that was what it took. A dancer is in love with dancing."

"Did you miss dancing when you stopped?"

"Oh yes, terribly. It was terrible for a long time. But I had no choice. There were problems with my knee and my back. I couldn't do the kinds of leaps and acrobatics I'd practiced all my life and was known for. Maybe I shouldn't have quit dancing without more of a fight, but you have to understand that when something is that close to you, it becomes your whole life. I couldn't do it well anymore and that killed my soul more every day. Do you know, even now, when I go to the ballet, I yearn to be up there dancing? It's strange, but I somehow feel guilty that I'm not."

"Not strange at all. That's how I feel every time I cover the ski events. Trust me, it hurts!"

"Now I think of myself more in the role of a choreographer, using my colleagues to create my own vision. I come to my work every day knowing what I want my film to be, and what I need to fit where. I work with my director and cameraman with the same energy a choreographer uses with her dancers. Sven is my premier dancer, working his camera like a premier dancer works his body, with technically pure moves. And all the others, the writers, the actors, the crew, we all have an artistic stake in my vision, my ballet. Except there is always one moment of breathlessness that is different for each one of us, our own special magic and music. So in a way, I'm still dancing in Barcelona."

"I've seen dancers like you were, Elizabeth. You watch them, and you know that it's totally their life. I saw a girl like that dance once in New York, a long time ago. She was too young and too thin, and yet, she filled the stage completely. She stayed in my mind for years."

"Maybe it was me," I joked.

"Maybe it was." He looked serious.

"Please let me pay," I pleaded when Steven took the check again.

"Not a chance." He quickly stuffed some bills into the waiter's hand. "I'm running your tab."

"Oh no, I'm working up to pay for the Tattinger."

We left the dock, and boated back on the streams of white moonlight lighting the water. The stars were only a reach away. We arrived at the mooring, knotted the ropes to the poles, walked up the hill to our pensión, said a friendly good night, and went to our separate rooms.

* * *

I woke with the sunrise and went for a run on the beach. This was me again, flying soaring. My shadow running beside me on the shore. The sweat was bristling on my body when I saw a figure running toward me from far down the shore. It was Steven in a sleek, blue racing bathing suit as in my dream. We ran toward each other, till we almost collided in the surf. Our bodies were warm and loose and shiny with salt. We held hands and continued to run down the shore. We'd gone about three miles when gray clouds began to roll in the sky, but we stayed on the beach. It was too beautiful to leave. The rain would pass. We slowed to a walk, exhilarated by the feel of the soft rain on our skin.

We'd hardly gone another half mile when the wind changed direction and the temperature suddenly dropped. Spiked lightning cracked through the sky and hail pelted us. We ran to the rocks for cover and slid into a cavelike opening. The hail turned into a heavy sheet of rain.

We were soaking wet and out of breath from running and laughing, hair matted to our faces, water dripping everywhere. I leaned against the wall of the rocks watching Steven. He fit so well into the outdoors. How natural his smile was here. All the pose of Rhett Butler and James Bond were gone. How natural we were together. If only it could be . . .

"Hope you brought the cognac," he joked. " 'Cause we're here for a while."

"I'd do better with a sweater," I shivered back.

Steven pulled me into his arms and tried to warm me by rubbing my shoulders and back. I felt the hard swell in his racing bathing suit and pulled away until I was standing before him against the rocks in my bikini . . . an old gnawing began to press into my mind . . . Give him what he wants . . . you must! You must! . . . You know what will happen if you don't . . . The tin sound of the rain beat on the rocks. Steven pulled me back into his arms and kissed the top of my hair. I could feel him pressing hard between my legs. The touch blasted into my mind and the memories I'd promised to forget two fisted behind it . . . "This is Steven, not the past. This is Steven, not the past," I repeated to myself like a mantra. You could love Steven. He could love you. But memories blocked out everything else, and the side of my face turned rigid on his chest . . .

. . . **The rain is beating furiously on the long windows of the drop living room . . . You can hardly see out to Riverside Drive . . . the panes are covered with steam from the apartment radiator. Nobody can see in . . . A girl with long blond hair, brushed out to perfection, stands in the center of a crimson Bokhara rug . . . She wears only a black lace bra. She would almost be able to fill it out . . . she's fourteen . . . But the bra is cut, exposing her nipples in their own circle of French lace. A man is sitting in the shadow on the brown couch . . . He instructs her . . . She walks to the window allowing him a full view of her taut girl buttocks, and smooth, pale legs. He speaks again, and she turns . . . Her arms wear black lace bracelets. He stands and walks toward her at the window . . . He's almost there . . . The look on her face . . . She's repulsed, repulsed . . . but fascinated . . .**

I bolted through the opening of our cave shelter and raced down the beach. The wind and hailstones chased, biting my legs behind.

"Elizabeth, come back! Come back!" Steven shouted after me. "We're in the heart of a storm."

Once in the open, I lost all sense of where I was and ran and ran unable to see for the rain. I screamed to the violent waves cracking on the rocks, trying to wrench the horrible pictures from inside me. But my voice was lost in the wind. I opened my mouth and the rain poured down my throat. I choked, I laughed, I cried, and ran until the mud pulled me down on the shore.

Steven came running out of the wall of rain. "Are you all right, I didn't mean to do anything to upset you . . . I'm sorry . . ."

I stood there sobbing.

"Please don't cry. I'd never . . . It's okay." He didn't know what to do or say to calm me. "Please . . . let me help."

I tried to raise myself from the mud, too weak to resist the gravity of pouring rain beating me back down.

Steven lifted me, shivering from the cold himself, and carried me the long way back to our pensión.

Bethy's voice walked along with us, raw inside me, "**You'll never hear me cry, you'll never hear me cry.**" I bit down hard on my tongue, until my tears stopped.

When we reached the pensión, Steven mercifully said nothing. I recovered enough to realize that it was almost too late for him to make his flight to Los Angeles. I hurried to my room.

In the shower, I turned up the hot water and made myself stand under it, scrubbing at my arms and thighs . . . *Your father raped you, Elizabeth . . . but you weren't a little girl anymore. You could have stopped him. You could have told . . . But you pretended it wasn't happening . . . your custom-made point shoes arrived exactly when you needed a new pair, the new practice outfits, him driving you everywhere . . . his Queen, enjoying his torment . . . You could have told . . .*

. . . I couldn't risk it . . . my ballet company . . . it was only the dancing and music that mattered for us . . .

You could have stopped him. Madame Verosha suspected. She would have listened to you . . . It was your fault, your fault, your fault . . . I turned off all the cold water and stood outside the scalding steam. I scrubbed at the skin of my belly and chest . . . *your fault . . . your fault . . .*

. . . **It's a late wintry Sunday afternoon, just getting dark. A private car is arriving at the Plaza. The doorman rushes with his huge doorman's umbrella to cover a fourteen-year-old girl in a French rabbit coat from the pouring rain. Her new suede pumps click on the drenched street. A dignified man follows behind her. Soon they're seated at the Palm Court promenade, coats safely tucked into the cloakroom. The music of violin** and harp surrounds them, and palms and flowers and crystal chandeliers ... The maître d' approaches. "As usual, monsieur? Cognac, pour monsieur, et pour the beautiful daughter, la plus belle ... ahh ... voilà ..." He waves an assistant to show her the choice of cakes he has prepared special for her today. She chooses and sits primly eating them with dainty bites. Her dignified companion puts his hand over hers that sits properly on her lap ...

Yes, I wore my private school manners, all the world saw that. They saw the fresh-as-a-flower young lady dressed in the long-sleeve green velvet dress that came gift-wrapped for her yesterday from Saks Fifth Avenue ... white lace high at the throat emphasizing her pink skin. She wore her hair neatly pulled back with only a wisp escaping ... Maybe her father acts a bit possessively, an observer would have noted ... but it's only a father's pride. Who would have believed that under-neath the green velvet and white lace, she wore the cut-out bra, feeling her nipples brush against the velvet ... waiting obediently for him ... who would have known what was hap-pening? how she feared him, how much she loved him.

"Elizabeth, are you all right in there? We have to get moving, right away." Steven was knocking at my door.

I turned off the hot water, but couldn't feel the difference.

Ten minutes later, we were in the car speeding down the road trying to beat the three hours' time it would take us to get to the Barcelona airport. I turned up the radio to fill the tension that neither of us dared to break. Steven's eyes were intent on the road and mine were inward to the truth ...

Then I was fifteen, and I could have told.

... Who would have believed you. "Look at her," they would have said. "Anorexic girls, they dream. Look how she shivers, even in summer." "Not him," they would have said, "a famous violinist." ... Remember what happened to you at your father's birthday party. Everybody was there in the drop living room to celebrate him. Everybody! A famous soprano from the Met was to sing. Your father would play for her. You were allowed a glass of champagne, but when nobody was looking you had another and another . . .

I was going to tell . . . I looked around at our polished antiques, and the people holding their champagne glasses, they were concert stars, intellectuals. They would help me . . . I'd read things, there were agencies . . . They had to know the truth about this house. I started to call them to attention . . . Please everybody . . . I want . . . I want . . .

"Bethy! Please sit down!" his voice boomed across the room. His voice would always stop you, stealing your words, your very breath . . . wouldn't it?

"I want . . . I want—"

"Bethy! Please," he cut you off again. He played loud notes on his violin, stretching them out, clearing the alcohol from your mind. "Bethy Dolly, can't you see that everybody waits to hear our great soprano. She is about to start her program right now. Do not make our birthday guests angry with you! Please be gentle for us and go quick to the kitchen and bring Madame a glass of water, set it by the piano for her."

I looked up at the drop living room again, without the alcohol driving me. It was a pit of cold faces and naughty whispers, and tapping of immaculate nails and clearing of perfectly groomed throats. What did they see as I stood before them, fifteen, five foot seven? I wore the black silk strapless designer dress he'd bought me for this special occasion. I was very thin but it was a woman's body. He was right, they'd only believe that it was my fault. I'd become a conspirator with him against myself.

. . . He played the sharp high violin chords again.

I ran from the room hearing loud clapping as the soprano's voice above it announced her program. They'd already forgotten me.

. . . Later that night he was furious with you. He beat you. You never resisted!

. . . Two weeks later, you were invited to audition for the ballet. You were too young, and you danced as if you'd never heard the word "ballet" before. You disgraced yourself.

But you were accepted anyway. Weren't you? Weren't you! Didn't you guess that it was his doing? You knew it was his doing! Didn't you? Didn't you? . . .

I didn't think, I don't know. I never talked to anyone.

But the other dancers knew it was his doing. You heard them whispering about it. Didn't you? Didn't you!

I heard them . . . but I turned away . . .

Steven was driving with both hands on the wheel, staring straight ahead at the road. I forced myself to begin to hum along with the radio. I focused my whole physical being on acting as if nothing had happened. But Steven's eyes were no longer interested in me. His thoughts were already somewhere else, distant, away from me . . . You could love him, I thought, but he doesn't love you. The weekend is over, and his thoughts are moving on. Los Angeles, in three weeks he'll hardly remember you, but you, you'll always remember. I continued to hum along with the music and Steven continued driving silently.

We arrived at the Barcelona airport, dropped the car at the rental return, and barely made the closing doors of the bus to the terminal. We didn't talk as we pushed our way to the rear exit to save some seconds. We were too late to check Steven's bags in at the curb, so we raced with them down the moving walkway to the gate.

"Please check me in, and tell them I'll be right there with the passport." Steven handed me a disorderly packet of papers, and rushed to the phones.

I did as he asked and finished his ticketing in time for the first boarding call, but Steven stayed on the phone. I walked to the magazine racks and watched him from across the concourse.

His mouth was close to the phone receiver, the left hand down. The conversation was important. An important story, or maybe his girlfriend. He took out a pad. Had he written down where to meet her tomorrow in California? Steven finished writing and looked through the crowd toward the gate desk, as if he was looking for me, but his eyes landed instead on a commotion of kids jostling each other. His eyes searched around again till they met mine at the magazine rack. I quickly looked down, then back to the magazines. When I looked up again, Steven was rapidly approaching.

"Will we see each other again, Elizabeth?"

I turned away. I wasn't ready to form words from my thoughts. Bethy's voice still pushed into my consciousness, sobbing, raw. If I started to speak, she might push through.

"Will I see you again?" Steven repeated.

I couldn't answer.

"Look, I know you're still upset about what happened on the beach, but please believe me, it was a misunderstanding, I wouldn't do anything to hurt you. Please, Elizabeth, talk to me? Will we see each other again?"

"No."

"Why not?"

"I can't."

"Why can't you?"

Don't! I warned myself. Don't say anything. It's right there. It'll all come out. Once you tell, these things burn their way faster than fires. He's got a good chance of becoming a full network anchor this fall. He'd never take the risk of being linked to you. You know how quickly he'd change if he suspected. Why should he care for you?

"Elizabeth, listen! I've got to know if I'll see you again."

"Thank you for a very lovely weekend, Steven." I struggled to find my voice. It came out low . . . Bethy . . . I slapped her back inside me, and forced the voice higher. "But you're going to miss this plane."

"Please, I hate to leave you this way . . . What can I say . . ."

"It's okay really, I . . ." I grasped for lightness. "Look, you'd better go, they're already boarding the women with children."

Steven's eyes narrowed, and the mouth became smaller, set without its smile in the square jaw.

If he'd only go, I could keep control. Bethy's tears threatened behind my eyelids. "The gate attendant's waiting for your passport." I pointed Steven away from me but he grabbed my hand and turned back.

His face searched mine. "Thank you for coming with me, Elizabeth," he finally said with a hint of a Western accent. He walked away from me and went to the attendant's desk to get his boarding pass. Then the old Rhett Butler posture returned, and without turning back, he swaggered through the gate.

I stayed and watched his plane until it disappeared in the sky.

Twenty-one

When I returned to Barcelona, I went straight to the front desk of my hotel. "I'll be checking out. Please prepare my bill."

"As you wish, señora." The desk clerk immediately rang his bell for someone to replace him and went to his computer to print it out.

Once in my room, I didn't answer the phone or look at messages. I went right to my closet. Anything . . . anything that was suggestive, tight, sexy, could give anybody any ideas about me, had to go, had to be destroyed. I took the little blue silk slip dress I'd worn to Mercedes's party, looser now that I was thinner, but still tight around the buttocks, and with scissors I stabbed at it until it was in pieces. The black dress, low-cut in the back, the fuchsia blouse, not tight but a provocative color, the white, light Indian cotton sundress that was see-through in the light. Yes, the short shorts from Venice Beach and the lycra tights . . . I stabbed and stabbed at them, then sat down to prepare myself for the vivid pictures I knew were about to lash through my mind. I couldn't pretend to forget anymore.

... I'm ten years old, coming into my bedroom. I'm wearing the blue baby doll pajamas Daddy bought for me yesterday. I close the door and carefully turn the key in the lock, quietly ... nobody could hear from outside. I sit in the middle of the room sobbing and trying to pull the pajamas off. I twist and tear at them but I'm trapped with his smell of sweat and cologne pasted to my skin.

In a frenzy, I pull the stuffed toys Daddy has bought for me from the shelf, little cards that were once attached to them fall to the floor with them, birthdays, Valentines. I take Lulu first, the brown bear, I always loved Lulu most ... I spread Lulu's legs wide and stab her with a scissor, again and again. I put the bears in the middle of the room ... my curling iron is smoldering on its stand from before ... I stab and sear at them with it until I can smell their fur, my flesh, burning ...

... The bears are limp, accepting their punishment. I take the white one with the Valentine hearts on the paws and pull the legs apart until I hear the rip in the middle. Valentine is no good anymore, she must be thrown out, destroyed. I go to bring the wastepaper can, the one with the tiger kittens painted on it, but the can is all white and the baby tigers are in the middle of the floor, dead. Their middles are torn apart and their blood is all around them. It is Lulu's fault, Lulu's. I stomp on Lulu until her face is torn apart ...

... I'm not crying anymore ... Methodically, I go to clean up the dead kittens. The blue baby dolls unlock from me and come off. I wrap the dead kittens in the lacy top. My hands are frozen, the fingers can hardly bend, but I work quickly. I pick up the dead kittens and place them inside the can. I wrap the mangled Lulu in the blue lacy bottoms and place her in the can on top of the dead kittens. Nobody can see the horrible dead things inside now. Just the lacy blue pajamas with his smell of cologne. I will tell Daddy they were ripped and had to be thrown out . . . Not unusual . . . no, not unusual at all.

. . . I go to sit on my bed. I'm naked. The freezing from my fingers is moving up my arm. I lean into the wall with my back . . . it is cold . . . colder. The more I shiver, the more I want to . . . Pneumonia! How wonderful it would be to be consumed by fever. . . . If I die, would I wake up with Marya? . . . I want my mother, I scream inside myself where nobody can hear . . . Please God, I want my mother. I stare diagonally across and up at the line where the wall meets the ceiling, it is so white, everything is white. I sit staring until the wall seems to disappear. There are no walls in my room, only the whiteness.

. . . I put my hand deep under the blankets and pull out Marya's hidden gun and hold it to me, caressing it exactly the way she did . . . I rub its coolness over my forehead and arms . . .

. . . A key is turning in a lock and Daddy is walking into the room. He wears a dark suit and holds his violin case.

I hold Marya's gun tighter to my chest.

Daddy stops and stands completely still. "Please give me the gun, Bethy Dolly," he cajoles me. "You know how much I love you. I love you, my little rose. Now come, my sweetheart, give me the gun.

"Bethy, give me the gun." He is standing very still.

Like a camera moving in, Bethy's features come into sharp focus. It's not the face of a little girl anymore. It's my face the way it is now. I raise the gun and point it at him.

Daddy carefully begins to walk toward me, picking his steps. "Elizabeth," he pleads, "give me the gun." . . . He is almost to me now. "You know how much I loved you. It was always only the dancing and music that mattered for us. You know how much you loved me."

I squeeze the gun's trigger, and the room explodes.

* * *

I found the right apartment that evening. As soon as the landlord left with the security, I locked the door and walked it again.

First the living room. Austere, facing the back, with a plain couch and a plain table. No distractions to greedily grab on to, no flowers, or crystal or cushion or tufting or pillows, or glass.

In the bedroom, only a small window, a simple bed, and an old wooden dresser. No mirrors here except a small one in the bathroom. What good were mirrors? I wouldn't see what was really there. Four solitary walls, a plain cell, where I could have the courage to look inside myself. Nothing would be right till then.

I paced the narrow corridor back to the living room. The apartment was almost a replica of the one I'd lived in when I danced in the ballet, as Bethy. All these years of self-deceit that I'd pretended to be Elizabeth. How could I have gotten so far away from myself?

First I convinced everyone else and then I convinced me. How many times had I seen this in scripts and novels, the characters protect the protection until the original horror disappears? Yet it happened to me. Whole parts of my life were carefully scratched from my memory. Marya? He never let me call her "mother." How did she really die? Only a carefully secluded child would believe her mother died so quickly from pneumonia.

But later, I never looked for the truth. Or did I and then look the other way? I left America, and when I returned, it was all another lifetime ago.

My head began to pound a familiar pounding. It had been years since I'd had Bethy's headaches, but I felt the emergency of them as sharply . . . take the medicine fast or it will be too late . . . I used to carry it with me everywhere . . . It has to be here . . . in the suitcase . . . somewhere . . .

"No, don't take anything," I shouted to the empty echo of the apartment like an accuser. "What happened to Marya? You've got to know. You've got to remember. You knew about the gun. She's your mother. How could you put her so far out of your mind? If you take the medicine, it will put you to sleep like it always did, and when you wake up you'll have forgotten.

"You could find out," I continued shouting. "There are coroner's reports, and people who would know how she died, the orchestra friends would know. You could find them easily. If you asked them about Marya . . ."

Marya's thin face and her Russian-accented voice came back to me as vividly as if she were in the room with me. *It pleaded, broken, "Leave her, Roland. How could you? She doesn't understand." I focused on her same hollow eyes as when she lay in bed with Daddy between us.*

The pressure in my head was closing around me. I rose to get some water and caught myself on the back of an armchair, making my way to the couch. The corners of my eyes began to blur with zigzag lines.

Eight o'clock, it had just been six. How had I been sitting this long in a straightback wooden chair? I had a cottony feeling in my mouth, and my tongue was thick. I stood and leaned along the wall the rest of the way to the couch.

Nine o'clock? It had just been eight. Must have dozed off again. That's what happened. I made my way to the bedroom.

Twelve noon? I'd never slept this long. Always got up at seven, didn't need an alarm. I was supposed to be at the set at eight, I'd better call José . . . The dial tone buzzed painfully through the center of my head, and I put the telephone down.

I looked in the bathroom mirror at bloodshot eyes in a pasty face . . . some food . . . a shower . . . some air . . . then I'll go to work. I started to put things away. There wasn't much, I hadn't taken much. But filling the two small closets took energy I didn't have. I leaned on the chairs . . . this closet for pants and this one for dresses . . . or the other way around. This one for dresses and this one for pants . . . and my notes and my papers and schedules . . . there in the bag, no, in the briefcase . . . Ahh here are the pills . . . must get the water . . . the stockings in the drawer . . .

I stumbled to the kitchen and put the cup to my lips but they were too uncoordinated to sip and the water spilled down my chest. I gulped the pills into my throat and pressed my head against the wall and caught myself falling. Better lie down . . . the plain bed with no ornaments . . . no pretext . . . through the hallway. I stumbled to the bedroom and fell into bed . . . falling . . . how wonderful is falling . . . but what if I fall too far . . .

Suddenly the phone was ringing.

"Elizabeth, it's me," the Count's voice crackled at me.

"I can't hear you," my voice stumbled through a dry mouth.

"I seem to be breaking up. I'm in the car," he said. "Wait, I will call back in five minutes when I'm out of this interference."

With difficulty, I replaced the phone into its cradle. How do they make these things these days that they don't fit? But why shouldn't it fit? Of course, I'm lying down, I'm at an angle. And it's dark.

The phone rang again. "Elizabeth, it's me." His voice was clipped and clear. "Can you hear me now?"

"Yes," I scrambled to reply.

"Is something the matter? Nobody has heard from you since last Friday, six days."

Six days? He must be mistaken? "I moved to an apartment," was all I could think of to say.

"Yes, yes, I know," he clipped at me impatiently. "Finally I went to your hotel, and pried this number out of them. Seems you left instructions not to give it. It took some pesetas. What is the matter with you?"

"Nothing is the matter." I sat up, disliking his tone. I struggled to harness my thoughts. "I was away for the weekend and then I moved."

"My esteemed partner ..." I could hear him smoking his Gauloise cigarette, "did you so easily fall under the spell of that notorious American journalist?"

"Certainly not!" I grasped my anger. "There have been New York matters. I left a message for you on Monday to tell the others. What? You didn't get it? Well these things happen. Sorry ... so sorry ... I thought for sure ..." A lie, a necessary lie.

"Well, no matter," he clipped on, showing he didn't believe me. "We must touch base right away. There is a problem with the money again. The French bank will want an update, exact facts and every figure before they release the second part of the financing for the film. It is their right and we must give it to them."

The ringing in my ears came to a halt. He's lying. He has to be. I spoke to the bank Friday. Nothing was said about this. These numbers are for him. I've acted strangely and he's nervous about me. But he's right. I would do the same thing. It takes little to lose millions with a film.

"Can you prepare it?"

"I can ... why not?" I replied. "They're entitled. Yes, I'll do it in the morning." But my mind started to race again ... the notes, my papers, the bills ... in the briefcase in the living room, no, in the closet, the pills, in the bathroom ...

"Elizabeth?" The Count's voice cut off my thoughts. "What are you saying? Or do we have some interference on this line. Are we disconnected?"

"Of course I hear you. An accounting for the bank ... I have it all here with me in the apartment ... it will take me only a few hours to prepare a report."

"Good. Good. Meet me at La Luna at seven tomorrow." It was more a demand than a request. "We will have an aperitif and talk about this, and maybe you will give your partner some numbers, heh?"

"Yes, La Luna at seven ... I'll be there ... we will have an aperitif."

"Elizabeth, what is happening there? Are you with a lover?"

"Of course not. You're calling me in the middle of the night. I was fast asleep."

"My dear, it is only six o'clock," he derided me.

"I was sleeping. I've had a touch of the flu. Thank you for waking me. This room is in the back, dark."

"Something does not smell right here. Maybe you are not okay, heh?"

"I told you, everything's fine. La Luna at seven. Thank you for your concern."

When I hung up and switched on the light, I was shocked to see two trays, one with a half-eaten omelette, and the other with soup and salad. Both had receipts from the twenty-four-hour takeout, with two different dates. The Bethy pills were beside them, and I'd somehow lost two days.

I woke again at seven in the morning, as usual, before the alarm went off, and made a strong pot of coffee. My head was still pounding but I was better. Maybe it had only been some bug after all. I carefully walked the length of the living room to make sure ... A little lightheaded still ... but ... a straight line ... there, everything's fine ... just groggy. The strong coffee will do it ... there, the briefcase, on the chair, look inside ... exactly, the papers, bills, schedules, projections, numbers, all neat and orderly.

I sat down at the plain brown desk, set up my laptop and went to work. There was no sound around me in the sparsely furnished apartment. Nothing was mine, no history and nothing of interest. No hint of future gaiety or grief, or sounds or sunshine in the street. It was exactly what I wanted.

The work took longer than it normally would have, but I was done, and left with the computer to find a place to print out the pages of accounting. Outside, steam poured up from the summer streets and the diesel fuel of the heavy traffic was choking. I immediately found a service for the printout, and stopped on Paseo de Gracia at a streamlined Formica and glass cafeteria, then on to Plaza de Cataluña, through the packed square of pigeons and people, to Ramblas de Cataluña and down the flower-filled center island promenade toward the seaport. At the foot of the Ramblas, a barrage of young blond German tourists with backpacks and sandals were crowding to watch a mime troupe performing in front of the displays of the craft peddlers. A left turn here and into the winding narrow busy streets of the Old Quarter, and I was at the Hotel Colón.

"Madam." The desk clerk handed me a neatly rubber-banded packet of mail. "And there is one more too that comes special delivery."

"How nice of you to accept it for me." It *was* nice. Usually you get a yellow slip telling you to go to a crowded post office.

He looked at me strangely. "But of course, I accept for you, señora, you give specific written instructions to accept for you still like always. If you wait one minute, por favor. Gracias."

"Thank you." I continued shuffling through new scripts and New York bills.

"Here, madam." the desk clerk returned with a Federal Express envelope.

I tore the flap away and found a letter from Steven. I held up the envelope to the light for a minute . . . the date was rubbed off. I carefully folded the envelope into my purse and left the hotel. Across the square, the cathedral loomed over me, crowded with tourists in the afternoon sunlight. To the side, huge tour buses waited for them with their metal tops reflecting the sun's hot glare. I wanted to go sit on the cathedral steps and read the letter, but I felt dizzy again, as if the world was too big, and the trip across the square would be too far.

I slid into the nearest café chair, put my scripts neatly in one pile on the side of the table in front of me, and Steven's letter by itself in the middle. I studied the handwriting on the envelope. Handwriting can be so personal, sometimes like having the person there. I opened it.

Dear Elizabeth,

I'm watching Barcelona disappear below me and it's difficult to express the empty feeling in me. I promised myself on the Costa Brava that I wouldn't put myself through the emotional turmoil of expressing my feelings to you. But as I look down on this beautiful city, I see your smile and something inside insists I write this letter. I feel our connection and know you feel as I do, but for some reason you won't let it be. During the drive from Costa Brava, I wanted only to hold you. I fought to look away from you.

When we first met on the plane in June, I said half kidding that you could be the love of my life. After this weekend, I know it's true. I don't know why I found it so hard to express these feelings face-to-face, but the thought of never seeing you again is too much for me to ignore.

All the while we acted as just friends, I pictured myself showing you the great ski slopes of the world, saw us in the sky together with the snow at Innsbruck, Mont Blanc, sitting in front of a fire together in Aspen while I tell you how much I love you. The pink of your skin, I could get lost in it.

What is love but a heightened state of being when the lover glows, has untold energy, and the world is the magnificent place it should be. The awful thing is that you and I have gotten used to seeing ourselves as finding love rather than seeing the found.

Elizabeth, these romances come along once in a lifetime. Let's not risk losing this. Whatever it is, you're the woman I love.

Steven

I read over Steven's letter again, stopping at the words, "Whatever it is, you're the woman I love." Then I picked up my mail, paid the check and left the café, walking through Barrio Gótico to Avenida Portal de l'Angel, through Plaza de Cataluña, on to Paseo de Gracia. I held Steven's letter tight in my hand. Let me see, I just tell you everything that happened, all about Bethy. And then you live happily ever after with me, the deeply troubled producer everybody's afraid to take a chance on anymore. *People* magazine could write how the former famous bachelor understood about how his network felt when every tabloid revealed his new wife's real past with her famous father. He did not mind stepping down at all. And he was so wonderful to her in her grief. How exemplary! I waved the letter, nervously weaving as I walked, until I reached the apartment. The clothes were still on the living room floor . . . I sat for a few moments appreciating the complete stillness. I felt almost invisible in here. Everything else was outside.

At La Luna, at seven fifteen, the Count was entrenched between two young women, a six-foot sleek Scandinavian blonde, and a lithe dark-skinned African beauty. The restaurant was one of those modern Italian tiled places where every sound is amplified. The designer-suited older crowd mingled with the younger patrons dressed in black. The air conditioning had no mercy.

"Elizabeth, here, I'm over here." The Count waved his little riding crop cane vigorously from between the press of the two beauties.

"Hello," I said, careful to make my voice steady and light. His companions left us to our business. I looked approvingly at the smiling Count. "I can see that it's a good thing I was a little late."

"And the numbers?" He got right to the point, lighting a Gauloise.

He carefully went through each number and every updated projection. He studied each column minutely until he was satisfied that everything was perfectly in order. Finally my partner's confidence and humor appeared to be restored. But there was one more thing. "Yves is here," the Count announced.

"In Barcelona? But why would he be here?" I asked. "Yves Bolanieu doesn't take idle pleasure trips."

"Idle or no, I can tell you I saw his long white Bugatti, or whatever it is, crawling like some shiny prehistoric insect thing through the Ramblas traffic."

"His car? He must be planning on staying."

"Not necessarily. He ships this car everywhere, staying or no. It has some kind of chrome anteater front, and the plates, would you believe the plates have his name on them. Your ex-boyfriend will not grow up."

"Well, we can't hold that against him. There are much more serious charges."

"Really?" The Count's ears almost twitched at the thought of some more lively international gossip to add to his plentiful arsenal.

"Not a chance," I smiled in rebuttal.

"But guess who it was who sits next to him, with her charm and smiles in the sunshine?"

"I can't guess."

"The flamenco dancer, that one who owns Club Las Cuevas."

"Mercedes?" This time I was very interested.

"Yes, that is her name. I thought I'd heard that you knew her very well."

"Don't pretend. You know that I know her."

"True, you two did cause quite a stir at a fiesta in Pamplona . . . for a certain bullfighter . . . a few weeks ago, heh? Finally, leaving a pensión too early in the morning for the train."

"How do you know about all these details?"

"Mi bellíssima, there is very little about the rich, the royal, and the famous that I do not know. It is a necessary part of my business."

"Your business? How is that?"

"I am not sure myself—but it is the secrets that always wind up making or losing money in the end."

"And what about Jorge? Do you know what happened there?"

"Absolutamente!" My raconteur put out the stub of his Gauloise and sat back to tell the story, but it was obvious he was bored with the unlucky Jorge, already yesterday's empty suit. "The Belgium police were indeed harsh on our Jorge when they found him with his millions of arms cache. They detained him for a long time." The Count stopped talking.

"And then? And then?" I prodded.

"Oh yes, ummm yes." Yves had the power now, but the gentleman Count would finish Jorge's trifling story for my benefit. "It seems there was more than one syndicate in more than one country. But your heart should not worry about Jorge, after how he acted to you."

"Prison could ruin him. I don't want that for him."

"Elizabeth, you have no need to worry. Finally through money from France, I don't know why France, but I have my suspicions, but anyway, the officials were satisfied and Jorge was allowed to leave."

"Where did he go? He isn't in Barcelona."

"As we speak, rumors have him somewhere in the Middle East trying to rescue his oil and gas business. Monsieur Bolanieu was really out to get him this time and seems to have done a good job there too."

"And Mercedes? How does she fit into all this?"

"Mi bellíssima, brace yourself. Jorge actually owns a large portion of her Club Las Cuevas, but now that there are creditors on him, we can only guess."

"I can't believe that of Mercedes, that the minute her good

friend and partner has a downfall, she would run to the arms of his lifelong rival."

"My dear, it is obvious how new to fame you really are. She only wants to save her club. She is entitled."

"There has to be another choice of investor for her besides Yves."

"But why does it matter to us, any of this? Because the film is all ours, our financing is sound, and the talent is there. Jorge is nowhere to bother us. And Yves Bolanieu? It is quite possible that he is here in Barcelona only as a Frenchman in love with a beautiful flamenco dancer. But see for yourself."

"What do you mean?"

"Our illustrious couple enters right now." The Count drew in the air with his little riding crop cane to direct my attention to the bar.

Mercedes looked spectacular in an immaculate summer white Chanel suit. You can always tell Chanel. I thought of that first night I saw Mercedes dance. She'd said to me, "Rodolfo and me, we dance in your film for no money. We dance the flamenco for love." The price of this outfit, down to the spotlessly new white-gold-chained handbag, was much more than "for love." Yves wore white also, a fine light silk Armani.

The Count continued talking, "And you will notice on the fourth finger of her left hand?" The riding crop cane seemed to gesture by itself in accompaniment.

"I certainly do notice." The light caught a large pear-shaped diamond.

They, however, seemed to notice only each other as they went to the bar.

The Count tapped the table with his cane. "I think this case here is actually very simple." Tap, tap. "To me, our Mercedes and our Yves look like a woman and man in love." Tap.

"But what about Rodolfo?"

"That," tap, tap, "is only a marriage of convenience. That is well understood. Rodolfo has his boyfriends, and Mercedes, she has had everybody." Tap, tap. "Like yourself."

"Excuse me," I bristled. "A few minutes ago you couldn't remember her name, and now you are sure I am her lover."

"My dear woman, when you are a business partner to me, it is my sacred job to know everything about who your lovers are. My money and my reputation cannot ride on your woman's emotions."

"Then why should you think that I am so safe?" I asked at this irony.

"Bellíssima Elizabeth, look who your lovers are."

"Doesn't look like such a good recommendation to me." I honestly had to laugh.

"But no, you are wrong." He pointed to the bar. "Here are two cunning people, smart . . . very smart. As well as successful . . . sí, very talented . . . and very beautiful."

"How does that recommend me?"

"Both lives did not start out that way."

"Wrong," I corrected him. "I think Mercedes and Yves have always been very beautiful."

"There you are right." The cane tapped its agreement again.

The conversation was getting ridiculous, but I was drawn in anyway. "But again, why is this good for you in business with me?"

"Because if your lovers did not have these characteristics, I would not trust your judgment."

This was amusing. "Maybe we ought to convince the banks to use your methods for their loans," I told him, "and they might not be stuck with such bad ones? How backward they are to look at credit ratings."

"They are bourgeois bankers." His tone derided the whole financial community. "They do not have the blood of an aristocrat who knows that family relations and relations of love say more about who is the poor risk and the good risk."

"Actually the banks consider me a rather good risk too. It's just in the movie industry they don't."

"My dear, you think I took the front for you with the French bank and put my money in myself, without knowing everything about you. Much, much more than only about the ballet girl who lost her heart once in Barcelona to too many men, and then worked hard and become lucky later. I know everything, everything. Heh?"

My heart stopped. No, it was impossible. No one in the world knew. I'd never told. He couldn't . . . he could know about every penny I'd ever made and every lover I'd ever had, but not about that . . . He's testing . . . trying . . . I'm too strong. He's probing for a weapon . . . just in case . . .

"Bellíssima, please do not look so horrified about simply a little history."

Just as quickly, I blurred it with lightness. "You make it sound as if there are spies everywhere."

The Count could see that I wasn't going to bite, but he went on anyway. "Some people, they do not survive, even though they pretend so well. Then they are not so safe for me as a partner. But you are a true survivor. It is a very deep part of you. So ingrained you do not even know that others do not."

"The movie business is shark-infested water, you learn that."

His look pierced behind my clichéd answer. "There is more interesting things here that make you survive so well . . . someday maybe we will talk some more about this, heh?"

"We don't have to," I grinned. "Ask anybody. They'll tell you I work too hard to be interesting."

"Yes, but maybe there are secrets they do not know, heh?"

"You're wrong again! You're reading too many magazine stories."

There was a flicker of reaction from the Count, almost invisible, but there. He was making a mental note. I'd protested more than once. He'd work to find out why. The Count stood with a smile at only the corners of his mouth. "But anyway, it is getting too late right now. The numbers you bring, they are perfect. We are in perfect shape, as the Americans say. I am glad to see you are better from your flu, and I must go." He folded the sheets of numbers I'd given him, and collected the riding crop cane.

I smiled my casual cocktail smile, both the watcher and the carefully watched, and leaned back too easily into the chair.

"And where are you off to this evening, sir." I once-overed his perfect classic-hued tip-to-toe ensemble appreciatively, in further hopes of distraction.

"So gracious you are! Ah but yes, I have the most exciting possibilities tonight with a beautiful young lady from England who comes to Barcelona to sing in the opera. She is beautiful, talented and as ambitious, and will appreciate my help immensely." For all appearances, the Count had slivered back into his bon vivant guise. He straightened the tie of his English-tailored suit, and purposely left the numbers he'd asked for on the table.

"Oh no," I stopped him, as he reached for the check. "Please let me." We kissed on both cheeks and he left.

I lit a Gauloise from the pack he'd left, ordered a Campari, and watched the smoke curl into the air. The man was eccentric, maybe cruel, but he was doing me a favor by telling me something loud and clear I already knew—in the movie business as in any other, nobody gives you the millions it takes to finance a film unless they're one hundred and fifty percent sure of your stability.

What if I started some kind of psychiatric therapy, and my secrets leaked out? That's how it always happens, somebody always hears something, and asks and asks and asks. They start looking, there are records, hospitals, people. They start writing, small articles at first. And who knows who sees them, and tells more, or what can happen? I'm not a movie star or entertainer, where these secrets would make me more interesting; and I could tell them on talk shows and in magazines to increase my visibility and allure in a perverse way. I'm a businessperson like any other businessperson who deals with banks and large corporations. I would be forever unstable in their minds. I'd risk everything I'd worked for all these years if anything ever got out.

I slowly crushed my Gauloise into the ashtray. Mercedes and Yves still sat in the bar section of the restaurant, completely involved in each other. They didn't see me. I put the money for the check on the table, and left through a side door without passing them.

Twenty-two

All next week, I went to my office, playing the neutral-colored, controlled persona I'd planned, but by Thursday, when I returned to the apartment in the late evening, I anxiously scanned the mailbox labels at the downstairs buzzer ... Yes, I was right, a Dr. Yárez, an internist, had his office on the first floor. There was no mistaking that the slight fluttering in my chest, which had started after the headaches, had become chest pains. Today I'd spent the hours shuffling papers from pile to pile in dread of the next fluttering because each time they came they were sharper. Finally they became stabs around my heart.

I slowly walked the stairs to the apartment, and wrote Dr. Yárez's telephone number into my appointment book, just in case. In the morning, the flutterings were gone, and I picked through the pile of clothes that were still on the living room floor for another colorless outfit and left. Maybe it would be all right. But by twelve o'clock, the chest pains were back, and I felt short of breath.

After an exhaustive physical examination, Dr. Yárez, a grand-fatherly-looking doctor, solemnly called me into his office.

"You're a young woman in exemplary health."

"But what about the chest pains?"

"Most likely the pains of anxiety," he explained kindly. "I know this surprises you, but I've seen this kind of reaction many times."

"Well ... what happens ... what can I do?" I felt a new choking sensation right below my throat.

The doctor carefully scrutinized my reaction. "Señora, maybe you'd like me to recommend a psychologist or counselor who could help you with some of the things I can see you're feeling that are causing this?"

He could see? So easily, he could see?

The doctor continued, quietly, sympathetically. "I think it would be best for me to refer you to someone with these kinds of specialties."

I almost laughed out loud at such irony. Sure, tell him yes and go to a "counselor," and watch your life broadcast all over Barcelona. "Bombshell Producer Tells All About Past of Sexual Abuse!" That would clear up anxiety chest pains fine. "I don't think so," I replied evenly to Dr. Yárez. "You see, I'm going home to New York in a week."

"In that case, I strongly suggest you see somebody there as quickly as possible. Emotional situations can cause the kind of frightening chest pains you have."

"Well, at least it's not my heart. I'm in the movie business you know, both conditions can be pretty common."

"Then that will be all for now." He searched my face seriously.

No! That couldn't be all! I needed to do something ... Wasn't there something ... The feeling of panic and suffocation was beginning again already. "Doctor, please, I need help ... I ... I ..." And later, I'd have the dreams ... the dreams ... "Doctor," I pleaded, trying to keep the emergency out of my voice. "I understand what you're saying, but seeing a counselor wouldn't solve it for me now." Calm! ... Act calm, reasonable. "Because there wouldn't be enough time. Perhaps just some Valium to get me through till I go home."

"No, I could not very easily give you Valium. The agencies watch these prescriptions very carefully. And my professional opinion is that it could get you into further trouble."

"But, Doctor." By now I was openly panicked, but I didn't care. "I can't work with this! Please believe me. You've never been on a movie set. This coming week is our most important week to the film. We're wrapping up. The pressure of everybody depending on me will be too much for me in this condition, and I can't stop. What can I do? Perhaps you can justify the prescription as precautionary . . . Please . . . maybe . . .?"

"There is no such thing as precautionary in this case," he replied sympathetically. "But I will give you a very low dosage of Valium, to take only before you go to sleep. With these difficult emotional situations, the physical body doesn't rest enough and becomes too overstressed. But," he warned, "I can only give you enough for this week and it won't be refillable." The doctor began to write on his prescription pad. He handed me the paper.

"Thank you very much, Doctor."

"Please, miss, I know you don't know me, and I see how hard this is for you, but . . ." He stood and walked out from behind the desk and came over to me. "See someone when you get home, as soon as you can. This reaction can be caused by simple day-to-day stress that builds up in a business like yours, and goes away by itself with a few weeks off for rest, or," he looked at me with the look of both a medical professional and a kindly man, "it can become very consequential to your health. Believe me, even with such good physical health as you have now, it can change."

"Thank you very much, Doctor."

"Try half a pill first. Sometimes it can be enough."

I left the doctor's office and ran upstairs, clutching his precious penned scratches. I laid the paper out on the windowsill to decipher what he'd given me. Five, only five milligrams of Valium, 2X ten pills, enough for five days only. If I split each pill in two and took them with wine, I could make them last for ten days ... but that would make only two and a half milligrams, enough to do nothing ... There are a million people you could ask to sell you all kinds of downers, I reminded myself ... No ... it'll get around ... and fast.

I knew a better method, a simple leftover skill I'd perfected to a science in my ballet days. I left the apartment to find a pharmacy, and walked into the first one I came to, a large bright all-purpose store, people in all the aisles. Two pharmacists were behind the counter, which meant one would always have me in view. I left quickly and walked down a side street.

Two pharmacies later, I found the right one, a small store with few customers browsing the shelves and one proprietor behind the counter. "Por favor," I cheerfully handed him the prescription.

He looked it over. "Sí, señora, cinco minutos."

"Gracias."

The proprietor took the prescription around the back counter to his bins of pills. I heard him typing the label there, and in five minutes he was back. "Aquí, señora."

"Gracias." I paid for the pills and watched as he filed the prescription in the tray I'd carefully noted before, on the other side of the cash register.

"Have nice day, Mrs." He was being cordial by trying to speak English to me.

"And you too, sir." I gave him an appreciative smile, and went to browse the nearby makeup brushes.

He returned to the back counter to finish his work among his bins of pills.

I waited and listened ... perfect ... his phone was ringing. "Hola." The pharmacist directed his attention to his caller.

I waited another moment ... the sounds of him typing the

label . . . his eyes would be on the keyboard . . . I quickly moved my hand over the counter to the prescription file tray near the register. The one on top would be my Valium. I smoothly grabbed it and left the store.

Four pharmacies later, I had the amount of pills I needed for now, and my prescription was still intact for the next time. I took the first pill the second the mission was finished, and went right back to my office.

"Here are your messages." The secretary waved a stack of paper in front of me.

"Thank you," I said, hoping she'd leave me alone to calm down.

"New York, New York, Madrid, London, London, Paris, Paris, Paris," she called out, reading off the origin of each call. "And your bank in Paris called several times."

"I'll call them right now," I said, but I wasn't calm enough to talk to anyone yet. I shuffled the messages from pile to pile until six o'clock . . . too late to return the calls, and the pains were back. One more pill . . . Of course I needed more than one to begin. And one more tonight . . . three times for just this first day. Outside, the steaming summer streets had become an oven. I rushed back to the apartment, turned up the air-conditioner, and sat in the dark.

"There'll be no dreams this night," I calmed my feelings of terror later as I approached the bedroom, sipping a glass of wine after the last pill. I changed the sheets, fluffed up the pillows, and lay down. Within a few minutes, the pains were gone, and I felt beautifully relaxed . . . Once I get through these next few days and the chest pains are gone . . . I assured myself.

And so the time went by, or I think it did. I felt that I'd been right about the pills, people needed them for certain times in their life when the stress threatens too hard. That's what they were for, weren't they? I wouldn't abuse them, I'd never lose control.

And as soon as the chest pains were gone, and the dreams had subsided, I did stop taking them, as I promised. But a strange thing happened when the dreams left—all my energy and drive seemed to have left with them.

In the early evening, I'd leave work exhausted and come back to the quiet of the apartment to rest but I'd never allow my eyes to close. Later on when the night lights of Barcelona came up, I'd go out to roam alone, anonymous in the crowds that thronged the streets, and cafés and bars of the elegant Diagonal, down the crowded Ramblas, and even through Barrio Chino, the Old Quarter of neon bars and ladies of the night. Pretty soon I would feel exhausted again and stop for a glass of Spanish brandy.

"Excuse me miss, madame, fraulein, señora," a million conversations were started by similar men from different countries interested in meeting a woman out by herself.

"Gracias no," I answered to every one of them, suitable or not, and returned to my sparse apartment and finally allowed sleep. Beautiful, exhausted, complete sleep.

In the morning I'd rise very early and tell myself how thankful I should be that the chest pains and the dreams were gone. The move to Madrid would go smoothly. We were only a little behind schedule . . . nothing to press about . . . And lately, there were lovely new dreams that made coming back to the apartment something to look forward to. In them, I was in New York and Steven Brandon was with me.

It was a Friday at seven P.M. when I opened my apartment door without much energy, and was shocked to almost bump into Steven with his hand on my buzzer . . . What . . .? I became confused. Had I conjured him up from the new dreams? I began to giggle nervously at the thought of it. What was Steven doing here, if indeed he was here?

"Elizabeth, are you okay?" Steven looked surprised himself. We were actually almost nose-to-nose.

"Of course I'm okay. What a strange question ... I mean, what are you do—?"

"Well, I ... I ... stopped by the set to see you three days in a row, and nobody knew where you were or how to reach you. The same thing happened at your office, and the screening room. I ..." Steven stopped, a little embarrassed to show how hard he'd tried to find me. He looked wonderful in a suit and tie. "I was concerned," he said. "It didn't sound like something you'd do. It didn't sound right. And nobody would give me your new telephone number. The whole thing was a big secret."

I smiled, he'd checked out everything, the perfect journalist, even in real life. *Twenty Seconds* or *Forty/Forty* ... or something minutes, or whatever it was ... "So how did you find me?" I asked.

"By the third day, I went to your old hotel and they told me how to get ahold of you. It wasn't that simple really, I had to work to pry it out of the desk clerk. He wouldn't give me any information. Finally, I had to threaten him with the rack if he didn't tell me."

"That translates as you gave him a couple of pesetas huh?"

"Only a couple, but ... who cares? The important thing was to find you. Did you get my letter?"

"Yes, today," I lied.

I watched Steven's face open into a smile, friendly without being familiar in spite of the letter. If he were married to someone else, you could still be friends with a man who smiled at you like that. It had no trace of guilt. Just him being there made me feel happy, brighter. He had the same effect on me that he did on Costa Brava. Maybe if I had more lipstick on. I hadn't bothered with blush, a little mascara, no, don't do it now ... that would look silly. Invite him in.

"I'm glad you're here, Steven. Please come in."

"I can't stay long."

"Neither can I. I was on my way out, but please come in." I closed the door and was surprised that my hand shook a little on the doorknob. I hoped he didn't see that.

"Are you sure you're all right, Elizabeth? You look flushed."

"I've had the flu, but now I'm better. Can I offer you a drink?" I went into the kitchen. "Ooo, I have brandy . . . Brandy's okay? What did you say? . . . Yes . . . barely moved in. Please excuse the clothes all over." I took the glasses from the closet and put them down on the counter. Seeing Steven made me feel an energy I'd almost forgotten I had. Its newness jumped like droplets of water in a hot-oil skillet. I was fidgeting . . . pacing . . . chattering . . . Yes it was true. I leaned on the sink. Get control of yourself, I commanded! Go back into the living room. Sit down, you'll be fine when you sit down . . . I came back to the living room with the brandies and sat down next to Steven on the couch. "I'm very surprised to see you. I had no idea . . . I . . ."

"Neither did I," he finished the sentence for me. "But the minute I got back, they had another assignment for me, and they turned me right around and sent me back. It's a big one, another steroid thing in the Olympic Village. I've been here working on it awhile, but I waited. I wanted to make sure you got my letter first before I saw you."

My skin felt too sensitive. My heart was beating too loud in my chest. Everything was happening too fast . . . Slow . . . slow down!

"Elizabeth," Steven was saying, "you know I would have come back without this new assignment."

I couldn't reply.

"I have to have some idea how you feel about me, about us. I don't know, I can't get a grip on it because you won't talk about it, you act one way and say another. I've got to know."

Everything inside of me went loose and I was bursting to

shout, "I love you." Open the windows and shout to the street. "I love you, I love you." It alarmed me. I couldn't feel this way this quick, just seeing him. Something new had happened here. You're not thinking straight, I told myself . . . the exhaustion, all your defenses are down . . . You're becoming exposed . . . Tomorrow you'll regret it. Be reasonable . . . "Steven, this is happening too fast for me," I finally said.

"Elizabeth." Steven was determined to say what was on his mind.

I raised my face to his.

He sat closer to me on the couch. "I heard what you said at the airport before I left for L.A. . . . but I swear, when I looked in your eyes I saw everything different. When I was in California, I couldn't get your look out of my mind. Now I'm seeing it again."

Careful! . . . Careful . . . don't expose, I warned myself, and instead of the "I love you" rising in my throat, I said, "Steven, I feel very much for you, but this is too quick for me."

"Let's spend some time, Elizabeth, give it a chance to—"

"My mind and my life are occupied by this film," I blurted out. "It's all I do day and night. The deadline is already here and we're not ready. Anything would be too distracting. On top of it, there's New York. I have to leave soon. We'll always be in different countries, different cities."

Steven's face had that awful hurt look he'd had on our picnic at Montserrat, and he looked down in the same quiet way.

I felt compelled to say something, anything, I didn't know what, I couldn't bear to hurt him, what was I doing? I tried to explain. "I have to think clearly, I don't have time, there are obligations, contracts."

"They're only excuses. That's not what I'm saying. Those things never matter to anyone in love."

We looked at each other.

Steven rose to leave. "I came back because I'd hoped you'd feel differently. But as much as I want to, I can't change the way you feel. I'm sorry, I misread things on Costa Brava." And he opened the door and was gone.

I stood on the other side of the door and the sound of its closing reverberated around me. It had been so fast. Almost a flash, another dream? Was it real? I couldn't tell.

What are you doing? I demanded. You don't even know what happened, what you said . . . You have no idea! . . . How could you let him walk out of your life like that again? How could you? He won't come back! Do you think he'll come back again? Don't you know he really loves you . . . you saw that. He came all this way. What more do you need? . . . But what if he knew? What if he? . . . what? what? what? Even Mercedes and Yves have love, but what do you have? Only your whats . . . and your more whats! He loves you! You love him! Don't let him walk away.

I opened the door. Steven was just reaching the bottom of the steep rickety stairway. "Steven," I said so low I don't know how he heard me. He turned, and suddenly we were both in the middle of the stairway. Steven bent his head and pressed his mouth to the palm of my hand. Something unfinished from Costa Brava caught us up. Nothing else mattered this moment. We looked at each other and knew conversation would be useless. It was unspoken. Why discuss it anymore? What I felt, what he felt . . . how could one truly know what the other felt? What did it matter? The airport? The ride? The café? The Avenida Palace? Montserrat? . . . Now he was here. I allowed myself to be folded into his arms, and folded him into mine. I led him up the stairs.

Piece by piece, we undressed each other silently in the sparse room. A small light from a ginger-jar lamp shone in from the hallway cutting into the dark. First the buttons and then the belts, my blouse fell from one shoulder and then the other, Steven smoothing his lips over the skin there. A shirt fell to the floor, and my hand smoothed over his chest and back.

Suddenly the smell of sweat and the cologne of another man filled the space, and I felt the suffocation of another time, but I pushed it away for these precious seconds, knowing it would be jealously back to claim me ... falling ... falling ... if I held on to Steven. ... Steven was kissing me, our first kiss, odd it should happen after all this time when we were already in bed.

"Elizabeth, I've searched the world for you. I knew it on Costa Brava, but now I'm sure."

Here it was, what one always reads about, when the lovers' bodies fit miraculously everywhere, in every detail: a shoulder dovetailing into the side of the chest of the other; the space between the breasts perfectly dimensioned to receive and envelop the side of the lover's face resting there; the skin of the inside of the thigh, like no skin that was ever felt before by either. Our hip bones locked into a groove in each other's body that was perfectly engineered for this moment in time when we would meet. Steven and I wrapped our legs around each other and proved that the predetermined measurements of each of our limbs, from ankle to knee and knee to groin, had been proportioned exactly right.

A tiny twist of my upper body and his mouth found the perfect place on my breast. Then lips locking, a slight lifting of the hips and Steven and I were joined. We journeyed across time—ancient seas no lovers had ever been to before. We knew each other's body as if it were our own, knew all the parts and into the mind. It was too compelling to be accidental; this is what the gods of love, Venus and Aphrodite, had promised.

It took such little time for the moment of explosioned ecstasy. Then a second of stillness, and Steven held me to him and joined into me again. For the first wondrous time, I felt more pleasure in a man's orgasm than my own.

Steven withdrew from me slowly and began to kiss my breasts and suck the hard nipples. I clung to him. His lips moved down the center of my body and settled, kissing and licking the rounded groove low on my stomach. The compulsion started in me again immediately, and I raised my hips to his mouth. His tongue moved down to that one perfect spot, the nerve center of a woman, and everything disappeared in the rush of perfect sensation you think you've known before, but can never anticipate the fullness of until you've met your perfect lover.

Steven and I lay together in the semidarkness of the room understanding that all other lovemaking that had happened before with other lovers was only a series of excited nervous thrills that physically happened and could make you feel passion, even a richness you thought was love, but was only longing, given so that when the day came that you found your perfect lover, you would know the difference.

The clock across from us said nine o'clock.

"Do you have to leave now, Steven?" I asked.

"No."

"I thought you said . . ."

"And you, Elizabeth? You said you were on your way out. Important."

"No."

We smiled in a conspiracy of knowing that nothing in the world could be more important than this moment together.

When we were feeling rested enough again to kiss and tease and touch the way lovers do I asked, "How did I ever find you, Steven?"

"You didn't, I found you . . ."

"But you said on the plane it was fate . . ."

"That wasn't exactly true."

"What do you mean?"

"Well . . ."

"There's something here."

"Don't make me say . . ."

"Too late now."

"I saw you sitting in the lounge at the gate. I said to myself, 'That woman is spectacular.' But you were checking your appointment book, completely engrossed. I said to myself, 'The last thing on her mind is you, Brandon.' I went up to the gate attendant and asked her where you were sitting. It was nowhere near me."

"C'mon, you're not going to tell me she changed everybody around just like that?"

"No, not just like that. The plane wasn't completely checked in yet. I showed her my passport and she recognized my name and picture. Then it was okay with her. After all, another story to tell at cocktail parties. How 'that womanizer Brandon wasted no time sitting himself next to a gorgeous extraordinarily talented film producer.' Sometimes it pays for a guy to have a bad reputation."

"You're wrong, I did notice you at the airport, but I made a point of not showing it, precisely because everybody knows your reputation." We laughed and kissed and snuggled some more. "But there's something else I want to know."

"Here comes trouble, I hear it."

"When you left before, so definitely, and I came after you, how come you were still there on the steps?"

"I walked very slow."

"You knew I'd follow?"

"I hoped."

"I've never met a man who was more romantic." I kissed little kisses over the planes of his face. "And a box office bad boy. All that, I'd never guess."

"I've never been romantic before. I've been mostly kind of a wise guy, I guess. This surprises me a lot more than you think."

"But your letter?"

"It came out like that. Trust me, you tapped into something, I don't know, it's like a jar of something, you turn it over and it just keeps coming. I've never written anything like that letter before. I guess I'm a lover who's been searching for his love. What should I do? Let it go?"

"No . . ." And we rose, locked in more kisses, to take a bath in the deep old-style bathtub in the bare cracked-tile bathroom.

Steven turned on the hot water. As the steaming vapors rose around us, the never forgotten scent of a certain Cognac hung in them, and strains of classical music that weren't there played silently to me . . . stalking, for another time. We climbed into the bath.

"Close your eyes, darlin'," Steven ordered, running a scrub brush down my back.

"Close yours, and guess what this is," I replied, rolling two hair rollers simultaneously on his back.

This lovers' game of guess what? expanded to include soap, and emery files and toothbrushes on arms and legs until the bathroom floor was soaked and we were kissing and laughing.

On the couch, the food we had ordered, tomatoes and ham and mayonnaise, passed riotously through lingering kisses. We gobbled pieces of crust, and pieces of cheese, and desserts of strawberries and flan and chocolate mousse.

"Can you take a trip with me tomorrow to Tarragona?" Steven asked, squeezing me tight as we left the mess on the table to return to bed. "It's a beautiful ride. Down the coast again, only the other way, and about two hours. I'd love to see it with you, ancient Roman ruins, walled cities—"

"I'll go," I hastily agreed.

"I love you, darlin'," Steven said, when our bodies were perfectly wrapped together again under the sheets.

"Tell me you love me, Elizabeth."

"I adore you, Steven."

"It's not the same thing. Tell me you love me."

I looked at Steven. I knew he wanted our romance to be happy and free. I turned out the light so he couldn't see the tears that were coming, and folded him to me to make love again.

Afterward, Steven lay vined to me in our perfect fit. I listened to him breathe, copying his rhythm into my own body, feeling above myself, fearless. But in my absorption, I'd been too careless, leaving the bedroom door open at an angle. My heart froze as I watched a shadow on the wall and I knew I'd given the stalking its chance to catch me . . .

. . . the room is white . . . a twelve-year-old girl lies in a bed watching the outside corridor through the angle of an open door, the men and women who go by and come into her room to feel her pulse and take blood for tests wear white too, doctors and nurses . . . The girl sits up . . . No, she's not ill, not ill at all.

Everybody here is too nice to her, almost solicitous . . . The admitting nurse had explained it very kindly to her. "You need a bit of a rest that's all. Your mother's death was understandably hard for you." Children's Psychiatric Pavilion, was what the door she'd been wheeled through had said. How long ago was it since she'd come here for this "bit of a rest"? She didn't care, she couldn't seem to care about anything anymore . . . except for her new secret she'd hidden under her pillow.

"Hellooooo." The curly-haired night-shift nurse entered her room with her night sedatives in a little pleated paper cup. "Hellooooo, well aren't you the lucky one. Going home tomorrow." No, the girl thinks, I won't be going home . . .

"And your father is sooooo charrrming," the night nurse coos.

. . . the girl looks through the door . . . outside in the corridor, other nurses are mewing and meowing in a circle around her father, who holds court in their center. Doctors in green surgical gowns with green masks dangling below their chins break through the circle to shake his hand, everybody always has something of a bow in their step when they approach him . . . The group retreats down the hall, circle intact . . . the girl directs her mind to her secret under her pillow . . .

The night-shift nurse smooths her bedcovers and walks to the metal closet against the wall of her room. She talks to the girl as she goes, "And your father has brought such beeyootiful going-home clothes for you to wear tomorrow."

... I won't be going home tomorrow, the girl thinks ...

The night nurse begins to give the new clothes her thorough inspection. She takes the white piqué summer coat with the fitted princess waist from the closet, and the flowered cotton dress, and frilly camisole and slip on a quilted sachet hanger. She shakes them out and looks them over carefully till she's satisfied that there are no pins or sharp objects attached to them. Then she neatly hangs them back. Last week, she'd been so sad to have taken away the girl's new hair barrette because it had too sharp an edge on its metal clip. "Good night, Bethy Dolly." The night nurse starts to the door, the nurses all call her "Bethy Dolly" now, and they hardly ever wait for her to answer anymore, they know she doesn't speak ...

As soon as the nurse leaves, the girl sneaks her hand under her pillow, feeling to make sure her secret is really there. Is it possible? Everybody would have said no, it was impossible, they're always so careful. But, yes, the girl probes her fingers along the sheet, and they're there, the secret six golden pins she hid two hours before as she heard the dinner nurse coming. She counts her cache carefully in her fingers, closing her eyes. Yes, it's true, hidden under her pillow are the pins that had attached the tags that said Lanz Original, and Jeunefille to the new clothes ... All during visiting today, the nurses had fawned and fussed over the girl's famous handsome father, milling in and out of her room. "Is his accent Austrian?" she'd heard them ask each other. "Yes a lot of violinists are Austrian," and in their oohs and aahs over her new clothes to please him, they'd forgotten to check for the tag pins till just now when he'd left ...

The girl turns away to the window so nobody can see her face through the door ... She pulls the covers over her and lies still for some time thinking . . . It will be light for two more hours, till almost nine tonight. Methodically now, without any emotion, she removes the pins from under her pillow. Still facing away toward the window, she carefully bends them straight and studies the map of her wrists. In her thin arms with their translucent skin, her veins stand out clearly . . . She's pleased . . . she'll wait another hour perhaps . . . she's thought of this before. And before and before! . . . She's heard that there are no nerves in the wrists, it doesn't hurt . . . her night sedative will take effect soon, she assures herself, and she'll feel even less . . . she'll press her six golden treasures into the veins of her wrist and in the morning she'll be gone . . . Yes, it's the right thing to do . . . she's known that for a long time, reassured it in her mind . . . She planned her details out all afternoon, while her father sat by the bed . . . She'll dress in the white piqué coat first. How will the coat look, so white against her red blood, will its diamond design soak through and become a blanket of wet red around her, or will its piqué whiteness be splattered and spotted and ribboned with red? . . . What will it matter? . . .

. . . The girl gets off the bed and starts for the metal closet where the piqué coat is . . . but she stops in the middle of the room . . . No! what if they hear the closet opening and catch her? . . . No don't wait! Do it now! . . . Yes! It's the right thing to do . . . She didn't expect she'd feel this terror welling in her. She scurries back to the bed and rolls herself up in a tiny ball under the covers away from the door . . . Do it now . . . Do it now . . . Don't wait . . . someone will come . . . it doesn't hurt in the wrists . . . it doesn't . . . remember when they took blood from your arm yesterday? . . . remember how it didn't hurt? . . . Do it now! . . . The girl presses the first pin into her wrist . . . see, it doesn't hurt . . . she presses it further and the blood begins to flow out, she presses the second and the third quick into the other wrist . . . and harder and deeper and her arms and the sheets are sprayed with blood . . . but now her arms are exploding in pain, and the pins slip between her fingers in their dark red coating . . . and she's screaming and pressing the pins into her veins and screaming and pressing and screaming and pressing the pins . . .

The morning arrived too bright and too sunny. Steven came into the bedroom. He buttoned his shirt and bent over the bed bracing himself with his arms on either side of me. "Here's coffee for you, sweetheart. Hope I didn't make it too strong." He reached for his tie on the doorknob. "I'm used to it that way, but I should've asked you. It is pretty black."

I closed my eyes . . . why did he have to wake me up to tell me about the coffee? I'd been wide awake all night, with all kinds of muscle aches, as if I'd taken ten ballet classes without warming up. And everything, right to my fingertips, was buzzing . . . Now, the minute I fell asleep . . .

"I have to go for a while, darlin'," Steven said, slinging the tie around his neck without knotting it. "But wait for me."

"I won't wait for you," I snapped at him, sitting upright. "Did you wake me up to wait for you?"

"Whaa?" He came over and put his arms around me. "I didn't mean for you to wait all day. I only meant—"

"What did you mean?" I slapped away the hand on my arm.

"Mmm . . . ? One of those tigers of the morning huh?" He laughed at my irrational behavior.

Only then did I realize how I was acting and why. The depth of the memories that had come back to me last night was painful in the morning light. Already I was pushing Steven away from me to protect them. But was the hospital scene real memory or the fantasy of a dream? It was too deep inside me to tell and already fading quickly as dreams do. I needed to know if it was true. I clenched my fists under the covers and tried to bring it back.

Steven was studying me as I hid my feelings from him. How

strange I must seem. "I'm sorry," I said, "I guess I'm an early-morning crank." Again I attempted to excuse my behavior as if it could ever be something natural.

But Steven accepted my explanation as if it were. And last night forgave all the strange ways I'd acted. "Will you let me finish now?" he said, willing to look the other way once more.

"If you'll let me go back to sleep," I muffled the words into the pillow, making them sound funny, making amends. If he felt everything was normal he'd leave, and I'd be safe to draw the hospital dream out into the open.

Steven went on. "It'll only take me a few hours to clean up at the affiliate. Then I'll transfer the story to another journalist. Then I'll come back here to pick up the love of my life and we'll go down to Tarragona as we said last night. We'll check out all the ruins—walled cities, castles, arches, cathedrals, the whole history of Spain—together."

I could hear the delight in his voice. My eyes felt too sensitive. I closed them.

"Sweetheart, you still want to go, don't you?"

"I do, I do." I hid my face deeper into the pillow. "I'm just tired. It's too early."

Steven's breath was on my neck as he bent over to kiss me.

I turned to him. It was no use . . . he wasn't going to leave me alone . . . I told myself, apologize again, and he'll leave. Then you can figure it out. A few more minutes and the dream will be gone . . . "Please forgive me for being a crank, my darling," I said.

"Forgotten!"

I opened my eyes halfway to see Steven bouncing out of the room like a cheerful kid. I felt awful for having acted this way to him.

"Remember." He turned around. "Twelve fifteen on the dot, downstairs ready to go—or else. I'll try to call before. But if I don't, be ready."

"Gotcha." I smiled a bit.

After he left, I lay there concentrating on the hospital dream, trying to bring back the colors and details of it. I'd been wide awake, it had to be memory. But I couldn't understand, the memory was broken. Was it true, I'd tried to commit suicide? I was only a little girl. What if they hadn't stopped me? My father had to have known what happened! He knew! They had to have told him.

I got out of bed and paced around with my hands clenching and unclenching. Go outside, stay inside, my mind kept me moving, not being able to accept that my father knew I'd tried to kill myself and still wouldn't stop what he was doing to me. Before, deep down, I had always somehow thought of his crime as a crime of passion . . . he couldn't help it . . . too much love can turn to agony . . . A little girl's thoughts had buried some romantic idea in the lavish care he gave to me . . . My Daddy bought me the best clothes, always the best restaurants, lessons . . . Now I saw the calculated violence of him . . . Yes, tenderly care for the victim, pamper her, keep the child victim alive or you'll have no victim. I felt a fury racing inside, searching backward to that time . . .

. . . Each day Bethy Dolly's bedroom was dark as she went over her plan in her mind . . . How quickly the time came . . . She rises from the bed and puts on her flower-quilted robe over her nightgown . . . Her robe, what does she need it for? Her bedroom window is covered by thick velvet curtains to keep out the cold . . . She hasn't opened them for the two weeks she's been home from the hospital. Bethy draws them tonight with a gold braided rope on the side of the window and looks out to the dark icy sky of winter . . .

. . . She tries to lift the heavy window open, but it won't budge, she's not strong enough. She tries again . . . Strange how calm she is . . . surely, she should cry. She tries again and the window screeches . . . A little at a time . . . She opens it enough and climbs up on the sill. Don't let him hear . . . The wind blows in at her as she looks down the twelve-story drop to the court-yard. She's not afraid. It'll happen quietly. Perhaps the fathers and mothers and children sleeping in the next apartments think-ing of their breakfasts and of clothes to wear to school and work and buses and trains and toys will never hear the noise of her body falling against the pavement in the night. She moves further out onto the window ledge. But what is this? There's an iron burglar's grate bolted to the outside frame of the win-dow. Its openings are too small for her to squeeze through. It wasn't there before she went to the hospital. She knows that. There was only a screen to keep out the bugs in summer. She looks through the iron grate down to the courtyard. No, the grating wasn't there before, she's sure. She lowers herself back to the floor from the sill . . . Yes, the living room windows. She hears him in his bedroom now, shoes scraping the floor, he's changing from his orchestra clothes, there is still time . . . She runs to the living room, and draws open the drapes . . . The smaller living room window opens easily and there are iron grates on it too. The icy air whips her as she stares through them down to Riverside Drive . . . she hears his slippers walking down the hall to her bedroom . . . there's no place to go . . .

I feel a little girl's trapped terror begin to turn into a pound-ing band tightening around my head . . . Yes, this was how it began, and then would come the headaches. I'd lose days. Flut-terings of pain were already starting in my chest. If I didn't stop them, they would quickly become the stabbing pains all over again.

My old survival strategy started . . . The Valium. Take them! No, I'd thrown them away. I'd been so sure the chest pains and the dreams were gone forever, I'd wanted to believe that. Another flutter of pain in my chest, already stronger. Steven would be back at twelve fifteen. No! I wouldn't let this take me over again. If he came back and found me this way, he'd want to know what happened. How could I explain it to him, I was only beginning to be able to explain it to myself. I couldn't. I'd lose him this time.

No, fight, I told myself. You love him. Don't lose! Get control! I ran to the bottom of my suitcase where I'd put back Bethy's headache pills and quickly retrieved them again. I had to make sure I wouldn't slip into Bethy's headaches and lose control. A flutter flew in my chest. The pills were powerful sedatives, but they were old. Sedatives lose their potency. These pills couldn't be as strong as they once were. They wouldn't affect me as much. Maybe I would become a little sleepy, that's all, but I'd be fine. I swallowed one of the tiny pills with Steven's strong coffee, then picked through the pile of clothes still on the floor. Bright colors . . . I must have kept some bright colors. Yes here was something red, a scooped tee, and the jeans. I grabbed a hairbrush from the floor and vigorously brushed my hair, keeping up my dialogue inside . . . What if I was sure that Steven loved me enough that I could tell him? Even so, how do you explain things of such enormity? How do you know how they'd be accepted? If he loved me enough . . . "Elizabeth," I stopped myself, "don't you know better, it was only one night of love. Don't bring things into this that might not be."

I showered and dressed and set to work. The apartment was easier to straighten than I thought it would be even though the pill was making me move slower. It wasn't how I wanted to be with Steven, I wanted to be honest. But already the details of the hospital room were moving far away from me. At twelve fifteen, I closed the apartment door behind me and turned the key. Suddenly I was downstairs on the street wearing the red tee, and Steven was giving me flowers and hugging me. It was still so hot out. But of course, it was summer.

"Have the coffee yet?" Steven said, maneuvering the same jeep we'd gone to Costa Brava in through the Barcelona traffic.

"Sure did, and I can't wait to get going. I love seeing these places with you. Costa Brava was magnificent." But I was already fighting to stifle a yawn from the pill.

Steven was jubilant. "For me, it was like I'd never seen it before. I feel like I'm winning the lottery to be able to pry you away from your work twice. I'm glad the film is going so well."

"Yes it is," I agreed, kissing him. To myself, I dreamily thought, As soon as we get out of Barcelona, I'll call and tell José I won't be available today to meet the Count at four. I can't bear the tension of talking to that man. Why should I? I'm just starting to feel right again.

"Well . . . everything went as I suspected this morning," an energetic Steven was updating me. "The athletes involved in the steroid mess had to withdraw. They gave a press conference and admitted everything. Poor kids. They'd do anything to their bodies to win. They swallow these pills without thinking. Interesting . . . the way they disassociate it. You'd never know anything to look at them, some of them are so young."

"But it's done," I said, pulling the subject away from anything connected to any kind of pill . . . Why had I taken Bethy's pill so fast? The pill was very old, what if the chemicals had altered, or it had become contaminated? Anything could happen, I could go into shock. No! I ordered myself to relax, the bottle was tightly sealed, and pills only lose potency with age. The dosage was weaker.

"Yes, it's all done," Steven agreed, "and now a vacation. I'm going to take the love of my life to see the wonders and beauty of Tarragona. What could be better?"

"What could be better?" I agreed and reclined the seat back. My eyes were starting to drift closed. I could hardly help it.

"Wait a minute there," Steven said. "I know I've put a lot of people to sleep but how will I live this down. We're not even out of the city yet." Steven was joking, but I could see that he was losing his humor about my behavior this time. I could hear the defensive swagger returning to his voice. "Hey, I'm supposed to be one of the most exciting guys in the world."

"You are, my darling! But couldn't I dream about you." I tried to sit straight up again, and show that nothing was different, but there was nothing I could do to change the fact that Bethy's mild pill was stronger than I'd anticipated.

Twenty-three

The terrain had turned as wild and rocky as Costa Brava. Craggy mountain ranges cut through by the sea, were on one side of us, with valleys and gorges on the other. Small white-washed towns were carved into the cliffs overlooking the sea. I sat up and looked around in wonder.

"Nice to have some company," Steven said. "For a while I thought I was making this trip alone."

"I'm sorry, but I was just so tired. Oh look . . ."

"I've been looking for over an hour," he answered coldly, but turned to look in spite of his tone.

A herd of goats was calmly following their shepherd along the sidewalk of a bridge. Bicyclists and strollers proceeded along in front and in back of them. In the center of the road we bumped and stopped in the congestion of automobile traffic and soon the goats had passed us.

"Why didn't you say you were too tired for the trip?" Steven wouldn't drop the subject.

"I'm sorry I fell asleep on you."

"Must be my personality."

"Please stop it. I really am sorry. What more can I say?" I

touched his shoulder and the side of his face, and the electricity started between us again.

We left the crowded walled town and rode past arches of a great Roman aqueduct. Bethy's pill had drained me, but I wasn't going to disappoint him. Steven was alive and interested in the history of everything. His voice zigzagged with the car around stone fences and thirteenth-century buildings with arched gateways leading into squares. We parked and walked through crooked streets, called Calle Santa Theresa, and Calle Dona Luisa. Then we were back on the open road again.

"You see that castle over there," the reporter in Steven wanted me to see everything, "the one with the pointed turrets, on the cliff?"

"Yes?"

"I did a story for *Life* magazine on this part of Spain years ago, and I used pictures of that castle. I still have them, and I'll show you when we get back—it was the first thing I'd ever done like that. I had such a great time with it that I almost felt guilty about taking the money."

We drove up a different cliff where I followed behind Steven along the walls of a monastery. Thankfully, we didn't stay long. And, soon after, we stopped for lunch.

In the ladies' room, I threw cold water on my face and the back of my neck, and held my wrists under the icy faucet until I worried I'd been away too long. The chest flutterings were starting again. I reached for my purse for the Valium . . . you didn't bring . . . Remember! . . . I sat down for a minute.

Steven stood when I returned to the table. "I was getting worried." He held out the chair for me.

"I had to wash my face . . . so hot!"

"You know, for a while I thought you might have left me for acting like such a jerk before in the car. I don't know what came over me."

"It was my fault for falling asleep like that. I wouldn't like it either, but I guess I'm still a little sapped from the flu."

"Why didn't you say so, I would've understood. We could've come another time."

"No, I wanted us to do this together now, very much. I'll be fine. It's perfect! Terrific! I just need some food."

We waited for our food . . . and waited . . . like you can in a small café off the road, somewhere in Spain. I drank glass of water after glass of water. Fans whirled above us making sounds that seemed too high-pitched for fans.

After lunch, I did feel much stronger. We walked along a dock and watched old men sitting quietly mending their nets. Their sons and grandsons unloaded the morning catch.

"Do you feel up to an Arab market?" Steven urged me, raring to go all over again in this antique world.

"Sure," I pushed myself, delighted by how caught up he was in our romantic surroundings.

We went through the Arab market, and into a twelfth-century synagogue. "Moorish architecture." He explained the history of the building as we walked out the back of the synagogue and followed the curving alleys inside the ancient walls of the town. Mustached men sat in the shade of cafés carved into the wall. Fans whirred above them . . . too many really . . . for such a small space . . .

I don't know exactly when the fever started. At first it was only one more queasy off-balance feeling, maybe tripping on the cobblestones, then a feeling of having dropped too fast in an airplane . . . "Shouldn't have eaten that spicy zarzuela for lunch." That made sense, one always has to make sense of the peculiar when on such unfamiliar ancient roads.

My wrists were beginning to feel like they weren't mine. Mine had strength and purpose, these were floating as in that child's game of pressing the back of the wrists between a doorway for a few minutes and afterward walking away and watching the arms rise by themselves.

Steven was talking to me, something about the Romans here in Sagunto in the earlier centuries. "First came the Carthaginians. You can see their influence in some of this architecture."

I nodded, squinting in the sunlight at the detail of yet another beautiful archway. But I really wasn't seeing. The sun was hurting my eyes through my dark glasses. I closed my lids against it and took a tissue to wipe the tears away, passing my hand over my forehead. Wet? I shuddered, realizing my whole body was covered in a cold perspiration . . . Different spices here I wasn't used to. Spices can make you sweat like this . . . I must be getting older, when I was younger, I could eat anything, anywhere . . . Remember the time in the old part of Tangier? . . .

Steven was talking. I heard the words, "Spaniards . . . Romans . . . conquest . . ."

"Yes," I agreed as enthusiastically as I could. "You certainly know a lot about Spain."

"I learned most of it doing that *Life* assignment. But I always loved this stuff. The only good marks I ever got in school were in history," a jubilant Steven was telling me.

A sudden contraction walloped the pit of my stomach, I fought not to double over.

Steven was looking into the lens of his camera. "Have you ever been to Israel, darlin'?"

"No, I haven't."

"It's a fascinating place. I'd love to take you there. Maybe we can go on an archaeological dig to the area around Masada. I've seen pictures of it there with whole cities built one on top of the other, just coming out of the earth. I've always wanted to go on a dig. I planned it out a couple of times, but I never made it. Something always made the thing fall through. See, darlin', that fate thing again."

I tried to listen, and to copy his festive mood—I tried very hard, but the sweat on my forehead was becoming stronger, alarming. I could almost smell it ... If I ignored it ... "Yes, Steven," I tried to say brightly, "I would love to go on an archaeo-log—"

"Watch out!" Steven caught me by the arm as I stumbled up a flight of broken stone stairs to the next level of the town.

"Haa!" I assured him. "Dancers only fall up the stairs! Did you know that?" I stood upright quickly and pulled the peak of my baseball cap well down over my forehead.

Steven looked closely at me under it. "Are you sure you're all right? You don't look like yourself. You look pale."

"Don't be silly. I'm fine! Oh look! This looks like an old fort at the top there. I know you'd love to see it, and I'd love to see it with you." I smiled, convincing him, but not myself. We began to pick our way up the steep and jagged stone steps with Steven protectively holding me by my arm ...

At the top we climbed over a dense but well-eroded stone wall, which had been built to surround what looked to be the remains of a fort.

Steven was as exhilarated as I knew he'd be. "Look out there, Elizabeth." He turned me to face out to the sea. "All these old forts were built in strategic lookout positions. From this point, you could see any enemy ship coming at you from anywhere in the Mediterranean. Everything for miles and miles. Look around you my love, at history."

I looked, but the wall, the fort, the outlines of everything were lost to me in a ferocious dazzle of blue.

Steven was circling the perimeter examining everything. "Would you believe this wall, a couple of feet thick at least, and on the other side of it, straight down, ninety degrees into the rocks. Nobody could sneak up on you here. They'd be picked right off by the soldiers holding their position on top, that is if they didn't get their ships cannoned away first."

I watched Steven, his camera out, already changing lenses to take close-ups of the remains of the gaping holes in the wall where the cannons would have been mounted. He was working, shooting from all angles, energized. This was the kind of work he loved, and I loved watching him do it.

"You know, darlin'," he called to me from the other side of the fort, "I think I'm going to do a photo story on this, like I used to. Not for money, not a chance, nothing like that, you don't get paid too much for this stuff."

"It doesn't matter if you like it."

"You can say that because you're a woman. If you're a guy money becomes the scoreboard that defines the difference of who you are. What you get paid the money for is being a network sports anchor, a jock sure, but still a very corporate type."

"You're too hard on yourself," I replied. "I don't think anybody sees you as such a corporate guy."

"Believe me, it's true. You don't know. Behind the cameras, it's like a bank with bosses, who have bosses who have bosses. And the bad part is I worked hard to serve time with this whole coporate thing."

"But why, if it's that different from who you are?"

" 'Money! You make money,' I told you how my dad drilled that into me when I was a kid, and I fought it. What I didn't say is that now I'm doing exactly what he would have wanted. When I worked as a freelance photojournalist, I guess I was still a kid and didn't understand yet how money works you over. I just knew I loved this stuff, and I did it. Smile, darlin', I want pictures of all the natural beauty up here."

I stood still and smiled cheerfully for the picture, then walked over to the wall and sat down on a remaining section that had crumbled itself away enough to form a low bench. The sea sparkled into the sky with such ferociousness it became a vast blue fire in front of me. Whitecapped waves crackled, disappeared, and crackled again. What if the stone under me crumbled away more and more, faster and faster, would I become part of the vast blue fire? Would I dare to be so free? I stood up, but felt another sharp pain, and Steven was beside me, with his hand on my shoulder, steadying me.

He lifted my baseball cap and looked at me probingly. "I'm worried about you."

"No no," I lied weakly, "please, don't stop taking your photos because of me. I'll be okay in a moment."

"Enough." Stephen was leading me. "I'm going to take you back to the inn and you're going to lie down for a while."

I let him lead me without protest.

Was it ten minutes or ten hours that I slept in the room with the white stucco walls and the light yellow curtains floating at the sides of the windows?

My eyes felt pasty and swollen. Everything hurt, arms and legs, my armpits . . . What if it was Bethy's pills gone bad? . . . No, couldn't be . . . It was one of those ugly but fast twenty-four-hour bugs, perfectly normal . . . you had to let it take its course. I was shivering under the flowered comforter. If only I had some water . . . I had to rest and drink a lot of water and take some aspirin, then I would be better. The buzz in my head . . . perfectly normal with this kind of flu. Tomorrow I'd be fine, and get back to work.

"You feel any better, darlin'?" Steven's voice came from the doorway.

I looked across at the open window, and the paintings of the ancient walled towns of Tarragona on the wall beside it, its cliffs and seas done in the bright primary colors of mass-produced prints.

"I think the fever broke," Steven said reassuringly as he walked toward me.

"What happened?" I managed to ask. My voice felt lumpy in my throat.

"Here, lie still. Try a little water." Steven was pouring from the brightly flowered china pitcher beside my bed. "You passed out, and the proprietor called a doctor. A nice fellow who gave you these pills. Antibióticos, he said." Steven was trying to be light for my benefit. "Don't alarm her," I could hear in his voice.

Pills? More pills? What did they give me? They didn't know I'd taken the others . . . Don't be silly . . . Enough time has passed . . . I tried to raise my head to drink the water, but it was too heavy, my neck hurt too much. Steven lifted my head and brought the water to my mouth . . . the water was warm . . . if only the water were cold.

When I lay back down I could feel that the pillow and sheet were bathed in cold sweat. I wrapped the comforter around me—clutched it to me in fright now.

"Here . . . just a little," Steven was saying as he raised my head again, this time to put a dry pillow under it. "Don't worry about anything, I'm here with you, my love. Do you think I'd let anything happen to the love of my life after all the time it took me to find you? I'm not leaving you for a minute."

I could see his efforts to calm me. They were too planned. Something had happened.

"You've had a bad time this last day." Steven sat down beside me. "Some food poisoning probably. But the fever has broken, and you got rid of most of it anyway. They didn't have to pump." He laughed. "A little messy but . . . good girl . . . you did it. You'll be okay. Just try to rest. I'll be right here, I've already told them in Barcelona."

"But you're on assignment."

"Don't worry, I've got a large staff back there that will take care of everything. I'm only the anchor anyway, it's no secret they do the real work, I just get the glory. If they need me, they'll call me here because right now I'm staying with you."

"But you could go if it's over." Talking was too much of an effort, I finished the sentence to myself—I'm only going to sleep. My arms and legs would not move . . . I should turn over. I sleep on my stomach . . . But no matter, too much energy was required. I would turn later.

In a dim light, Steven was bathing my forehead and cheeks with a wet towel, and removing the crusts from my eyes . . . No, let him, don't fight, it burns too much to open them. Steven was running the wet towel over my arms and legs . . . shivering . . . Cold, wet . . . the sheet was being changed . . . like in a hospital . . . they roll the patient to the other side of the bed, and carefully arrange one side. Then they roll the patient back over the done side and arrange the other. How clever. They tuck in the ends and the patient has hardly moved. How did Steven know how to do this? *The comforter again . . . but where are its flowers? Now it is green, and the yellow curtains hang gray in the twilight. The wind rushes in . . . The air around me hurt. It had to be replaced. Got to open the window . . . onto Riverside Drive . . . see the smashed body of a girl on Riverside Drive . . .*

. . . Red, white and blue, the dazzle of starbursts, and circles and shakings of light exploding toward me . . . watching the Fourth of July fireworks from a roof of an apartment house on Riverside Drive . . . climbing up to sit on the ledge, with Daddy holding me tight by the thighs . . . legs hanging over . . . his hands pressing in . . . moving up . . . teasing . . . taunting . . . then falling, falling . . . the people looking down at the smashed body of a girl on Riverside Drive . . .

It must have been some hours later by the darkness outside that I saw Steven's form sitting, outlined in the moonlight through the window. Had he been sitting with me all this time? Did he really care that much that he'd give an important Olympic assignment to another journalist, to stay here and make sure that I'd be all right? I didn't deserve that. He walked over to the bed, talking to me. "I have to go out and make some telephone calls to the States now, darlin'. Would you believe their phone here doesn't have long-distance service? Well, we wanted rustic for the weekend—we got rustic." He thought I was sound asleep

but still he made jokes to cheer and reassure me. "Look, darlin',
Mrs. Fernández, the proprietor's wife, is going to be glued right
outside the door until I get back. She assured me so many times
that she wouldn't move, I even learned some Spanish from her
repeating it so much—she's raised 'nine children and two hus-
bands and she knows exactly what to do with a fever!' " Steven
sat down very carefully on the side of the bed and cradled my
head, lifting it. His voice became softer. "So be a good girl now
and drink a little water for me before I go, doctor's instructions,
okay, and when I come back we'll do it again."

With my eyes closed, I sipped a few drops of water from
the cup he held for me.

"There, that's my love. Try. Come on, sweetheart, a little
more water." He tucked the covers around me again, pulled the
window down a bit against the draft and left the room.

As soon as the door closed, I began to cry. I'd never had a
man touch me this caringly before. They always wanted something from me and it was told immediately in the touch. I needed
Steven's love in my very core. I couldn't survive without it. And
I'd found it without looking. I was a wonder with him. I wanted
to take care of him too, make sure he was happy . . . I wept with
the longing for it . . . if only I hadn't fallen so far . . .

. . . I'm standing at the top of a steep hill looking down on
a city block with Steven's yellow jeep parked at the bottom in a
corner. Already I can make out Steven's form distinctly, even
though he's too far away for me to see. I recognize him the way
you recognize a person you love. You see them walking toward
you from blocks away, although they're crushed into the middle
of a crowd. You know their outline and movement so well. You
feel the smile come on your face . . .

. . . Steven is sitting in the jeep . . . I see his profile. I notice
the way his head leans on a slight angle to the left and the curve
of the neck. He must be reading a newspaper while he waits for
me, yes there it is, propped on the steering wheel. I walk slowly

enjoying every precious second of watching him . . . Every once in a while he looks up—looking to see if I'm coming . . . I see the sure lines of his even features and the texture of the short hair in relief against the canvas hood of the jeep . . . His left arm leans out of the window with the shirtsleeve rolled up. Already I understand the curve of his arm as it shows from the shirtsleeve and its tan color and the feel of its skin, slightly roughened with a down of blond hairs. I know the miracle of that arm reaching for me and wrapping me at night, and its sweetness handing me coffee in the morning. I love this arm as I love every part of him. How it swings rebelliously at his side instead of holding the handlebars of a bicycle or the steering wheel of a car as it should. I will always watch that arm with awe and delight. I can see that Steven's wearing a cotton shirt with a collar, and I know it'll be tucked into tan chinos neatly with a belt . . .

. . . Steven looks up again and I start to walk faster to him . . . One foot in front of the other, I'm going so fast, I'm rolling out of control and now I am at the bottom of the hill . . . but Steven's jeep is not at the corner anymore . . . "Steven," I call out, running across the street to the next corner, but the yellow jeep has moved yet again. I run to my lover across the next street, to another corner . . . but still the jeep moves away from me to the next. I'm out of breath running . . . Steven's torso does not move anymore, but sits frozen, looking down, in the moving jeep. Finally I'm catching up behind it. I run even faster . . . This time, I'll catch up, I think, as I come up beside it and playfully touch-tag the door. As soon as I touch it, the door opens and Steven steps out . . . His back is to me in his light blue cotton shirt and tan chinos. "Steven, it's me, Elizabeth," I call, reaching to touch his shoulder, but his torso turns with such force that I'm thrown back and I look into my father's face framed by its thick dark hair, dark eyes under their great brown brows, and his full mouth catch me in their field. My father smiles at me and mocks me, holding out Steven's shirtsleeve arms to me . . . making me cringe away from my lover ... But it's only his trick, as the shirtsleeve arms are replaced by his own in a dark suit. My father's voice is pleading, gentle to me, "I love you, my Bethy Dolly, my little rose. Come, Bethy, come home with me now. You know you will. You know it can be only us, always. You know you won't ever tell anyone. You can't. Come, Bethy!" He opens the car door and leads me in ... Inside the car, it isn't the yellow jeep, but my father's green Mercedes with its wood-paneled dashboard. His perfectly polished wing-tipped shoe shows out of his suit trousers on the gas pedal. I huddle away from him into a ball on the leather seat and press toward the window. I'm wearing the hospital white piqué coat with its six golden buttons ... It's splashed and ribboned with blood. I thrust out my wrists. "No! No! I'm not Bethy Dolly. No! I'm not Bethy! I'm not her!"

I shot awake hearing a little girl's voice, "I'm not her! I'm not her!" The voice was inside, I couldn't make it come out of me, but I could hear it clearly as if I had. I listened to the little girl over and over desperately denying herself, "I'm not Bethy," but I couldn't feel any feelings of her. She was detached. Outside my window, I could see the muddy brown of the sky. It must be five thirty in the morning. The night demons were always at their strongest at this time, but soon it would be light and they'd be gone. I knew well how to fight them.

But this morning was different. In this moment of uncommon weakness from my fever without enough strength to quickly dress myself in the camouflage of Elizabeth, in this short moment of unprotected terror, I began to understand what had always eluded me. I held my night demons to me, elongating the moment, and let my key unfold before me slowly. I didn't rush it, and somehow I feared it less. In the weird quiet calm of those who have been weakened and drained by fevers, perspectives can be flattened, intensities diminished, and the world seems clearer. Too weak to don protection, there's a clarity of the senses. The years and years of emotions piled on emotions till they'd become a ferocious tangle of wires that crissed and crossed and hid their beginnings and endings were beginning to unravel. I understood something for the very first time—I'd always thought I'd never told because I was hiding my truth from the world, that if I told, great iron doors would lock on me forever. But all the time it was only to hide it from myself.

I whispered my key out loud. "I'm not Bethy Dolly. I'm not her." And again, "I'm not Bethy." Yes! it was so simple to see. How could I have missed it . . . if I never told, and nobody ever knew, I could always pretend it wasn't true, couldn't I? . . . I could always run away from myself and never be her. Who could prove otherwise? And so I did run. And as time ran with me, I locked out anyone who would ever be close enough to find out. I was locked behind my own great iron doors where I wouldn't know, wouldn't remember, wouldn't feel. I would never allow a real love to come near. Oooo . . . my father knew me well, he never doubted how safe he was with me. No matter what I said or threatened, when it came the time, I would always run away and never tell. He could do anything with me he wanted. Would I follow his lead again and deny myself my life as Elizabeth too?

Outside, I could see the light barely starting to come up in the stillness. I watched it, whispering again, "I'm not her!" The dark muddy brown of early dawn lightened my window, and allowed a deep muted green of the trees to show in its shadows. I whispered it again, "I'm not Bethy!" It was close to six but I held tight to my night demons. I needed them to make me feel Bethy inside me before my strength returned to protect me.

As the sun lightened the world outside more, Steven looked in on me again, opening the door carefully. I pretended to be asleep. He tiptoed to the bed and felt my head. I didn't dare look at him or move, trying to breathe evenly. "Good girl," he whispered. "Cool as a cuke. You're going to be fine by tonight. So get good rest, I've made reservations for us to dance at the king's ball. When I told them you were here, and we were in love, they decided to have one. I love you, Elizabeth." He kissed me lightly on the eyelashes and left. I allowed myself one peek. Oh what wonderful longing I had for the life we could share.

As soon as he left, I checked my forehead too, and my arms. He was right, I wasn't sweating anymore, the fever had broken. It was almost full morning. I raised myself in the bed, getting my bearings. The sun was coming up fast. The curtains in their early-morning pale yellow swayed calmly at the sides of each window. The air smelled sweet. The flowered pitcher was on the night table. I poured water into the cup and pulled myself up to sitting. Still lightheaded, I made myself say it all out loud to affirm what I knew was true. "My father, Roland, was safe in his evil depravity with all of us. He would easily kill the women who loved him to protect himself. My mother, Marya, took her life because she couldn't tell and she couldn't live with knowing. He never stopped her. With her gone, the threat of his being exposed was gone too. Bethy Dolly tried to take her life and failed, but she died for him a little more in her heart every day without questioning it. Finally as she grew into a young woman she succeeded, by giving up her identity. Roland's secret remained protected. And me Elizabeth, he never knew me, he never dreamed who his perfectly controlled Bethy Dolly would become. Should I let him reach out from the grave and pull me after him too? Should I so willingly go, unquestioningly letting him kill the love inside me?" He would make me fill its place with emptiness to protect his secret ... No, Steven, don't ever come close to me and find out. No, Steven, don't love me so much, and I'll never love you, and nobody will ever know ... My father beat me at fourteen when the boys began to call. I didn't protest. He was right, they might find out. Now I was beating myself in his place. It was my time to take back my life from my father.

It was morning and its strength of smells and breezes, and the brightness of the sun nourished me to strength, but not the strength I needed to overcome the iron fears trapped by a lifetime of hiding. Quick, I had to think this out before the day returned, catching me up in its denial again. In no time I would be regretting this special unprotected moment, and every dangerous thought I was thinking. And I'd never let it happen again. Already I was beginning to ponder the great chance I would be taking if I told Steven. What if I was wrong, what if he didn't love me, what if he told. I couldn't go back. But if I didn't act now, I'd allow the great doors to lock on me again. I'd always be lying and hiding away from Steven's love, always afraid to give it back. Our love would die. Our life together could never be.

I'd have to take my greatest risk quickly before the morning grew much more. Who would have ever suspected that it would happen here, that I would let loose the thing I'd kept secret for thirty years, here in this simple tourist inn, somewhere in Spain, in a bed many other travelers had slept in, and like me stayed only a few hours before continuing their lives. But mine would be changed forever.

I was determined. I didn't know what I'd say to Steven or how I'd begin. How do you tell the man you love, words about yourself that you'd never said your whole lifetime . . . what would happen when you dared to let such secrets loose? What bitter rust would flow from you first?

I could have called out to Steven and he would have come to me, but I waited, not knowing what to expect, sitting in the bed for another hour. The fear locked and unlocked in me until finally Steven entered the room. He walked across the tile floor to me, beaming that I was sitting up and looking alert. "What amazing improvement! I should have gotten you a nice juicy chocolate éclair to celebrate instead of this fresh pitcher of water and three plain dry little crackers. Sorry, doctor's orders." He sat down on the side of the bed and hugged me. "Mmmm, why didn't you tell me you were going to deck yourself out like that in this extraordinary peignoir and look so beautiful." He hugged me again as I sat in the old torn print nightshirt he must have borrowed from the proprietor's wife.

"I . . ." I stopped myself. Already I was finding myself being drawn into his humor, already searching for a clever answer to give back, already moving away from what I'd decided . . . my camouflage was falling over me quickly . . . my father would be pleased . . . But I wouldn't let him have me this time . . . Now! I told myself. Now!

"Steven . . ." I began.

He looked surprised at my different demeanor.

"Please let me tell you something I feel you should know. I want to tell you about myself, not about dancing in Barcelona, but how I came to be there and who I really am." I gasped for air. My breath came fast and I could taste the emotion sour in my throat. My reflexes began a swallowing movement in my throat to pull it back . . . you haven't said anything, I thought, you still have a chance to change your mind . . . it will be unbearable for you . . . already you can see that. But the secret valves had already opened and the first rust had already begun to flow out. I began a low wailing, "My name is Bethy."

Steven didn't ask me any questions, he just held me tight.

"Steven," my wail grew louder, "my name is Bethy, my father raped me when I was very young. I worshiped him and could never believe how much he'd hurt me, and what he'd done. So I didn't. I think some years went by after that, I don't know, and it didn't happen again. I believed that maybe it never happened in the first place, that it wasn't true, I loved him so. But then after my mother died, it happened again once, and then more regularly. I still could not accept it as true. When I was twelve, I tried to take my life rather than believe it, but they stopped me . . ."

Steven held me quietly. The wailing had stopped but other sounds came from me, a kind of a rasp that made me shiver.

After a while, I began to speak again, but my voice sounded as if I was hearing it from behind a door ... "A year later I ran away. The police finally found me crawling on the ground inside the bushes of the park, hiding out of sight of their flashlights like a little animal. I was terrified. They brought me home in the police car, I could have told them then, but I didn't. I thought if I did they would lock me away forever. When the police left, my father took me to his bed, but he didn't touch me again for some weeks. I thought I was safe, and that our life would be good from now on. I never spoke with anybody." The rasp cut off my words again, but I fought through. "What if what I'd done came out? When it started again I shut myself away from any friends. I knew nothing more of life except my dancing. As I grew older, I was expected to perform in sex like a woman, and I did."

Steven silently bundled the covers around me and rocked me ... I shook under them. I could feel the swallowing movements starting again, pulling my words back, my throat caught numb in its whisper. I wanted terribly to stop what I was thinking, doing, betraying ... yes my father was reaching to me, pulling me to him ... he'd punish me later ... I would deserve it ... But my new will kept me going, I wouldn't let him have me this time, I was going to break free ... I stopped trembling on the outside, outside, I spoke.

As my words started again, they came out more evenly and my voice became stronger. "... Nobody could ever suspect. My father was a famous violinist, and as his daughter, I lived what looked to be a privileged life. Noted people of the arts and academics came to our house and sat in the living room. I learned early on to live outside our truth. I took their hats, I took their coats, I served them tea. I allowed them to compliment me on my dancing, they'd seen me at the Young Dancers' concert. They said I was a beautiful gracious young lady, how pleased they were to meet me ... I said nothing. They would never see the horrible wretched girl who wished for death at night in the dark. I hated her! She deserved everything! I was not her! I was different! I was the dancer!

"As I grew older and was accepted to the ballet company, my father could see that I'd be working closely with other dancers every day, and they might become friendly, I might tell. To guard his crime against me, he threatened that he himself would tell my ballet company. I would be unmasked to the other dancers, the choreographers and the directors too. Everyone would know it was my fault. I lived in fear every morning on my way to rehearsal that the moment I would walk in the door, everything in my life would be over. I'd shake terribly, struggling to hide my fear until I could slip into the rehearsal hall and see that everything was still the same as when I left yesterday, and I would be safe as the dancer for another day. At night, I accepted him completely. 'Please, Daddy, please,' I'd beg him each night, 'please don't tell, I'll do anything, please.'

" 'Aah, eventually, it will come out about you. It cannot be hidden.' He tortured me on a string, controlling me completely until I was seventeen.

"It was about that time that my father became ill, and lost his strength. I heard the doctors say the words 'stroke,' 'liver,' 'complications.' They called other doctors. I didn't know what anything really meant, but I took care of him faithfully, serving his meals, writing his correspondence and taking his calls for a year. I brought him books to read and washed his clothes and bedclothes, and gave him his medicine. Still, he got weaker and weaker.

"Then one morning a very strange thing happened. I'd made him toast and his strawberry tea and packed my rehearsal clothes to leave. I came into his bedroom with the tray and put it before him. He was propped in a sitting position listening to classical music on the radio. The room was dim. I opened the blinds only halfway so as not to jar him in his weakness. 'Thank you, Bethy Dolly,' he said ... And I looked at him, at this famous, robust man who'd grown so rapidly old in these last months. His thick dark hair had become sparse and gray on a translucent scalp. The teeth were yellowing and the glowing skin of the face and neck was sallow and loose. The pajamas had grown too large for the small shoulders. The large-boned muscular body had become so frail against its pillows and lost in form under the great comforter that it had almost lost its gender. Except for the stubble of white whiskers that had been let loose on the face, a visitor who didn't know him might have wondered if it was an old man or an old woman lying there. All his distinguished visitors and his orchestra friends had stopped coming weeks ago. The vitality and great will were gone from this hull and husk of a body, and with it something else had gone too. As I sat there, I tried to remember the first time, and the second time, and the third time, but I couldn't remember anything. Where did it go? I tried to remember last year, last spring. I knew it had all happened but I couldn't remember.

"All that morning at rehearsal, I was distracted trying to remember the details of our sexual encounters but all of them were gone from my mind. By the afternoon I'd told the rehearsal director that my father was worse and needed me at home. With great respect he excused me. I jumped in a taxi for the nine short blocks to our house—I had to get back to know if it were true. I tiptoed into his room and stood by the door watching a small thin yellowed soul under a great comforter. I know now that that was the moment I finally ran away in my mind and it would be easy now for me to leave."

Steven had said nothing. I stopped talking and the quiet hung like a fog around us. Steven's arms were around me as they'd been, but I realized they weren't holding me anymore. How long ago had they stopped? What had happened? Steven moved away from me, and the covers dropped from my shoulders. I sat alone. I reached to him but he sat further away from me pressed to the wall, rigid, numb, and then he stood from the bed and walked to the other side of the room, as far away from me as the room would allow. He buried his head in his hands, he couldn't look at me any longer. I watched him pace up and back, up and back, but only on the other side of the room. Some line had grown down the middle, cutting him off from me. Hidden, my secret had been a barrier between us. Out in the open, it was a solid wall.

But I'd come too far to let it end this way. I rose from the bed and stood on my side of the room holding out my arms for Steven to come back to me. Steven sat with his head in his arms. I crossed the room and stood away from him at the window holding out my arms again. He bent and shrank away from me as if I'd threatened to strike him. I realized what a terrible mistake I'd made.

Jolted, I went back to the other side of the room and walked around the bed. What destruction I'd brought to myself this morning. The secrets had tricked me. They'd been waiting all these years for this. One small enchantment with romance, and I'd been deceived into thinking it was right to tell, that Steven would understand, we'd be close. That I'd still have his love. I circled the edges of the table where the flowered pitcher he'd lovingly brought me the water in stood. The secrets had tricked and sneaked from me. As my father had promised, "Eventually it will come out about you." I'd ruined myself.

Elizabeth, haaa, how grand she'd been, a film producer, smart and wealthy, but now it was over. How quick, in a flash, like the emperor who'd lost his gold clothes, she was me again, Bethy.

I felt a strange relish in wanting to unveil more to Steven, everything, all the lovers ... Haaaa ... Oh I could disgust him about his Elizabeth, the "love of his life."

Bethy whirred all around me, egging me on ... I'd tell Steven everything about the Elizabeth he'd loved. I wanted to see his revulsion, the disgust on his face. A journalist, he could tell the world . . . I crossed the room to him once more and ripped his hands from his face to see his look of hate for me, but what I saw instead was his look of love. I saw Steven's tears for me. It sickened me. How could it be love? Pity, yes! Pity, it had to be pity! But never love. My masquerade was over and there was a strange, horrible and wild relief to it. I was uncontrollable, wanting to retch the awful green slime of who I really was. He could beat me, slam me to the floor, stomp on me, but not that look of love.

"Elizabeth, my darling, I understand—"

"No, not darling." I jumped at him with the strength of a madwoman and began to beat him with frozen hands. The whirring around me was almost a wind pushing my fists down like hammers . . . Yes, beating the man who loves you. If he would not debase me, I would debase myself.

Steven grabbed my fists and shook me until my head rattled and every bit of energy drained from me. Holding tight and pushing each other away we struggled across the room until he threw me on the bed. I tried to get up but he pushed me down.

"Elizabeth . . ." His voice choked above me trying to get out. Finally it was a hoarse whisper. "It happened in my family too. My sister Paula. I knew what my father was doing to her. I knew it all along. But I was only a child myself. Maybe if I had told someone, I could have saved her. But how does a child tell?"

I lay still with his hands gripping mine. Or were mine gripping his? The knuckles were white.

"Elizabeth, I never told anyone before. Like you I ran it inside me. I could never speak the words out loud. Even now, I look at our family pictures trying to pretend it didn't happen. But it's told right there in those pictures. Anyone who looked at them would see my father always in the middle, a dignified man, with all of us, his smiling family, close around him, except for Paula always on the end, a little away, never daring to touch, wearing the minimum smile a child has to wear in a posed photo.

'A shy child,' someone might say and go on to the next loose stack of pictures, and the next. Where's Paula? they might wonder. There aren't too many pictures of Paula! After she turned ten, my father made sure she wasn't seen.

"Paula was my older sister. There was Paula, me and Daisy, my little sister. Paula had something wrong with her arm, and one leg was shorter than the other. My mother seemed to hate Paula, and I couldn't understand why. She used to chase her with a stick, until Paula ran under the bed, dragging the shorter leg. It didn't slow her down. Paula knew how to escape. Daisy and I stood on the side by the door, watching in terror. We were very careful to never get caught doing anything wrong, we obeyed everything we were told to do without any questions. What if it happened to us?

"My father would beat Paula for lying. I never understood why she lied about everything. Once, I lied too, because I knew they would beat Paula again if they knew she'd stolen the money from my mother's purse. So I lied and said it was me who did it. Paula had taken me to the movies and bought me candy with the money. It was a double feature of Abbott and Costello and Tarzan. We stayed twice through, and Paula laughed even more the second time. When we got home my father was waiting with the strap.

"He began to beat Paula. The strap pounded her. I thought he would kill her. I screamed and tried to run out of the house to get help, but he caught me and beat me too. I was on a little bed against a wall. I tried to cling to the wall to get away, but the wall was unrelenting and cold, it pushed me back until I submitted to his strap. The blows didn't hurt after a while. The humiliation and his betrayal stayed with me always.

"And then one day I saw it. Through the lacy curtained French doors off the living room leading to my parents' bedroom. My mother was away playing bridge. It was a Saturday afternoon and I'd come in early from baseball practice, and as I passed the

French doors, I heard a choking sound on the other side, and dared to look through a corner of one of the bottom square little panes.

"I sat transfixed, not believing what I was seeing. Paula was on her knees in front of my father. He had both hands on her head. In shock I realized his penis was in her mouth. Paula was choking, gasping, retching, but he held her head in a vise, thrusting into her throat. Her head was back as if her neck would break. She seemed like some twisted fragile bird who'd broken its wings and was gasping to find flight again. Her whole body jerked in spasms.

"When he finished, my father left her there vomiting and gasping. I hid deeper in the corner behind the blue armchair. I could hear the shower starting to run on the other side of the wall, and the toilet flushing.

"Then Paula came out of the room limping on the shorter leg, and trying to smooth her dress over her knees, and rubbing her hands and wiping at her face all at once, and looking around and listening before she started to run. She didn't see me hiding in the corner. I couldn't let her see that I knew. How can you unmask something like that? What about my mother? It would destroy her if she knew. Who would I tell? What would happen to my family? My father was a banker. He would lose his job. What would happen to us? He was a generous contributor to charities, a supporter of the church, and an officer on the board of our athletic program. Who would believe me? Maybe I'd been mistaken?

"I didn't see Paula that afternoon, and she didn't come down to dinner. My mother brought her a tray.

"On Sunday, we all went to church. My father and mother wore their Sunday best. Paula, me and my little sister, Daisy, sat very quietly in church. We weren't allowed to speak to anybody when we went to church—except to say, hello, ma'am or sir, please or thank you.

"Paula started running away, but they always found her, and brought her home. My father would beat her with my mother standing on the side, egging him on. She hated Paula, but she was very tender to Daisy and me. I thought she knew because she sent Daisy away to boarding school. My father protested, but she was insistent.

"Afternoons in my house became unbearable. My mother and father would both be at work, and Paula would invite the boys to our house. She was a plain girl of fifteen with a bad limp and that something with her arm, but the boys would come anyway, and they would smoke and drink and laugh and Paula would take her chosen ones into her room. Afterward they would sit and smoke some more and put their hands on her breasts.

"She didn't know I was there. She thought I'd gone out to play ball, but I was afraid if I left the boys would strangle or kill her, so I hid in the kitchen till they were gone. Then I would come in as if I'd just come from the ball game, and Paula and I would open our books at the kitchen table to show that we were doing our homework."

I stared at Steven—all-American Steven from a small town in Colorado. Blue veins stood out on his neck.

"I was an accomplice to Paula's destruction, Elizabeth. I could have helped somehow. But how could I? I couldn't tell on her, and I couldn't tell on my father. And what would have happened to me?

"Paula ran away for the last time when she was sixteen, and I was thirteen. My father went out looking for her that night. She already knew the roadside bars. He found her drinking with a trucker and tried to bring her home. She ran into the man's truck. My father jumped on the running board, and the man pushed him off into the road. My father lost some teeth in the fall. I know this because he rocked me in his arms later sobbing. He'd never hugged me before, but he was so distraught. 'My Paula, my baby, my Paula,' he kept sobbing into my body. I was grief-stricken with confusion. I couldn't believe he felt this way, but he did.

"Paula called the next day to tell me not to worry. While my mother kept her on the phone, my father went to trace the call. I grabbed the phone back. 'Run, Paula, run. They're tracing the call,' I whispered into the mouthpiece at the risk of my life. Paula hung up, but my mother didn't say anything to my father. Then we both knew that she knew.

"Paula disappeared from the face of the earth. The police tried for years, but they couldn't find her. 'Sir,' I'd hear them tell my father, 'these things can go this way. These problem kids are real clever. Hate to tell you but we usually find them when there's a crime or a death. Then they turn up sure enough, and not that far away from where they started.'

"Daisy and I weren't allowed to talk about Paula to anyone, ever again, and somehow people never asked. I could see them whisper when they saw us but stop when we approached. We went to church every Sunday as usual, and nothing was ever said. Daisy stayed at boarding school, and I began to go to my mountain every day. I'd pretend Paula was there and talk to her. I knew someday I'd see her again.

"Recently, Paula telephoned me. I cried so much from happiness that she was alive. She called me from a drug rehabilitation clinic in Colorado, where she'd been for four months. Do you know, Elizabeth, the amazing thing is that Paula is only now beginning to remember how my father sexually abused her. She repressed everything after she ran away. The beatings came back to her first. What really happened is coming back to her in bits and snatches of pictures and dreams. Of the fifteen women in her group only one remembered everything. Paula's therapist explained to her that the human mind's protection mechanisms are extremely strong. She's dealt with an unbearable trauma by scratching it from her consciousness.

"Paula looked me up to ask what I knew, to make sure this

wasn't some fantasy that came out of her therapy. When she began to remember what happened, she realized that I always knew."

"What about Daisy?" I could barely ask.

Steven collapsed in weeping. When he spoke again it was a cracked pitiful sound, deep in his throat. "That is my worst guilt. When Paula told Daisy, Daisy said, 'I thought I was the only one.'" Steven looked at me, pleading. "If you could have seen Daisy, she was a little kid, with a beautiful face, like an angel. She was so quiet, she never bothered anybody or caused any trouble . . ." His mourning of what happened to Daisy overtook him.

It hurt me more than anything to see Steven suffering like this in front of me. It seemed deeper than my own pain. I went to him and put my arms around him.

He folded me into him. "You aren't alone, Elizabeth. There are more than you know. It happens in families like ours, not just to children of the ghetto. You were a victim, not an accomplice. How does a child tell about this? Look at it with a child's eyes, not the adult eyes you have now. I love you, Elizabeth, I love you very much."

I left Steven's arms and sat in a wooden chair, watching him cry. Steven knew all this about me and yet he loved me. I sat here with my face swollen from fever and tears, and he loved me. My hair was caked with days of sweat and dust from the road, and he loved me. I'd acted like a madwoman, and truly I was, and he loved me. I'd been sick and delirious, and he'd cared for me. I'd told of disgusting things, who I really was, my own betrayal, and he'd stayed at my side.

Steven saw me watching him, and straightened, holding back his tears by pressing his eyes. I knew the heartbreaking things of his life that he'd carefully kept hidden, and I loved him. I knew the image he'd pretended to the world was there to hide his horrible guilt, and I loved him. He sat weeping like a weak child and I loved him. His perfect TV features were distorted and swollen and I loved them. He rocked in his grief and I knew he had years to go before he would make peace with himself, and I wanted to stay by his side.

Tell him you love him, the voice inside me said. Tell him, the voice grew stronger. You love him. Why don't you tell him. It's over . . . now you can tell him . . . Remember love . . . The voice inside was different. It had always been Bethy's. Now it was my voice. "I love you, Steven," I said and went back to him, lifting him to stand facing me.

"Elizabeth," he said, "the first time I saw you, at the airport, I had to meet you so I sat next to you on the plane and we talked. When I saw you in the café afterward, our first day in Barcelona, I wanted very much to know you better, but you were already with someone else. When I saw you behind the camera so engrossed in shooting your Olympic film, I was determined to be with you. In Costa Brava I couldn't help it, I began to fall in love with you. Today I couldn't be more sure that I'll always love you. Hiding a secret, you build a fence around yourself and it quickly becomes a concrete wall. You make yourself live behind it where nobody can cross. You give up hope that you'll ever break out. You're always alone, acting a part so that nobody ever suspects. Today, hearing you tell something so deeply forbidden about yourself, I realized the courage of the person you are. You gave me the courage to break out too. I'd never had that courage before."

"I never had this courage before either, Steven. Before this morning, I always felt that what had happened to me was a disease I could never be cured of. I was too weakened by it. You gave me the courage to try."

"Elizabeth, before this morning I was weak too. Do you realize that out of our weakness, our love can start, here, now, with incredible strength and honesty. Do you realize that?"

We looked at each other. Never had two lovers professed their love with such tear-stained swollen faces, and through the bare honesty of such red and watered eyes. "Yes, Steven, I love you very much," I repeated. And we held each other and cried.

Twenty-four

Paris, September 1994

I think it will take a long time to reverse the injury that Steven and I have both done to ourselves. Oh, I don't blame myself anymore for what happened to me as a child. I know now I truly believe that I was a victim, and I can't change anything of what happened to me by turning back the time. I'm not a person who moans and cries and seeks sympathy either. I put my own victimization in perspective, knowing that many of the human race have amazing capacity to heal when you consider the survival and strength of innocents of every nature in war, famine and disease. Some are not so lucky.

But how do I reverse the rigid habits of protection, habits of shutting myself away from any real love that would ever be offered to me? I know now that I did that by myself, willingly. Understandably so, you may protest. And I agree with you, but still it's so. At forty, I finally understand the mechanism of love and that it's each person's birthright, but I also understand how honestly and fearlessly open to it you must be to have it come to you. I couldn't allow love into me before, and I have to fight still to take it, even though I've been gifted to glimpse the ferocious joy that openness to love brings. But then it's very difficult to find love, not only for me and Steven, but for anybody who feels they have anything of themselves they must hide. My loves before Steven—Luíz, Yves—had only been selfishness, or desperately, addictively needing a lover who will claim that you're perfect. That's what a shut-away soul needs—it constantly needs to reassure itself.

It's been over a year since Steven and I have moved our base of business and our love to Paris. True, we live in the city of lovers, in the center of the arts in Europe, and that, I have to admit, increases our chances. But why should it not, we've paid the price.

Two months ago I gave up my studio in TriBeCa. As a filmmaker, Paris is ideal for me; and as a reluctant but acknowledged specialist these days in low-budget films, I didn't see the need for paying two rents. Paris offers the absolute of creative communities, far away from New York and Hollywood, although I can't say that similar sharks aren't swimming here too. But there's abundant open water to swim away. Earlier this year I began to shoot new footage in France, in Giverny . . . new colors, new feelings for me. Living in Paris inspires my work daily in ways I haven't thought of before. You may think it's because of the incredible bridges and art and architecture here, but I know it's because Paris allows me to work quietly at a time when I need to be quiet to heal.

Steven still keeps his apartment in L.A. for his daughter, who is in school in Switzerland and often wishes to visit her friends back home. He's given up his money-making, suit-and-tie network job for the insecurities of photojournalism. He not only has much less money now, but he constantly loves to risk his life in the most dangerous places. You've never seen a man so happy.

My Paris day starts at eight A.M. in our three irregular-roomed apartment walk-up we rent on Rue Dauphine on the Left Bank.

Our bedroom is so small that the bed takes up most of it and seems to extend up the muted peach and gray stripes of the wallpaper into the beamed ceiling. I open the windows to a little terrace which wouldn't support anything except our geranium pots and go back to bed to listen to the day begin. A few cars honk by and voices and footsteps on the pavement float up. It's beautiful.

Steven, who's been working since seven in our larger room, which is still very small, is at the doorway, leaning over the bed to rip the blankets off me. "So, darlin', are you going to be ready for the coffee sometime today?" He finds my jeans and tee somewhere on the narrow space of floor around the bed and hustles me into them. We touch and look at each other as I button the jeans . . . We'll make love later this morning, we think . . . Sex is one of the great miracles we share together, but neither of us have really good reflexes to honor it properly before the coffee.

Downstairs at Café Bucci, we stand side by side at the pewter-top bar where Steven quickly downs two espressos and I slowly put my hands around a steaming cup of café au lait. Our next stop is a few blocks away at the open air market of Rue de Seine, where we buy ham and a baguette for our first business meeting of the day. We sit on the banks of the Seine, our favorite breakfast conference room, and lay out the details of our current and future projects. There aren't too many Parisians walking the Seine that early, it's very private. We sit across from the Louvre, or a favorite building that looks to be a massive old castle floating in the Seine, and consider how lucky we are.

Today we're deciding if Steven should go to the interior of a country in Africa that I've never heard of to do a photo story. He's excited, nobody's done it before. I try to dissuade him, predicting danger and disease. He wants to go very soon, will I help him arrange it? I protest that now would be the worst time. He decides, "I'll go before it gets cold." I try to have him put it off longer. He promises—or threatens me, I don't know which—

that come the winter, he's determined to be here to teach me to ski. The French Alps are only a train ride away.

With that settled for now, I get up. "Time to go to work. I have to be at the editor's at nine thirty to look at dailies."

"Shall I go with you?" he offers.

I'll invite him to the editing room today, but I usually don't. He's too uncritical, he loves every frame I shoot. I know he really does, but I'm wary of falling into my old habits of loving a lover who flatters me in my work. My work is such an organic part of me, I'm still vulnerable to loving for reassurance. I need my love for Steven to always be totally unfettered. Steven's said that I also like his work too much. I think he's wary too.

In the late afternoon we go back to the apartment on Rue Dauphine. We'll finish calls, then perhaps a nap, perhaps make love, perhaps a walk. Later in the evening we'll finish our calls to the States where it's still midafternoon, or go to the theater or do nothing.

But at six o'clock we always go to a café with the other Parisians. A funny thing happens at six o'clock in Paris, it gets brighter. It's like a whole other day is beginning and the cafés fill up. In Paris at six o'clock, somehow the sun comes out all over again.